Beyond Sleep

Willem Frederik Hermans

Beyond Sleep

TRANSLATED
FROM THE DUTCH
BY

Ina Rilke

The Overlook Press
WOODSTOCK & NEW YORK

This edition first published in the United States in 2007 by
The Overlook Press, Peter Mayer Publishers, Inc.
Woodstock & New York

WOODSTOCK:
One Overlook Drive
Woodstock, NY 12498
www.overlookpress.com
[for individual orders, bulk and special sales, contact our Woodstock office]

NEW YORK:
141 Wooster Street
New York, NY 10012

This translation was made from the most recent, 27th impression of *Nooit meer slapen*,
published in 2003 by De Bezige Bei; this is identical to the 15th impression, published in
1978, which also contains the author's postscript, appearing here on p.311.

Library of Congress Cataloging-in-Publication Data

Hermans, Willem Frederik, 1921-1995.
[Nooit meer slapen, English]
Beyond sleep / Willem Frederik Hermans ; translated from the Dutch by Ina Rilke.
p. cm.
I. Rilke, Ina. II. Title.
PT5844.H526N613 2006   839.3'1364—dc22   2006048743
Manufactured in the United States of America
Hardcover ISBN 978-1-58567-538-8
Paperback ISBN 978-1-58567-988-1
10 9 8 7 6 5 4 3 2 1

I do not know what I may appear to the world, but to myself I seem to have been only like a boy playing on the sea-shore, and diverting myself in now and then finding a smoother pebble or a prettier shell than ordinary, whilst the great ocean of truth lay all undiscovered before me.

Isaac Newton

Beyond Sleep

1

The porter is disabled.

The oak reception desk at which he sits, staring through cheap sunglasses, is bare but for a telephone. His left ear must have been ripped off in the explosion that caused his disfigurement, or possibly it was burnt in a plane crash. What is left of the ear resembles a misshapen navel and offers no support for the hook of his dark glasses.

'Professor Nummedal, please. I have an appointment with him.'

'Good day, sir. I don't know if Professor Nummedal is in.'

His English sounds slow, as if it's German. He falls silent, doesn't stir.

'I made an appointment yesterday with Professor Nummedal's secretary – for ten thirty today.'

Automatically I glance at my watch, which I adjusted to Norwegian summer time upon arrival in Oslo yesterday. Half past ten.

Only now do I notice the electric clock above his head, also indicating half past ten.

As if wanting to dispel every vestige of doubt in the disabled porter's mind, I bring out the letter given to me by Professor Sibbelee in Amsterdam and say:

'Actually, the date was fixed some time ago.'

The letter is from Nummedal to Sibbelee, mentioning today, Friday 15th, as a possible date for a meeting. *I wish your pupil a good journey to Oslo.* Signed: *Ørnulf Nummedal.*

I unfold the letter and hold it out for the porter to read. But he doesn't move his head, only his hands.

On his left hand the fingers are missing, and all that remains on the right is a nail-less stump and the thumb. The thumb is completely unscathed, with a clean, well-kept nail. It almost looks alien to him. Not one finger left for a wedding ring.

His wristwatch has a small metal cover, which he snaps open with his thumbnail. There is no glass beneath the lid.

The porter runs the nail-less stump over the dial and says:

'It is possible that Professor Nummedal is in his study. Two flights up and second door on your right.'

Open-mouthed, I put the letter back in my pocket.

'Thank you.'

Why I thanked him I don't know. The cheek! Treating me as if I were just anyone, someone who'd wandered in off the street without having an appointment.

But I suppress my rage. I'm prepared to have pity on him, like his employer, who evidently sees fit to keep him on despite his inability to perform simple tasks, such as receiving visitors without treating them as though they can drop dead for all he cares.

In the meantime I have counted the treads on the two flights of stairs: twenty-eight each with an interval of eight paces across the landing. From the top of the stairs to the second door on the right is another fifteen paces.

2

I knock. From inside a voice calls something I don't understand. I push open the door, rehearsing my English phrases under my breath: Are you Professor Nummedal . . . Have I the pleasure . . . My name is . . .

. . . Where are you, Professor Nummedal?

The study is a vast oak-panelled room. My eyes seek out the professor and locate him in the farthest corner, behind a desk. I advance between two tables laden with half-furled maps. To the side of the small grey figure behind the desk looms the white rectangle of a drawing board in upright position.

'Are you Professor Nummedal?'

'Yes?'

He makes a half-hearted attempt to rise.

A shaft of sunlight falls on his spectacles, which are so thick as to appear opaque. He raises his hand to flip up the extra pair of lenses hinged along the top of the frame. Four small round mirrors are now trained on me.

I step up close to his desk and explain that I telephoned his secretary yesterday and that she told me to be here today at this hour.

'My secretary?'

His English is very hard to distinguish from Norwegian, which I don't speak, and his voice is as ancient as only a voice can be that has said all there is to say:

'I do not recall my secretary saying this to me, but perhaps it was her intention. Where does you come from?'

'From the Netherlands. I'm that student of Professor Sibbelee's. I'm going to Finnmark with your students Arne Jordal and Qvigstad.'

3

My hand reaches into my inside pocket and once more draws out the letter Nummedal wrote to Sibbelee.

I find myself unfolding the letter, as I did for the porter. 'Well, well. You is a Nedherlander, you is . . .'

I chuckle by way of assent and also to show my appreciation for his near-perfect pronunciation of the Dutch word.

'Nedherlanders!' he goes on. 'Clever people. Very clever. Can you follow me? Or do you prefer to speak German?'

'It is . . . all the same to me,' I say.

'Niederländer,' he retorts in German, 'a highly intelligent nation, they speak all languages. Professor Sibbelee writes to me in a mixture of Norwegian, Danish and Swedish. We call that Scandinavian. Take a seat.'

'Thank you,' I say, in English.

He sticks to German.

'I have known Professor Sibbelee for many years. Let me see, when did I first meet him? It must have been before the war, at the conference in Tokyo. Yes. The year I presented my paper – which has become a classic, if I may say so – on the milonite zone in Värmland and its expansion into Norway. Vielleicht kennen Sie die kleine Arbeit?'

He pauses for a moment, but not long enough to compel me to confess my ignorance of the said opus. Then, brightly, he continues.

'Sibbelee opened a debate about it at the time. Things got quite heated. He could not agree with a single argument I put forward. Can you imagine? Such a to-do! Sibbelee is thirty years younger than me and in those days he was very young indeed, very young. The passion of youth!'

Nummedal bursts out laughing. Even when he laughs the creases in the far too ample skin on his face remain for the most part vertical.

I laugh along with him, although I'm a bit concerned about his memories of the very person who recommended me to him.

Can he see what I'm thinking?

'Das sind jetzt natürlich alles alte Sachen! All water under the bridge, now. Sibbelee changed his tune eventually. He even worked here at my institute for a spell. I can't for the life of me remember what sort of research he was engaged in. One can't remember everything. In any case, he spent quite some time here. The results didn't amount to much, as far as I know.'

Exit Sibbelee, down the hatch. I can sense my mentor's nemesis rubbing off on me. Wouldn't it be better to take my leave now? But the aerial photographs?

'I am eighty-four years old,' Nummedal says. 'I have seen a great deal of scientific work done to no avail. Warehouses filled with collections no-one takes any notice of, until the day they are thrown out for lack of space. I have seen theories come and go like wild geese or swallows. Have you ever eaten braised lark? Incidentally, there is a restaurant here in Oslo where they serve gravlachs. Have you heard of it? A sort of salmon, not like smoked salmon – well there is a similarity I suppose, but more delicate, more subtle. Raw salmon, buried underground for a time and then dug up again.'

His voice has grown more subtle, too, to the point of being inaudible. The skin of his neck droops slackly in his too-wide collar, and when he purses his lips in deep thought the folds seem to travel upwards, unimpeded by his chin, to corrugate his whole face.

Silence.

On the desktop before him are papers and two large stones. Also some small porcelain bowls containing smaller stones dusted with cigar ash. Across the papers lies a magnifying glass the size of a frying pan.

'Professor Sibbelee asked me to pass on his best regards to you.'

'Thank you, thank you.'

Another silence.

My tongue is a hand groping in the depths of a black sack for some way of steering this conversation to my purpose in coming here. Nothing tactful comes to mind. Plunge in at the deep end, then.

'Did you, by any chance, manage to get hold of those aerial photographs for me?'

'Aerial photos? What do you mean, aerial photos? Of course we have aerial photos here. But I do not know whether anyone is using them at present. There are so many aerial photos.'

He doesn't know what I am talking about! Could he have forgotten his promise to Sibbelee, that he would give me the aerial surveys I need for my fieldwork? I have a feeling that further explanations of my need will be counterproductive, but I can't think of anything better. I can hardly give up without having tried every tack.

'Yes, Professor, the aerial photographs . . .'

'Is it the entire collection you wish to see?'

'There has been . . . there was . . .'

My left hand is down between my knees holding my right, which is bunched into a fist. My elbows press against my sides.

'There was mention of a set of aerial photographs I could use for my research in Finnmark.'

I am not sure what I just said rates as correct German, but I can't imagine there was anything Nummedal would have any difficulty understanding, and I articulated the words clearly and without faltering.

He draws a deep breath and says:

'I consider Qvigstad and Jordal among the best pupils I have ever had, and I speak of a period of many years, you understand. They know all about Finnmark.'

'Of course. I have only met Qvigstad briefly, but Arne strikes me as someone from whom I can learn a great deal, which makes it all the more a privilege for me to accompany him.'

'A privilege, sir? Indeed it is! Geology is a science that is strongly bound to geographic circumstance. In order to obtain results that amaze and impress, one must practise geology in areas with something left to discover. But that is the great difficulty facing us. I know a fair few geologists who went looking in places where no-one had bothered to look before because it was assumed there was nothing there. They never found anything either.

'May I let you in on a secret?' he goes on. 'The true geologist never completely forsakes his gold-prospecting forebears. You may laugh at me for saying this, but I am old. Which gives me a certain right to romanticise.'

'No, no! I know exactly what you mean!'

'Ah, so you know what I mean. But for you as a Dutchman, the concept must be somewhat unpalatable. Such a small country, densely populated for centuries and with scientific standards known to be among the highest in the world. I can well imagine the geologists in Holland having to stand on each other's toes, and being sorely tempted in the process to palm off a stray toe as the incisor of a Cave Bear!'

'The country is small, admittedly, but the soil is exceptionally varied.'

'That is what you people think, just because there is a geologist with a microscope on each square metre. That does not change the fact that there are no mountains. No plateaux, no glaciers, no waterfalls either! Marshland, mud and clay, that is all! It will end with them counting every single grain of sand, I shouldn't wonder. To me that is not geology. I call it bookkeeping, hair-splitting. Verfallene Wissenschaft, is what I call it, verfallene Wissenschaft.'

My laughter is both civil and sincere.

'Oh, Professor, they have also found coal, salt, oil and natural gas.'

'But the important issues, my dear sir. The big questions! Where did our planet come from? What is its future? Are we heading towards a new ice age, or will there be date palms growing on the South Pole one day? The big questions that make science great, the questions that are the true function of science!'

Pressing both hands on the creaky desktop, he rises.

'The true function of science! Do you understand? Coal to burn in the stove, natural gas to boil an egg for breakfast, salt to sprinkle on it — mere household words, as far as I'm concerned. What is science? Science is the titanic endeavour of the human intellect to break out of its cosmic isolation through understanding!'

8

2

Nummedal comes out from behind his desk. He keeps his fingertips in contact with the desktop throughout.

'I propose taking you on a little tour of the environs of Oslo this afternoon. Where are those maps . . . ?'

He moves towards one of the long tables covered in maps.

'That would be very nice,' I say.

I spoke without emphasis or reflection.

What if I had said I had to continue my journey northwards this afternoon?

He flips down his extra glasses and holds one of the maps up close to his eyes. What if I come right out and tell him the only reason I called on him was to get hold of the aerial photographs?

His jaw sags.

What if I tell him I've already booked a seat on the plane to Trondheim? That I must leave in fifteen minutes?

But what if he takes offence, and lets me go off to Finnmark without the photographs?

I step closer to him. We stand side by side at the long table. The map in his hands has been rolled up for a long time, the corners curl inwards. Nummedal leans forward to spread it out on the table and I help him hold down the springy paper.

It is a heliotype print. Could it be an unpublished map, one he has picked out as a special favour to me?

No, it is an ordinary geological survey of the Oslo district. He says:

'I must have a better copy somewhere, in colour.'

As he moves down the table he upsets a pile of papers, spilling them across the floor. I squat on my heels to retrieve them.

'Oh, there is no need!'

Looking up, I see he's holding another map, a cloth-backed one this time. With my hands full of papers, I straighten up. Nummedal takes no notice.

'Here it is. Come along now, let's go.'

I lay the papers on the table and follow him.

Which map has he got now? While I hold the door open for him, I see it is the coloured version of the geological survey of Oslo. Does he really have no idea why I am here?

'This one is mounted on linen,' he says, 'but not in the proper way. It can't be folded.'

And he hands me the map.

The corridor. We move towards the stairs, me on his left with the roll under my arm.

'I was in Amsterdam before the war,' Nummedal says, 'I visited the geological institute there. Splendid building. Fine collections from Indonesia.'

His right hand trails along the wall.

'Losing the colonies must have been a terrible blow for geologists in your country.'

'It would seem so on the face of it. But fortunately there are plenty of opportunities elsewhere.'

'Elsewhere? My dear young man, don't delude yourself! Other countries have their own geologists. The science is bound to suffer in the long run if your geologists have no alternative but to set their sights abroad.'

The thirteenth tread of the second flight down.

'Maybe,' I say. 'Still, you know, nowadays, with all the new international organisations, and borders becoming so much easier to cross . . .'

'All that looks fine on paper! But where does it leave the profound insights and natural affinity with the big questions, if people receive their training in a tiny, flat country of mud and clay without a single mountain?'

Just as well he doesn't expect an answer.

'You must admit,' he explains, unprompted by me, 'that tectonics is the branch of geology *par excellence* with scope for mental constructs of genius. Is there anything more challenging than drawing inferences about the interior structure of the Alps or the composition of the Scandinavian Shield from a handful of observations and measurements?'

We have not reached the bottom of the stairs, but he halts anyway.

'In a place like Holland you never have solid rock underfoot! When you arrive in Holland what is the first thing you see? The control tower at the airport with a sign saying: Aerodrome level thirteen feet below sea level. What a welcome!'

Laughing, he completes his descent, but once more pauses in the hall.

'You would think the floods of 1953 had taught them a lesson. Other people would have left, they would have moved beyond the reach of the sea! But not the Dutch! Where could they go, anyway?

'Sir, I will say this: if an entire population specialises itself, generation upon generation, in surviving in a country that is strictly speaking the domain of fish, then those people will end up inventing a special philosophy of their own, in which the human dimension is totally lacking! A philosophy based exclusively on self-preservation. A world view that amounts to keeping dry and making sure there's nothing fishy going on! How can such a philosophy be universally valid? Where does that leave the big questions?'

Interjections come to mind: what good did universally valid philosophies ever do anyone? What are the big questions anyway? Isn't survival a big question in a world fraught with danger? But the prospect of having to say all this in German is too daunting,

The clock in the vestibule indicates five past midday and the porter is nowhere to be seen.

Nummedal goes over to the reception desk, rests his hand on the top and sidles towards a cupboard, which he opens.

He takes out a walking stick and a hat. The stick is white with a red band beneath the handle.

Blind boss of a blind porter.

3

Out in the street I feel like a dutiful grandson accompanying his half-blind grandfather on a stroll because it's such a sunny day.

But it is he who draws me to the restaurant.

It's a large, posh restaurant. Or was. Now there are pink plastic chairs and small tables without tablecloths. The walls are panelled with hardboard in pastel shades, teak-finish chipboard and formica with perforations.

There are no waiters to be seen, just girls collecting dirty dishes.

Background music: 'Skating in Central Park' from the Modern Jazz Quartet.

I steer Nummedal carefully between the tables and chairs to the long counter.

I take two teakwood trays and place them end to end on the nickel-plated bars along the front of the counter. Nummedal is by my side, his white stick hanging on his arm. The stick swings in front of my face with each wave of Nummedal's arm to attract the attention of the staff behind the counter. A whole row of scrubbed blondes wearing green linen tiaras.

Nummedal and I are in a queue of hungry customers, all of whom slide their teak trays along as they load them with dishes from the counter. But Nummedal is so agitated that he forgets to move on, causing a pile-up behind him. He makes a baying sound from time to time. *Frøken!*

Frøken!

Not one Frøken takes any notice. The Frøkens are busy replenishing the servings on the counter. Frøken hors d'oeuvre pretends not to hear, Frøken bread rolls ditto, Frøken soup isn't listening, nor is Frøken meats.

What does Nummedal want, anyway?

Why does he need assistance? Why can't he take his pick from what's available? And if he can't see properly, why doesn't he tell me what to get for him?

My poor senile grandfather making a fuss over nothing. Nummedal . . . his name reminds me of the old Dutch word for 'nothing'. Could that be what his name means?

Now and then I give his tray a nudge with the side of mine. We are reaching the desserts and still haven't picked anything to eat. We'll have to go back to the end of the queue if we're not careful, and shuffle past the counter all over again. I haven't dared to put anything on my tray, not even a glass, knife, fork or paper napkin.

At one point Nummedal refuses to budge at all, causing a gap in the line. Shall I help myself to a portion of pineapple and whipped cream, just for something to do? The people ahead of Nummedal have already gone past the cash register. I look round anxiously in case we're causing a disturbance among the hungry patrons. No lamentations from them, not even a sigh. Dapper Vikings! Noble race of unhurried giants! Nummedal is still baying.

I can now make out a second word: gravlachs!

*

The girl in charge of the pineapple and whipped cream has heard it too. She leans forward to Nummedal, shakes her head, draws herself up again and calls back to the girls we have already gone past.

The word has also been heard on the customer side of the counter. Everyone starts looking for gravlachs. They're still in the throes of selecting, inspecting and sniffing when the word gravlachs returns to the whipped-cream Frøken after passing from tiara to tiara. It is now presented in the negative.

Nummedal exclaims loudly, thankful that his question has been understood, apologetic about placing an impossible order.

'No gravlachs in this place!' he declares in English.

'I understand. It's not important.'

Next he apologises for not having spoken to me in German, and repeats: 'Kein gravlachs hier!'

'Ich verstehe, ich verstehe,' I say.

Quickly I seize a bowl of pudding and set it on my tray. Arriving at the cash register I see mugs of hot coffee. Nummedal has left his tray behind, he has taken the coffees and is now paying for both of us, without checking his change.

A man leaves the queue and approaches me. His head is square and his spectacles are perfectly round. He points to the furled geological map tucked under my arm. He smiles and makes a little bow.

'I understand you are a stranger here . . . This is a very bad restaurant, you know, where they don't have gravlachs. In Oslo one can never find what a foreign visitor wants! I am ashamed of my native city. You must be accustomed to so much better in London. But you have a map, I see? Is it of the city? May I take a look?'

Balancing the tray on my left hand, I reach for the map with my right and pass it to him. He's going to have to wait in line again, just because he wanted to help.

He unrolls the map.

'There is only one restaurant where you can get gravlachs. I will point it out to you.'

'Won't that be too difficult on this map?'

It's on the tip of my tongue to tell him it's a geological survey. What will he think when he sees all that red, green and yellow, with the city itself no bigger than a potato sliced in half?

His finger is poised to trace the direction. The map springs back, I want to be of assistance, the tray balancing on my hand teeters.

It teeters in his direction. The coffee spills over him in a tidal wave, the pudding clings in evil little clots to his suit, the bowl shatters on the floor, but I manage to keep the tray from falling. He holds the map aloft with outstretched arms. I look round to see where Nummedal has got to. He's seated at one of the tables, stirring his coffee.

'No harm done! No harm done!' cries the man who wanted to help, waving the bone-dry, unsullied map.

I take the map from him. Pushing me out of the way, two waitresses set about wiping him down with a sponge and a towel.

More helpful Norwegians gather round.

One of them has fetched a pudding for me, another coffee, and a third brings a salad with pinkish slivers of fish.

'Lachs, lachs!' he singsongs. 'Lachs, lachs! But no gravlachs! Too bad!'

I ask how much I owe them, looking from one to the next, get no reply. I try again, but stammer so badly that their pity only increases. *Can't speak a single foreign language*, they reckon. *Came all the way from God knows where to eat gravlachs*.

Hoping and praying they won't come after me, I turn my back on them and take the loaded tray to the table occupied by Nummedal.

A Frøken kneels on the floor to mop up the spilled pudding.

Nummedal says: 'Haben Sie die Karte?'

I spread the map on the table, taking deep breaths in anticipation of the next ordeal.

Nummedal pushes his spectacles up on his forehead, fumbles under his clothes and draws out a magnifying glass on the end of a black cord. He holds the glass just above the map, as though searching for a flea. He cranes his neck as far as it will go. His head looks ready to come loose and roll over the table. Muttering, he slides the magnifying glass with one hand while trying to point with the other. The map curls up maddeningly. I make myself useful by securing the corners with the ashtray, one of the mugs and my two dishes. But I'm not listening.

Had I been taught by private tutors all my life, I would be illiterate today. Never have I been able to concentrate when people start explaining things to me on a one-to-one basis.

Ever seen the heart of an animal cut open while still alive? The malevolent pulsating within the splayed monstrosity?

That's how it is for me when I have to listen to someone explaining something – a sense of time being pumped through empty space. Almost suffocating, I gasp: Yes, yes. Sitting still is an enormous effort, as exhausting as a three-day hike.

*

Nummedal is showering me with information I didn't ask for. I need his aerial photographs, not his vanity. Beads of sweat trickle down my breastbone, which begins to itch; my eyes goggle out of my head. I see and hear all, but don't register.

May queens appear behind the counter wearing burning candles in their hair.

With open-heart cleavage, the Frøken mops up the mess I made on the floor. Her honey hills, her beehives.

I curl my lips away from my teeth and slowly open and close my jaws.

Nummedal has found some detail on the map which he considers of paramount importance to me.

He puts down his magnifying glass, takes off his spectacles, pulls a white handkerchief from his trousers and begins to polish each of the four lenses in turn. In the meantime he preambles:

'In fact the Oslo district extends from Langsundsfjord in the south, which you can't see here, up to Lake Mjøsa in the north . . .

'Tectonics . . .

'Deposit of the Lower Palaeozoic . . . Drammen . . . Caledonides . . . Archean substratum . . . two synclinals . . . litho-tectonic structure . . . shale . . .'

I make noises, bend over the map so closely that I can distinguish neither dots nor lines, say:

'Yes, yes!'

And exclaim:

'Of course!'

But I'm close to exploding with despair at not even catching enough of Nummedal's exposé to be able, later on, when he points everything out to me in the field, to tell him how right he is.

Then at least he might form a more favourable impression of me than of my mentor Sibbelee . . . and give me the aerial photographs, which is all I want from him.

'Are you really going to show me all that? Won't it be too much trouble?'

'Being in Oslo and not even taking a look around the Oslo district! Out of the question.'

'I am very grateful for your . . .'

'Ja ja, schön! That is what all you young people say! Shall we go now? I have finished my coffee.'

But I haven't. Out of feigned respect I haven't touched my food. I stuff my mouth full of salmon and pass Nummedal his white stick. He walks off, unsurprisingly leaving the map behind for me to carry.

At the exit the man who wanted to help comes up to me again.

'Gravlachs!' he cries. 'There is only one restaurant where you can get it, but it is closed in June. No gravlachs in the whole city! I do apologise. You are not used to this in London. Or are you from New York? This is typically Norwegian! They never get anything right here! This would never have happened in Paris. I'm sorry. I'm sorry. No alcohol in restaurants. No striptease either! Good luck to you, sir!'

4

The asphalt rises and falls. There are few cars about and the pavements of Oslo are lined with grassy ramps.

A white, columned palace in the distance where the king resides.

Down a flight of steps. Underground station. Electric train.

One of the oldest electric railways in the world, supposedly, with carriages made of vertical oak planks, varnished and meticulously secured with brass screws.

Nummedal and I sit facing each other at a small window. The tunnel is quite short, and soon we are riding in the open. The track is carved out of rock. The train gives a high-pitched hum in the bends as it snakes upwards.

The city lies below.

Nummedal has stopped talking, and I rack my brains for something to say.

Everything that comes to mind is unspeakable: . . . how is it possible that you, all of eighty-four years old, can still be lording it over a university lab . . . what a diehard you must be . . . entitled to your pension for at least ten years if not twenty . . . assuming the retirement age in Norway is sixty-five, although it might be sixty given that the socialists have been in power for such a long time . . . but

he chose to remain at his post, loyal and irreplaceable . . .
rules have no doubt been bent to make this possible . . .
the incomparable Nummedal! . . . I wonder how long he
has been practically blind? . . . Honorary doctorates in
Ireland, Kentucky, New Zealand, Liberia, Liechtenstein,
Tilburg. Praiseworthy, indefatigable in old age . . .
enviably so . . . or such a harridan of a wife at home that
heaven and earth must be moved to spare him the bless-
ings of *otium cum dignitate* in her company . . . or else
some sourpuss housekeeper . . .

I consider his clothing . . . old, but neat. Old people wear
out faster than their clothes. Why is that? He has on a type
of ankle-boots you'd be hard pressed to find in the shops
nowadays. Sturdily re-soled. A fastidious type.

I reckon he designed his glasses himself. Had them made
in the instrument workshop of the university, of course. I
feel a sudden rush of pity . . . I'd like to say to him with
tears in my eyes: Listen here, Nummedal, Ørnulf. I know
what you think, but you're mistaken. There is no hereafter
presided over by some little old man even older than you,
with all the honorary doctorates and all the same principles, albeit on a more exalted level. Once you take the big
step into the utter darkness that might fall any moment –
a stroke, for instance, causing a flash flood in your decrepit
brain – there won't be a little old man saying: Hello,
Ørnulf, it has been my pleasure to see how you got on
over the years, how you stuck to the university instead of
taking things easy at home, how you received a pre-
announced visitor from abroad with a mixture of arro-
gance, irony and bonhomie. And how you took him to the
mountains to show him you're not past it yet, so he can
tell the folks back home: Nummedal's still going strong.

Tough as old boots. Could still teach every young man a thing or two!

He swings one leg over the other. His liver-spotted hands rest on the handle of his white stick, swaying from side to side with the cadence of the train.

'Judging by the time,' the geologist-cum-Adenauer-lookalike says, 'we should soon be going past an area where the Silurian is clearly exposed. Keep your eyes peeled. You can't miss it if you're careful. Look, over there.'

He points to the wooden slats between the windows, but I can distinguish the Silurian rock anyway.

My thoughts begin to drift again. What do I want? I want him to give me the aerial photographs . . . How am I to get through to this very old man, who's long past caring what anyone might have to say and who feels no compunction at putting people in an impossible position, assuming he still knows what he's doing?

Perhaps it's Sibbelee who is most to blame. Sibbelee should have presented my case differently. Should have said . . . well, what? He should have asked for the photographs to be sent to Holland! But Sibbelee was not to know precisely which aerial photographs exist of the terrain I am planning to write my thesis on. Besides, wasn't it a mark of courtesy on my part to collect them in person?

Suddenly it hits me where I went wrong!

I should have fallen to my knees upon entering Nummedal's study. Humble, but eloquent! Help me, I should have cried, sate me with knowledge! I shall write ten scientific articles and make sure your name occurs a hundred times in each! I shall mention your name in everything I publish to the end of my days, even if the subject has nothing whatsoever to do with you or your invaluable research. I have friends on advisory committees for honours lists . . . honorary doctorates . . . obituaries . . .

Obituaries??

But it's too late now anyway . . . I have let the perfect opportunity for attack pass, and now I am under siege. Cowering on the defensive, stuck fast like a warped axle in a damaged hub.

In a fix I can't squirm out of.

5

Nummedal is an excellent walker.

Out here, in the bright sunshine, his eyesight seems a lot better, too.

We climb higher and higher, and Nummedal takes every available short cut between hairpin bends, striking up foot-paths sloping at close on thirty degrees. His pace is steady, his breathing unlaboured, and he holds forth on geological subjects as he climbs.

At appropriate moments I respond with affirmative grunts. I can tell from his intonation when is a good time to come out with an 'of course' , 'quite so', 'of course not', or even the occasional 'ha ha!'.

I am still carrying the rolled-up map. Each of my arms aches in turn, after ever shorter intervals, as I have to keep the arm securing the map from pressing against my side to avoid creasing it. Now and then I hold it at one end between thumb and forefinger, but when I do that I can't let my arm hang down because the map would trail on the ground. I lag behind Nummedal and hold the map to my eye like a spyglass. Have to stop myself using it as a trumpet. Oh God! What misery, I would wail.

The mountainside is interrupted by a small plateau. Here a tall ski tower has been erected, from which a wooden slide protrudes like a tongue made of logs. We go inside, climb up countless steps, and arrive at last on a platform with parents and children leaning over the parapet admiring the views.

The tower is situated near the tip of the fjord. You can see nearly all of it from this height, with the sprawl of the city on the left and dark forests on the right.

'Und geben Sie mir jetzt die Karte!'

I unroll the map. He flips up his extra lenses. Points. Flips the extra lenses down again. Speaks. Taps on the map with the back of a pencil. Points into the distance again. He's giving a lecture. I dare say he's been coming here with his students these last sixty years.

There's a French saying: not knowing which leg to dance on.

I don't know which leg to stand on.

I lose all grip on my thoughts: like birds fleeing a cage when the door is left ajar, they take wing into the landscape.

The fjord is deep blue, while the blue of the sky so far north seems almost too timid to call itself blue. Craggy mountains, toy-town houses. A world-famous panorama. Seeing this and dying – by whooshing down the slide made of logs, which stops abruptly above a round lake. In winter the slide is covered in snow, of course, and the lake frozen over. How many times do I whoosh down, ski-less, snow-less, while Nummedal pontificates? If only he'd given me the photographs – how happy I'd be to listen to his every word, how enchanted by the wonderful scenery.

When finally he comes to the end of his lecture I see that the map has been the wrong way up all along.

6

We take the same train back. We have been together all afternoon, but he is as remote as ever. Rambles or excursions of
this nature usually end with the professor telling jokes, bad-
mouthing colleagues, or telling you about their dogs, cats,
children.

Not so Nummedal. Looking at his watch through his
magnifying glass, his mouth turns down in disgruntlement.
He has run out of topics of conversation and can't wait to
be rid of me.

Evening is very long in coming.

We climb the stairs at the terminal station and find
ourselves in the centre of Oslo once more.

Nummedal flips down his extra glasses.

He is about to take his leave, because he stands still.

I thank him very much for putting himself to all that
trouble.

But the pleasure was all his – as if I didn't know that
already.

'Herr Professor!'

I have to force the words out of my throat as if I've
choked on a lump of coal: 'Herr Professor, do forgive me
for going on about this, but could we come to some arrange-
ment about the aerial photographs?

'Aerial photographs?'

'The aerial photographs of Finnmark. I realise you can't lay your hands on them from one moment to the next, but what if I call at your office tomorrow, some time in the morning, perhaps your secretary could . . .'

'I don't have any aerial photographs for you. Aerial photographs! Of course we have aerial photographs at my institute! But aerial photographs for you to use in the field – how could you think . . . ? We don't go out and take those photographs ourselves, you know.'

'But Professor Sibbelee said . . .'

'What does Professor Sibbelee know! How can Professor Sibbelee make promises about my aerial photographs? If you want aerial photographs, you must go and get them from the Geological Survey in Trondheim, which is where they are kept. It is on your way up north, anyway. Pay a visit to the Geological Survey! Østmarkneset, Trondheim. Direktør Hvalbiff! He will be pleased to see you. They have just moved into a splendid new building, of which he is very proud. He will be delighted to give you a tour and show you everything! Hvalbiff is your man. I will telephone at once and tell him to expect you.'

Nummedal proffers his hand.

'Goodbye, sir, I wish you the best. Do give my regards to Arne and Qvigstad! And do call at my office after you have finished work in Finnmark. Don't forget.'

He flips up the extra lenses.

'I will relieve you of that map, shall I? Goodbye!'

He steps to the edge of the pavement. With two lenses on his forehead and two before his eyes it's as if he has armed himself with four headlights.

He points his white stick into the rush of traffic. Drivers

step on their brakes. He crosses to the other side. The street seems to close up behind him.

Now what?

It would be remiss of me not to send Sibbelee a postcard.

From a revolving metal display I select one with care: a colour postcard of the ski tower. I head back to my hotel, holding the card by a corner, flapping it absently from time to time as I ponder what to write on the back. Nothing appropriate comes to mind, because all I can think of is what I really think: . . . your note introducing me to Nummedal hasn't been much help. He's old, nearly blind and possibly not fully aware of what's expected of him. He kept me busy all afternoon, but not before airing his low opinion of Holland.

For you, my estimable mentor, he has little regard. Apparently you took issue with him in your youth, for which it seems he is still seeking revenge. After some carefully worded comments slighting your scientific achievements, he took me under his wing and talked of nothing but his own exploits. None of this had anything to do with the purpose of my mission, but I listened patiently. To the end he treated me as if I were an admirer come to pay homage. But all that time he must have known the only reason I called on him was to collect the photographs. I . . .

Where is my hotel? Shouldn't I have reached it by now? My surroundings are completely unfamiliar to me. Nothing remotely like where I'm staying. There aren't even any shops around here. Dead to the world, this neighbourhood, an unlikely place for a hotel. From my inside pocket I take the small street map I found in my room last night.

I've been going in the wrong direction! I always get lost, always. How many times haven't I lost my way in foreign cities?

It takes me another hour to locate my hotel, and still it isn't dark. Back in my room, I order a whisky. Sorry, sir, not allowed. As a last resort I drain a large glass of water, sit down at the small bureau and, with my mouth opening and shutting like a fish out of water, I scrawl on the back of the ski tower postcard:

> Dear Professor Sibbelee, a quick greeting from the North, although not yet the High North. I met Professor Nummedal this morning; he asked me to convey his best regards to you.
> I am very grateful for this valuable introduction. Professor Nummedal gave me a warm welcome and took the trouble to take me on an instructive tour of the environs of Oslo!
> For the aerial photographs he directed me to the Geological Survey in Trondheim.
> Alfred I.

The only space left for my signature is in the bottom left-hand corner, and I consider it a lucky twist of fate that there is no room for the rest of my surname.

7

Scandinavian countries have numerous qualities to recommend them, one of them being the strength of their sanitary installations.

The shower is a bristle brush of water. I stay under it for a long time, as if I could slough off the entire wasted day. Start all over again. But when finally I turn off the taps, I ask myself: Was it really a wasted day? Maybe Nummedal's intentions were good. Maybe he genuinely tried to obtain the aerial photographs for me, without success, and simply wanted to make up for it by taking me on that tour. Maybe telling me to go to Trondheim was the best advice. Maybe his gruffness was due to embarrassment at not keeping his promise to Sibbelee.

I return to the bedroom dripping wet, twiddle the knobs on my transistor radio. I can actually receive a Dutch station here. Let me see. There's someone talking into a microphone.

It's a professor of physics, giving a lecture. Fascinating Facts from the World of Science and Technology – in terms comprehensible to the layman.

Sounding a note on the flute, he says, requires an air speed of a hundred and twenty-five kilometres per hour.

*

What was that? A hundred and twenty-five kilometres per hour? That's hurricane force. I have that kind of figure on tap, promising young scientist that I am.

You need to blast the air with your mouth at a speed of a hundred and twenty-five kilometres per hour for the flute to produce a sound.

I never realised that, and yet I played a fair number of flutes between the ages of seven and fourteen.

My first flute was a plain celluloid instrument. I could play the national anthem on my flute, but one day I held a magnifying glass to it to find out whether it would burn. It caught fire, I dropped it on the floor, the flames went out for lack of fuel, but my mother was deeply shocked. She gave me a recorder made of ebony. Not long afterwards I found out that the flutes they played in real orchestras were of the transverse type. My mother said transverse flutes were very expensive, too expensive. That was long after my father died, but my grandfather was still alive, and he gave me a flute he had played himself as a boy. A big transverse flute with six openings and eight valves. It was made up of four segments screwed together end to end, with rings of ivory marking the joins.

First we'll see how you get on by yourself, then I'll decide if it's worth your having flute lessons.

I wanted to be a flautist, a professional flautist in a big orchestra. My mother didn't like to say no, but she was not pleased with my chosen career.

It was six months before I was able to get any sound out of the big transverse flute. At the market I bought an old book of flute studies. By the age of fourteen I was playing quite well, but then I made a fatal discovery. The flutes they played in real orchestras were quite different from the one I had. They were so-called Böhm flutes, a variety invented by one Theobald Böhm, and they didn't have six openings and eight valves like mine. The technique was quite different, too. My flute wasn't even good enough for the school orchestra. I asked my mother, who seldom refused me anything, to buy me a proper Böhm flute. But my mother said: 'Do you know you'll have to start again from scratch? And I hope you realise that people don't become world famous for playing the flute. The violin, yes, or the piano. Flautists mostly play the accompaniment in big orchestras. It's the best they can hope for, and even then all they get to do is perform music they didn't compose themselves.'

Her last point tipped the balance. I took to collecting rocks, because becoming a biologist like my father did not appeal to me. Instead of a flautist I would be a scientist.

And, yet, in all those years playing the flute I never stopped to consider the speed of the air passing through it, let alone how that speed might be measured.

Water in my ears, a towel over my hands, I stand there, shamefaced. An enquiring mind seeks to measure and count.

I have even made a habit of counting my paces, in imitation of Buys Ballot, who formulated Buys Ballot's law. (If a person stands with his back to the wind in the northern hemisphere, the area of low pressure is found to his left.)

Wind . . . but it was someone else who had the idea of measuring the wind passing through a flute. Not me.

Just as I'm about to change the station on the transistor, the professor observes that the speed of the air current in whistles was calculated by Christiaan Huygens – all of three hundred years ago.

I switch off the radio and climb into bed. I can't get to sleep. At this extreme northern latitude the sun doesn't go down far enough. The windows are blacked out with curtains, but it's impossible to forget the daylight outside.

At half past four I'm still awake. The bus from the S.A.S. office to the airport leaves at eight. If I fall asleep now, I may not wake up in time. But I don't fall asleep.

At five I give up and get out of bed, open the curtains and take another shower. By the end I feel drowsier than before, but there isn't much point in lying down again. Naked, I sit on my bed and consider. I decide I might as well pack my suitcase now, and go over the contents of my rucksack again.

Hiking shoes, hammer, sleeping bag, water flask, mug, new notebook, camera, films, the geological compass Eva gave me in my first year at university. It's quite large, with a rectangular base, precision degree scale, sights, clinometer, spirit level and mirror.

I snap it open and peer at my reflection. Eva had said the mirror made it a funny sort of present. She had said: 'I didn't know geology was a science that makes you look in the mirror all the time.'

She was twelve at the time, my little sister.

Not only was she the first person in my experience to define geology thus, she was quite right where I was concerned.

Over the years I must have taken the compass from its

case ten times more often for a quick glance in the mirror than for taking measurements.

The mirror is so small that when I can see my nose and eyes in it, my ears are invisible. And when I look at my chin I can't see my eyes. Even holding it at arm's length doesn't allow me to see my entire face.

But I would hate to part with the little mirror.

If you ask me, the history of mankind falls into three significant stages.

In the first, man didn't recognise his own reflection, any more than an animal does. Show a cat a mirror and it reckons it's a window with another cat beyond. It hisses, prowls around the mirror. Loses interest eventually; some cats ignore their reflected image altogether.

Man was no different to start with. One hundred per cent subjective. An 'I' that could question a 'self' did not exist.

Second stage: Narcissus discovers the mirror image. The greatest sage of Antiquity was not Prometheus, who gave fire to man, but Narcissus. Henceforth the 'I' sees a 'self'. There was no demand for psychological insight at this stage, for man was to himself what he was, namely his mirror image. Whether or not he liked what he saw, his self did not betray him. I and self were symmetrical, each other's mirror image, no more than that. We lie and our reflection lies with us. Only in the third stage were we dealt the blow of truth.

The third stage begins with the invention of photography. How often do we think our passport photos do us justice? Hardly ever! In former times, when people had their portraits painted and they didn't like the result, they blamed the artist. But the camera can't lie, as we all know. So it is revealed to you over the years through countless photographs that you aren't really yourself most of the time, that you and your self are not symmetrical, indeed that you exist in a variety of strange incarnations for which you would refuse all responsibility if you could.

The fear that other people will see him as he appears in the portraits he disapproves of, that they might never see him the way he likes to see himself in the mirror, has caused the human individual to fragment into a general plus a band of mutinous soldiers. An I seeking to assert itself amid the constant clamour of alter egos. This is the third stage, in which self-doubt, previously a rare state of mind, flared into consternation.

Roll on psychology.

At least my compass assures me of one soldier I can rely on, one who'll stick with me through thick and thin, who'll write my thesis for me *cum laude* and who'll gain a professorship one day. When the newspapers ask for his picture I'll go on taking his portrait until I've got one that's just right. But this morning he's red-eyed for lack of sleep – and I have such trouble sleeping as it is. His chin is stubbled, because I haven't shaved yet.

I have my shave and get dressed. I pack my rucksack and suitcase with deliberation. The items I will leave behind in Alta can go in the suitcase: white shirts, electric razor, etc. Into the rucksack go my notebook, thick socks, ballpoint, pencils, hammer, ever-useful polythene bags, hiking shoes, sleeping bag, transistor radio. Steel measuring tape? Can't find it anywhere. May have left it at home. I make a note in my diary to buy one in Trondheim. *Steel measuring tape* I write beneath *Østmarkneset*, where the Geological Survey is situated.

Before going down to breakfast I give the bathroom a last once-over, as well as the wardrobe, the bureau and the bedside table. No, nothing lying around. I even check the drawers and cupboards I didn't use, just in case. I can't stand hitches of any kind. Leaving things lying around, landing in situations unprepared, being tongue-tied — what could be worse? I will not accidentally fall to my death in a mountain chasm like my father, and if I do fall I will have to be prepared. Losing my footing will not take me unawares. I will manage to hang on to something, or else to break my fall.

I have already put my suitcase and rucksack out in the corridor, and just as I make to shut the door behind me, what do I see?

Something on top of the coat rack. It is the postcard I wrote to Sibbelee last night.

Discovered in the nick of time!

8

At the first call for the flight to Trondheim I make my way calmly to the aircraft and board with a friendly greeting to the stewardess.

I stow my mac and camera in the overhead luggage net, sit down and yawn. For the next hour or so there is nothing for me to do other than doze, and I let my eyelids droop. Not heavy enough – they lift again.

The seat next to mine is vacant. I am by the window, looking out on to a wing, so there is nothing much to see.

The stewardess walks past with an armful of newspapers. I pick one at random and leaf through it.

Almost involuntarily, I begin to read.

DUTCH EXPEDITION RELIES ON SHERPA CELEBRITIES

It's a report about that Himalayan expedition – the one Brandel is on.

We make our first camp beside the airfield of Pokhara, close to such Himalaya giants as Annapurna (8078 m), Machhapuchhare (6997 m) and Lamjung Himal (6985 m), whose ice-capped summits dominate the entire region . . .
All we have to do now is wait for Wongdhi the

Sherpa-sirdar who left Kathmandu eight days ago with a team of a hundred porters.

The term 'Sherpa' is generally taken to mean a high-altitude bearer or mountain guide, no doubt due to the name Sherpas have made for themselves on previous Himalayan expeditions, but in reality it refers to a specific tribe.

Experience

Wongdhi is only twenty-nine but has already earnt an excellent reputation on the Himalayan circuit. Recently he accompanied our French friend Lionel Terray on the ascent of Jannu in Eastern Nepal, a height just short of 8000 metres, and it is interesting to note that Wongdhi, unlike Terray, did not use oxygen. He also took part in the Women's Himalayan Expedition to the summit of Cho Oyu, an undertaking which ended tragically when the leader, Claude Kogan, was overtaken by a giant avalanche together with Claudine van der Straeten and three Sherpas. One of them was Wongdhi, the only member of the party to survive. In broken English he described how he was able to dig himself out with the aid of his penknife, which he always carries in his top pocket. Several of his fingers were damaged by frostbite and later amputated in France.

Omelette

We have another Sherpa celebrity in our midst . . . Danu the cook. All expeditions nowadays vie for the services of this young man, known for his extraordinary cooking skills and exceptionally good humour. For Danu the high point of the day doesn't arrive until evening.

When we settle down to enjoy a moment of leisure after a gruelling day, he starts rushing around to attend to our needs. Tea is usually served within five minutes, often accompanied by a delicious omelette . . . almost better than back home!

At times I had the impression Danu simply made for the nearest cottage and snatched the kettle from the hob . . . so as not to keep the sahib waiting! In short, Danu's a great guy!

Loyalty

A minor incident that occurred during this expedition may serve to illustrate the Sherpa mentality. As Brandel and I lay sleeping in our tent near a mountain hamlet, some child started pelting our tent with stones from on high. Immediately the Sherpas came running to chase the little blighter away.

Soon after that, having drifted off again, I was woken by a scuffling sound close by . . . it was Danu, lying down across the opening of the tent in his sleeping bag, his pick at the ready to protect his sahibs should the need arise. The fact that it rained during the night was immaterial: Danu remained at his post till daybreak. It is clear why the Sherpas are so highly esteemed for their loyalty and devotion.

Weight

The porters or coolies are mainly recruited from the area around Kathmandu, where large numbers of men have made portering their profession. The wages here are considerably lower than in Pokhara, where local men may be hired by the day in between their other occupations. Loads of thirty to thirty-two kilograms are normal during expeditions, but the porters are capable of carrying more than twice that weight, if necessary from early morning till late at night.

It is by no means unusual for a porter to carry a load of seventy kilos and more over long distances into the mountains, although it is a very slow process. We saw the most astonishing demonstration of load-carrying at the airfield in Pokhara. Included in our equipment flown in from Kathmandu was a crate weighing one hundred and twenty-five kilos. None of the adult men volunteered, but a lad of about seventeen hoisted it on his back and carried it up the slope for about two hundred metres. Afterwards he was weighed by one of our doctors – thirty-seven kilos!

Setting out
As regards our ascent of Nilgiri, we can rely on trusty Sherpas such as Wongdhi, Dorjee, Danu and Mingma Tsiring putting on a good show when it comes to setting up high-altitude bivouacs, and more than likely at least one of them will accompany us to the summit.

Trusty Sherpas putting on a good show . . . I've had enough of reading the paper, so I lay it down on the seat beside me . . .

Sitting in a plane always gives me a sense of being conveyed somewhere without actually travelling. Out of the window I can't see anything but the wing, nor is there much to be seen on the back of the seat in front of me. Where else but in Western civilisation would they invent a means of transport requiring no more than passing a couple of hours facing the back of a seat fitted with a little net containing sturdy paper bags in case of air sickness?

A far cry from the loyal Sherpa! The loyal, mountain-climbing Sherpa who is prepared to carry burdens four times his own weight for the convenience of his sahib! Who's going to help me carry my burden?

Arne wants to borrow or hire a horse in Skoganvarre to carry our gear for us the first part of the way – twenty-five kilometres. That's all, after twenty-five kilometres the horse will have to go back. There's nothing for horses to eat where we're going. So back it will have to go after just one day.

From then on we'll be carrying several weeks' worth of rations and all the other stuff we need on our own backs. No horse. No loyal Sherpa sleeping across the front of the tent in the pouring rain to protect his sahib. No Danu the chef, whose services are so much in demand. Danu of the extraordinary cooking skills and cheerful nature, Danu who doesn't stop at house-breaking to get hold of a kettle of boiling water! Merely to serve his sahibs a nice cup of tea at the end of a weary day!

I have no idea how much weight I'm capable of carrying on my back, when it comes down to it. Twenty kilos strikes me as a fair weight. Twenty-five? Possibly. Stupid of me not to have done a dry run at home first. Loading my rucksack with as much as I think I can carry, then weighing it. Subtracting a percentage from the total weight to allow for the fact that I won't be carrying it in short bursts, but for hours at a time over rough, rock-strewn terrain, up hill and down dale.

On the other hand, what good would it do to know exactly

how much I think I can carry? The likelihood is that our combined baggage will be divided into three equal loads. And I wouldn't want to carry less than my share, in any case.

I've never actually been on an expedition like this before. I've had some experience camping, but there was always some village nearby to buy food in the evening. *There's a first time for everything, Mama.*

Of course, Alfred. No use blaming me for having missed out on sporting activities.

I was never one for sport, I have to say. Had I not chosen a career that obliges me to travel I'd have been a real scholar holed up in a study. As it is, I have no choice. What else can you do in a study besides study other people's books?

I am not interested in finding the kind of rock samples everyone else has already put in little boxes. No, I'd go further and say: I am not interested in finding rocks that have always been on earth. What I really want to find is a meteorite, a lump of stone deriving from space, preferably composed of matter never hitherto encountered on earth. The philosopher's stone, or, failing that, a mineral that would be named after me: *Issendorfite.*

What was the date of that newspaper? The day before yesterday. But the article could have been despatched from Nepal three weeks ago.

Brandel has never been a close friend of mine. He's different in all sorts of ways. Likes a lot of action. Always eager to take a risk. The main reason he went to university was to give his love of sport an academic edge. Won medals for long-distance skating, a skilled alpinist by the age of seventeen. Did two hundred kilometres an hour on a motorbike: *going so fast that the trees along the road blurred into a hoarding.* Never read a book to the end if he didn't have to.

It could be that Brandel is reaching the summit of Nilgiri at this very moment. Let's see, my watch says five to nine. By my reckoning it must be about three p.m. in Nepal.

So it's possible.

Brandel's summers from the age of seven were spent in Switzerland. Scaling mountains like a chamois. Yodelling, too. Didn't drink or smoke. Switzerland! I've never been there myself, unless you count the time I travelled through on a night train.

A load of thirty to thirty-two kilograms is normal. I suppose I should be able to manage that. I wonder what my daily food intake actually weighs. Would a sandwich weigh fifty grams or less? I haven't a clue. Don't reckon I can carry sixty kilos, though. I weigh just over seventy kilos myself. How much was it that young Sherpa weighed? Thirty-seven kilos. And he carried one hundred and twenty-five kilos uphill over a distance of two hundred metres. In excess of three times his own weight. In my terms that would work out at two hundred and twenty kilos. A pointless calculation. A three-tonne truck weighs something like ten thousand times as much as a Dinky toy, but that doesn't make it ten thousand times stronger. If a man were, relatively speaking, as strong as a flea, he'd be capable of dragging a railway carriage behind him single-handed, but no-one can do that.

In my mind's eye I see Sherpas filing past. Sixty kilos suspended from a wide band around the forehead, backs so

43

bent their hands almost touch the ground. Crooked legs, incomprehensibly spindly like those of donkeys.

I could of course reduce my load by leaving behind my transistor radio. Saves three hundred grams.

Brandel is a friendly sort of chap, always ready for a laugh, never gets into arguments. An inveterate optimist. People like that are beyond me, but I believe they're quite content. A bit like dogs, really. A dog's life: proverbial misery. Yet most dogs are optimistic.

And why shouldn't Brandel look on the bright side? He's got Wongdhi the Sherpa-sirdar and one hundred porters to convey his toothbrush and pyjamas to the summit of Nilgiri.

As for me, I have just wasted a whole day trying to get some conceited, near-blind old codger to give me the aerial photographs I need.

9

Trondheim strikes me as the kind of place I could grow fond of.

Russet wooden warehouses along the waterfront.

All the buildings here are made of wood. It's odd to see trams riding in the streets. There ought to be a law against trams in wooden towns. Not a real town. More like a replica, fashioned not by carpenters but by cabinet makers for display at some world fair.

But I have no time to lose. The plane to Tromsø leaves three hours from now, and I still have to lay my hands on those photographs.

In the taxi I keep an eye out for the sights of Trondheim. I see a large cathedral with copper-green roofing. Also a red-and-white communications tower.

Sunshine, clear blue sky. I don't feel in the least drowsy, and just now, when I told the taxi driver I wanted to go to Østmarkneset, he understood me even though I don't know any Norwegian and had to guess at the pronunciation.

We drive across a long bridge, after which the town rapidly thins out.

The road isn't even metalled any more. Rolling hills. Tall

spruces. Here and there a row of new wooden houses, no longer the work of craftsmen but of machines.

The taxi pulls up. The driver turns to me, reaches over the passenger seat to open the door on my right and points to a half-finished structure ten or twelve storeys high.

'Geologisk Undersøkelse,' he says.

I can see why he can't drop me off any closer. Surrounding the block is a zone of potholes, primed radiators, felled trees and sawn timber. I pay him and get out of the car.

Although there are bricks in ample supply, there isn't a bricklayer in sight. But then, as I draw near to the building, I catch sight of two workmen struggling to right a sheet of plate glass the size of a small football pitch.

I wave at the men, calling out:

'Geologisk Undersøkelse!'

I can see myself reflected in the glass between them.

One of the men doesn't react, both his hands being occupied, but the other frees his left hand briefly to describe a circle in the air.

I set off in the indicated direction, walk around the perimeter, find my path blocked by bushes, don't dare go back, push my way through the bushes and find myself in a kind of forecourt with a parked jeep and a vehicle on caterpillar tyres.

Some warm-up for my meeting with Direktør Hvalbiff!

I pause to dust myself down. Anyone watching? No.

This part of the building appears to be finished. It has windows and even a small door.

There's nothing to stop me entering, and I step into a narrow corridor. Finding the secretary's office is my next challenge.

One I needn't rise to. A figure emerges from a laboratory filled with throbbing machines. He comes towards me, smiling. He has white wavy hair and wears a bow tie. I give him a meaningful look, thinking he must be Direktør Hvalbiff in person.

'I'd like to speak to Direktør Hvalbiff, if I may,' I say.

All innocence.

And I *am* innocent.

'Direktør Hvalbiff? He is not in today. I am Direktør Oftedahl, of the Statens Råhstoff laboratory.'

'Isn't the Norwegian Geological Survey in this building?'

'Not in its entirety, or rather not yet. But maybe I can help you. Come with me.'

I go with him, down the corridor and into his office. He seats himself behind his desk and motions me to a chair.

'Our building is by no means finished yet, as you can tell. What did you want to see Direktør Hvalbiff about?'

'Professor Nummedal made an appointment with him on my behalf. I'm from Holland, doing postgraduate research. My thesis will be about the soil structures of Finnmark. I was supposed to pick up some aerial photographs at Professor Nummedal's office, but he didn't have them. Professor Nummedal said I could get them from Direktør Hvalbiff, here in Trondheim. Professor Nummedal said he'd telephone Direktør Hvalbiff to tell him I was coming.'

'Telephone? From Oslo?'

As though eager to redress any oversight that might have been committed, he picks up one of the two telephones on his desk, asks something, says something, of which I can only make out his concluding words: 'Takk takk'. He replaces the receiver.

'They don't know anything about a phone call. Direktør Hvalbiff was here briefly yesterday, then went straight back to Oslo. We are in the process of moving, you understand, and most of the property of the Geological Survey is still in Oslo. Both our departments will be housed in these new premises.'

He begins telling me about the new building. Direktør Oftedahl's English sounds flawless to my ears, and apparently he considers mine good enough not to propose switching to another language. He talks at length. He's not in the least concerned about my having come all the way here for nothing, nor about whether Hvalbiff did or did not react to a putative telephone call from Nummedal.

Oftedahl's face is red and fleshy, with white bushy eyebrows like overhanging eaves, but the scars on his neck draw and hold my attention. The bow tie is far too small to hide them. All the way up to his jaw his throat looks as if it has been scooped out with a large spoon. I can't imagine what kind of operation this could have been – but then what do I know of operations? It doesn't look as if there could be much left of his larynx or his tongue, but there must be, because he has a strong, deep voice, and, given his clear diction, there can't be anything wrong with his tongue either.

'Is there any chance,' I ask, when he's run out of steam about the problems of relocation, 'that the aerial photographs have already have been moved here? I can't think why else Professor Nummedal would send me to Trondheim.'

And in my mind I add: Professor Nummedal was positive that the photographs were here.

*

Oftedahl rests his forearms on the desk and eyes me intently for a moment or two, then says:

'Possible. Possible. Let us have a look.'

He stands up.

I get up too and move to the door while Oftedahl comes out from behind his desk.

Beside the door hangs a framed photograph, a portrait with an autograph: *Roald Amundsen*

'Amundsen,' I say, while Oftedal holds the door open. 'Is the signature real?'

'It certainly is. Do you know why Amundsen was successful? He wore clothes made of animal skins, with the fur on the inside. He didn't wear anything underneath. Capacious, warm clothes, you understand, warm and yet well ventilated. Whereas others, such as Shackleton and Scott, wore thick shirts and woollen underpants. Their clothes got drenched in sweat, froze solid in places. It was impossible to get them dry. But Amundsen was fine. That is why he was the first to reach the South Pole.'

We go down the corridor, turn a corner and find ourselves in another corridor, low-ceilinged, wider than it is high.

'It doesn't bear thinking about,' Oftedahl muses, 'the way explorers like Amundsen had to relieve themselves – at fifty degrees below zero, ha ha! It must have been a very quick business!'

The corridor, lit by concealed ceiling lights, has moiré rosewood panelling and a parquet floor.

*

'So you studied geology,' Oftedahl says, tearing himself away from Amundsen and the South Pole to focus on me again. 'Interesting. My training was as a geophysicist. My department keeps track of every significant geological finding. I feel like a warehouse steward at times, and then I regret not being a geologist. I spend too much time in the office with paperwork. Fieldwork is better, more romantic. Geologists are the last explorers in the world.'

He laughs.

'But do watch out! Better not step on the planks, just use the beams. The builders are months behind schedule, as usual in the construction business. All this ought to have been finished long ago.'

The parquet flooring comes to an end. No more partition walls either. Nothing like a corridor or passage. We cross a floor surface that is no more than an unmade-up layer with concrete pillars between one slab and the next. At the far end of the space is a stairway of raw concrete, up which we go.

'What brought you to Norway?' Oftedahl asks as we arrive on the next level, which is in the same unfinished state as the one below.

'I met a Norwegian student in Amsterdam called Arne Jordal, who told me about Finnmark. We decided to take a trip there together this summer. He has been there before, so he can show me the ropes. We'll keep each other company, but we're researching different subjects.'

'Good, good. There is someone else who will be in Finnmark this summer, a petrologist by the name of Qvigstad. He works at the Geological Survey.'

'Yes, I know. Arne Jordal wrote to me that Qvigstad would be coming along. They both studied under Professor Nummedal.'

He nods, and I grin, because at least he's heard of the expedition I'm joining. No fear of him taking me for some impostor, then.

We arrive in another section of the building, which is for the most part finished: concealed neon striplights in the ceiling, rosewood panelling, parquet floor. Oftedahl opens a door.

The room is unfurnished and still smells of new wood and paint. There's a telephone in the middle of the floor. Oftedahl strides towards it, crouches down, lifts the receiver, dials a number. I wander off to the glass curtain wall, on which someone has painted two large Os with whitewash, and beneath: *Jane Mansfield*

A white ship steams across the fjord. White steamer, blue water, blue sky, slopes with black fir trees like wet raven's feathers stuck in the ground. The white steamer has a yellow-banded smokestack.

Behind me I hear Oftedahl saying something in Norwegian, pausing, saying some more, pausing again.

'Mange takk.'

He replaces the receiver. I turn round to face him.

We leave the room together. I hope his telephone conversation in Norwegian was about the aerial photographs, expect him to broach the subject at any moment, but he keeps silent as I accompany him down the corridors, to what purpose I don't really know.

'Your new institute is wonderfully situated. The view is terrific.'

'This sort of view is fairly common in Norway. Do you know Professor Nummedal well?'

'I only met him yesterday, I had a letter of introduction from my professor in Amsterdam.'

'I see. Nummedal is a nationalist, a chauvinist, you know. You don't speak Norwegian, so you wouldn't have noticed, but he speaks Nynorsk. He comes from the Bergen area.'

Oftedahl laughs, a bit like the way people in Holland laugh whenever partisans of Frisian have their say.

Yet more concrete stairs.

'Nynorsk,' Oftedahl says, 'is one Norwegian language. There are two, and that with a population of under four million. As if two languages weren't enough, there is a campaign underway to promote the use of Samnorsk as a third.'

I have lost track of which level we are on now. My shoes are covered in white dust. The windows are still missing up here, and I shiver in the cold air. We step over loose planks and beams, avoiding puddles of rainwater.

'Direktør Hvalbiff and Nummedal do not see eye to eye. It is probably just as well Hvalbiff is not here to receive you. Because if he were here I doubt he would have given you the photographs you want, even if he knew where to find them.'

Once more we arrive at a section of the building that is finished. The doors to the offices are open. Some desks are already occupied by secretaries. A grey lady comes towards us, as if summoned by Oftedahl.

They talk. She must have been the person on the other

end of the telephone earlier. Oftedahl steps aside and introduces me to her.

'We are very sorry,' he says slowly, 'but we are in the middle of organising our archives. I do not know my way around yet, and besides not all the material has been moved here.'

I feel my cheeks flush with joy. Aha! A glimmer of hope! So not everything has been moved yet, but my photographs are bound to be here already. I can't imagine Nummedal sending me all the way to Trondheim for nothing. Of course he must have telephoned. Hvalbiff just wasn't there to receive the call, and thank goodness for that, if he hates Nummedal so much. On the other hand, there could be any number of people already working in these wonderful premises. How can Oftedahl, head of a different department altogether, know whether anyone took a call from Oslo yesterday?

The three of us proceed down a corridor. Scatterings of chairs, ranks of steel filing cabinets. Towers of crates which we have to squeeze past. The grey lady ushers us into a room furnished with two desks and littered with boxes.

She takes a box from the top of a pile and opens it.

The photographs are stored upright.

'Go on, take one.'

I try to do so. But the box is so tightly packed with them that I can hardly get my fingers in. When I get hold of one at last I cause a tear in the corner as I pull it out. Flustered and stammering, I study the photograph feeling as if I'm committing an indiscretion.

Sure enough, it is an aerial photograph. I recognise the ocean, with a snippet of coastline, a serrated stripe in the lower right. There's a little clock to be seen in the upper right, indicating seven past three. In the upper left an altitude meter the same size as the clock indicates the height at which the photograph was taken. Impossible to decipher without a magnifying glass. There is also a number in the margin. I turn it over to look on the back. Stamped: *Ministry of Defence*. Nothing about the location.

'Isn't there a list corresponding with the numbers?' I ask.

In the meantime I inspect the label on the box. Just as I feared: only numbers, no names.

Oftedahl says:

'A list corresponding with the numbers? That will be an entire card index, I expect.'

'Quite possible,' the grey lady says. 'This has never been my department. I didn't notice any filing systems when I unpacked the cases. And Frøken [*unintelligible*], who is in charge of this, is in Oslo.'

'Ah, problem solved,' Oftedahl says. 'I suggest you give Frøken [*unintelligible*] a ring in Oslo, ask her to take a look in the catalogue so she can give you the numbers of the Finnmark photographs, then you will know which box they are in.'

Starting back to the corridor, he says something in Norwegian, then motions me to accompany him.

He draws me into another room on the same floor. Inside, on an oak table, stands an old-fashioned display case, likewise made of oak, containing a large scientific instrument with elaborate brass fittings.

'Do you know what this is?' Oftedahl says, as if he's forgotten completely what I'm here for. Instead, he launches into an enlightenment session for my benefit.

'The great Heiskanen! I know geophysics is not your speciality, but I am sure you know of him.'

*

Only now do I notice the Rotary cogwheel on the lapel of Oftedahl's jacket, and then, on his right hand, a wedding ring as well as a signet ring set with a stone the same colour as his bow tie.

'It was with this gravimeter,' he says, 'that the great Heiskanen conducted his fundamental research into the isostatic uplift of the Scandinavian Ice Sheet. The great Heiskanen! Surely you've heard of him? Ah, geophysics is up and coming! Gravimetry, seismology, magnetic field measurements! In a word, geophysics is the earth science of the future! As for geology, it is, in a sense, becoming outdated. As there are dead languages, there are sciences that will one day become dead sciences. You know, once the basic principles had been discovered, there were not that many more discoveries to be made. It became an applied science, a bag of tricks enabling us to find out, or rather to *guess*, what the invisible substratum looks like. But along with the new geophysical techniques we have developed a sort of radar, as it were, which allows us to see right through the strata of the earth's crust. So why go to all that trouble with tents, hammers, maps and notebooks? An interesting life, yes, but less so for someone who knows he is wasting his time, who is aware that far better methods exist. When it comes down to it, the traditional geologist is little more than a glorified bookkeeper. Compared to a modern geophysicist he is just about as up-to-date as a bookkeeper using pen and ink instead of a computer! Without geophysics the supplies of oil and natural gas would long have run out. Or, on a simpler level, consider how aerial photography has revolutionised our knowledge of this planet! Not only can you see everything a hundred times better on an aerial survey, you can see a hundred times more than someone standing on the ground in the middle of the bushes or up to their knees in mud. Ah, here's Frøken [*unintelligible*],' he says, and switches to Norwegian.

She must have slipped in through the door which Oftedahl left ajar. I didn't notice her at first, so I'm a bit taken aback.

She holds her hands piously folded in front of her chest. But her hands are empty – no catalogue, no aerial photographs either.

When she has finished replying to Oftedahl she steps up to me to shake my hand: 'Goodbye, sir.'

Oftedahl escorts me in person to the main entrance, which, since I missed it on my way in, is from my perspective the main exit.

As we go down marble staircases, Oftedahl explains that, unfortunately, he cannot be of any further assistance to me. His secretary called Oslo and was told the catalogue has already been packed and could even now be on its way to Trondheim. It is definitely not in Oslo.

'Is there anywhere else,' I say, and I know I'm only saying this not to lose all sense of hope, 'I mean, do you think I could get aerial photographs anywhere else around here?'

'Anywhere else? You do know that aerial photographs are classified material, don't you? It's the same all over the world. Only exceptionally are they are made available, under very strict conditions, for specific scientific purposes. Besides, the ones you want are of Finnmark, so close to the Russian border! A load of nonsense, probably, because why would the Russians want to steal our photographs? They can take their own. But that's the way it is. I recently met a professor of economics who thought you could buy aerial photographs at the newsagent's, just like postcards, ha, ha. People can be so ignorant.'

He laughs, sighs, and concludes with:

'So sorry your efforts have been wasted. I hardly dare suggest you return in a fortnight. The catalogue will certainly have arrived by then, and we will have unpacked the cases, too. But yes, of course, I realise that your time is limited. Well, well. Goodbye to you, sir, it has been a pleasure. Good luck. Have a good time in Finnmark!'

The hallway is lined with mirrors on every side. Pressing one after another to see whether they resist or give way, I leave my sweaty fingerprints all over the glass. Once I have located the door I turn round for a final look.

Oftedahl is nearing the end of the passage. He turns to the right, and I see him in profile against an illuminated stairwell. The lower jaw and the missing throat.

One day his whole head will be reduced to a fleshless skull, but for now not even his voice betrays that part of him has gone already.

10

I am curious about what my neighbour is reading.

Swivelling my eyes, twisting my upper body as unobtrusively as possible (has he noticed? . . . No I don't think so . . .) I try to make out what sort of book it is.

In between short bursts of reading he puts the book face down on his lap and spreads his hands on top. He has an anchor tattooed on his right hand, his white shirt is creased, but clean. His cheap tie is roughly knotted, his suit old-fashioned but seldom worn. Spotless, but badly pressed. Obviously a sailor. Wears sweaters and overalls on board, so his good suit lasts for years.

When he's not reading he stares into space, chewing a wad in his cheek.

There's another tattoo on his left hand, but I can't tell what it represents. The hand slides off the book. It's a Teach-Yourself-English book for Dutch learners.

'Are you going to Tromsø?' I ask him.

'Are you Dutch?'

'What did you think?'

'On business, are you?'

'No, no, I'm heading further north. Family visit.'

*

This untruth escapes me before I know it, which I regret, as I don't fancy telling lies any more than going into details about my trip to the high north.

'Seaman, are you?' I ask quickly.

'I'm replacing a cook who jumped ship in Tromsø. I hate flying, you know. It's the shipping line – they send you.'

He turns the book face up again.

'English is so difficult. Can you make sense of that?'

He points to a line. It says: 'Does Alfred go to the races? No, he doesn't.'

'Why is it "does" and not "goes"?' he asks. 'I don't get it.'

'It's only a manner of speaking,' I explain. 'When the English ask something, they use "do" to activate the verb. Not like the Dutch.'

'Where's the sense in that?'

'Well, I can't help it, that's just the way it is. In English, when you ask a question like that you begin with "do you ..." or "does he ...", followed by the verb in the infinitive.'

Infinitive ... I bite my lip the moment I've said it. Why can't I explain anything without sounding pedantic?

'Right,' he says, 'know all about it, do you? I can tell you're an expert.'

'The English say "do you smoke?",' I continue (he did ask, after all), 'they don't say "smoke you?" like in Dutch. They see smoking as something you do, they make you do the smoking, as it were.'

'Well, you're wrong there,' he says, 'what they say is "have a smoke".'

He takes out a packet of North State, which he waves under my nose.

I accept his offer and light up.

'North State,' he says. 'Here in Norway they call them South State.'

'Really?'

'You do smoke. Me not smoke. Me tobacco,' he says pointing to his cheek.

I grin.

'How do you say this in English?' he asks.

I may have all the answers, but I don't have aerial photographs.

'To chew tobacco,' I say.

'Too choo tobbacko,' he echoes slowly. 'Do me a favour and write that down for me, will you?'

I write the words down, first in the correct spelling, then in a Dutch phonetic version.

'I can see you've had plenty of schooling,' the seaman says. 'If I'd had half the education you had, do you reckon I'd be up in this plane being taken somewhere I don't want to go? Not likely! I'd be my own boss. Can't sleep at night for thinking about stuff like that. How I'd feel if I'd had the opportunity to do a bit of learning.'

He turns to his book again. Flips the pages.

He keeps asking questions. Eager.

All those little things he doesn't know and I do – they are so much part of me that it is years since I felt any satisfaction at knowing them. But that doesn't alter the fact that I haven't got the photographs, and that there's no-one I can get them from now.

The sailor is unrelenting in his praise of my prodigious knowledge. My gloom lifts a little. It is the first time in my life that I feel pride at knowing English.

He doesn't let up until I've accepted all his remaining cigarettes.

Hearing the stewardess making the landing announcement over the intercom, I suddenly realise that I forgot to buy a measuring tape in Trondheim.

11

As plant cover diminishes and forests peter out the further north you go, buildings become lower and settlements more scattered. Is this a general rule? Perhaps. Perhaps not. What business is it of mine?

I must wait until tomorrow to continue my journey, and have nothing better to do than dwell on such truths.

Here in Tromsø you hardly notice when it's evening. At this time of year the light never fades completely. This is the empire on which the sun never sets. Hold on, I think to myself, that's a sentence I can use when I write my mother a postcard.

I walk down a street with pale blue wooden houses. It's broad daylight, it's not a public holiday, yet no-one's at work because it's half past ten in the evening.

People are out and about, roaming the streets, no-one seems ready for bed. Youths just like the youths in a Dutch backwater grope the same sort of girls, who comb their hair as they walk. What is different here is that their ice creams come in big cones, much bigger than the ones at home. There are very few cars, if any. A tranquil dream-town, where the sound of footsteps prevails!

There is a souvenir shop with reindeer hides, traditional Lapp costumes, reindeer antlers, doilies, boat-shaped sleds, postcards of Technicolor Lapp families, bear skins. A stuffed polar bear stands guard by the door.

Everyone strokes its fur in passing, me too.

A father hoists his young son onto the bear and aims his camera.

The ironmonger is shut. Mustn't forget where it is. I'll come back in the morning for that measuring tape. It's easy to locate – the shop is on a square that slopes down to the water.

In the middle of the square is a bronze statue on a rectangular base, a bluish figure in arctic clothing.

I'm looking at the statue from behind. Who is it? I walk up to it and read the name on the plinth:

ROALD AMUNDSEN

Facing the fjord, the conqueror of the South Pole looks over the water to the black mountains beyond, their peaks laced with white snow even at this time of year.

He stands with his feet wide apart, as though permanently braced against the storm. Bare-headed, though. His hood rests in ample folds around his neck. His anorak is as long as a nightshirt and the thick tubular trouser legs overlap the tops of his boots.

His forehead is high, the hair on his bony scalp cropped short. His moustache is bushy and dignified, and it is hard to visualise it encrusted with icicles, which would make the explorer look far less serene. Maybe not so hard, after all.

The stories about explorers I read as a boy come floating back to me in gory detail. Amundsen surviving by eating his own dogs. The dogs, in turn, eating each other. Shackleton eating ponies. He used ponies instead of dogs, which caused insurmountable food problems; the more ponies he took with him, the more insurmountable.

And then there was Scott.

Scott. Battling to reach the South Pole in his frozen thermal underwear, his toes frostbitten, but his heart pounding in his throat at the idea of treading on ground that had never been trodden by man . . . Ground? Snow then. And treading on snow heretofore untrodden by man is something anyone with a back garden can do in winter.

What else was new?

A gaze cast skywards to a zenith never before observed by man? What sight would meet those eyes? Not stars, because in January it never gets dark in Antarctica.

So what did Scott get to see at the South Pole? The Norwegian flag flying from a ski pole planted in the snow. Note attached: *Greetings from Amundsen and good luck to you, sir.*

So he turned back. His companions died one by one. Scott himself slowly froze to death in his tent, in his thermal underwear which hadn't been dry for months. Unlike Amundsen, he didn't have jerkins made of turned animal skins. Until the very end he continued to write up his diary. It was found afterwards and published in a special issue of *The Earth and Its Peoples*, which I read when I was fourteen.

'For God's sake look after our people.'

Scott's words, written at death's door. I wonder if it ever entered his mind that they might one day be published in a magazine. I expect it did. Maybe not, though, maybe he always wrote in that vein. Most people don't write down what they're really thinking. Not: my half-frozen thermal long johns stink to high heaven. Or: at fifty degrees below zero our urine freezes into reeds of yellow glass in the snow.

That is not the way they write. They keep the flag flying, even if they're not the first to plant it at the South Pole.

Poor Scott. If aerial photographs had existed in those days . . . But they didn't, not in 1911. They do now. But not everyone has them.

I stroll along the waterfront, past fishing boats with orange steel balls on deck and hulls painted in primary colours. Screaming gulls swoop over quays strewn with fish offal. It is a quarter to eleven and the sun has fitted me with long, dark shadow-skis.

Spanning the fjord is a bridge two kilometres long and so high that an ocean liner can easily pass underneath. I make my way up the ramp. It isn't steep, but it's a long way and quite tiring.

A large vessel draws near. Leaning over the side of the bridge, the sun on my face, I lose myself in the ship passing below. Standing at the rail is a figure wearing a hat, who looks remarkably like Arne. I give him a wave, you never know. He waves back, but that doesn't mean anything, because people on ships always wave back. People using different modes of transport always wave at each other. Besides, it's an American ship, and there's no reason why Arne should be arriving by sea at all.

Reaching the other side I decide to take the cable car to the top of the cliff: *fem kroner, takk, tur og retur.* I soar right across the tree line, after which the slope is bare. The gondola is filled with peaceably drunk Norwegians. I wish I could tell them how congenial their company is.

The gondola slides under a projecting roof and shudders

to a halt. Upper terminal. All the passengers get off, but they don't stray far over the rugged surface of forbidding rock.

Tourists stand huddled together, lifting their faces to the sun. The rounded crags are bald, with here and there a patch of moss. Inky clouds in the distance are tipped with white, making them look like another stretch of mountains, immeasurably higher than where I'm standing now.

An American woman paces restlessly about, her head covered in a rigid auburn hairdo. Catching sight of me she comes over and starts talking to me as if we have met before.

'I'm going to be stuck here until midnight! We can't go back down before, because of the midnight sun. His dearest wish is to see the midnight sun in Norway. That's all he cares about lately, even when it's raining. Until now there's always been a cloud sliding over the sun at the very last moment. I can't understand what he sees in it. We've already been to Spitsbergen – hunting cruise, you know, ten days there and back. Arctic safari they call it, two and a half thousand dollars, all in. It was awful, believe you me! D'you know what they do? There's no need to leave the ship at all. You just stay on board. The ship goes up to the edge of the ice. The crew shoots a seal and makes a bonfire on the ice. They throw the seal into the fire. Then the polar bears show up, attracted by the smell of burning seal-fat. Those bears are very tame, they go up on their hind legs and paw the side of the ship. And then everyone starts shooting. They call that hunting! Jack wanted to shoot a bear with a bow and arrow! I told him: Jack, you're crazy. You're just like Fred Flintstone – you know the one, from the cartoon series on television? So I say to Fred, I mean Jack: You should've been born in the Stone Age. A bow and arrow, that's crazy!

But he says: It's more sporting. More sporting indeed . . . what a dummy! He shot three arrows, but that didn't kill the bear, of course. It looked almost human, a great big darling teddy. It sank down on its backside and tried to pull out the arrows with its teeth. I've never seen anything more horrible! Can you imagine? The red blood on that white fur. In the end the captain finished him off with a bullet. Crazy old Jack wanted to do it himself, but the captain said, very politely: Just leave it to me, sir. And right he was. You can be sure I won't be using that bearskin back home. Not in my bedroom, anyway. Which reminds me. I'm forty-one and you, honey, are about twenty-three I guess, and I can see you're not Italian, or I'd say let's leave him right here to enjoy his midnight sun, while you and me go down in that cable car and find a hotel.'

She laughs. No, she wasn't a beauty when she was young either, although she's quite slim and shapely. If she hadn't made that remark about me not being Italian, then I . . .

'Is it twelve yet?' she asks. 'I haven't got a watch.'

I push up my left cuff and show her the time: five minutes to go.

'Thank God for that,' she says. 'Oh well, maybe a bit of staring at the midnight sun will do him good. He hasn't had much sunshine in the night, I have to say. Know what I mean? But he's only got himself to blame, you know, too eager for his own good . . . Boy, oh boy!'

She swings round towards a cluster of tourists.

'Jack, Jack, it's midnight now!'

I consider telling her that although my watch indicates twelve, that doesn't mean it's twelve o'clock solar time. But then I realise that I don't know the exact geographical longitude of Tromsø, so I won't be able to tell her at what time the sun will in fact reach its lowest point. Telling her she's got it wrong and not knowing the right answer myself – perish the thought.

So I mutter:

'There's a gondola leaving in a moment, and there won't be another one for half an hour. I can't wait that long. The sun is the sun, also before midnight.'

And I take my leave from her at three minutes to twelve.

I go down in the cable car and head back to the bridge.

Making my way across I keep my eyes on the American ship I watched earlier as it passed beneath the bridge. It is now docking. *City of Chicago, Chicago,* it says on the stern.

For the next twenty minutes – the time it takes me to cross to the mainland – my eyes don't leave the ship. Passengers with luggage swarm over the decks.

The nagging doubt at the back of my mind swells into a conviction so strong that I can't help acting on it. I continue down the ramp quaking at the knees. Drawing level with the ship, I have a full view of the decks. A gangway has been lowered to the pier. People are disembarking.

The man I waved to earlier could very well have been Arne! There could have been a change of plan, some hitch, happens all the time. It's due to a succession of hitches that I haven't got my aerial photographs, so why couldn't something have gone wrong with my appointment with Arne?

We were supposed to meet up in Alta, but who knows what has happened: he could have sent a message which I never received, suggesting another meeting place. Such as here in Tromsø. I must get to that ship as quickly as possible.

The bridge forces me to make a frustrating detour. Being

so high in the middle, it extends a long way over land before reaching ground level. I have no choice but to follow it to the very end, and all this time passengers are leaving the ship.

Arne could easily have disembarked by now. Where will he go looking for me? There aren't many hotels in Tromsø . . . The least I can do is find out if he's on the passenger list.

Having reached the end of the bridge at last, I double back towards the pier. I come across a straggle of passengers, the last to leave the ship.

No Arne. My next thought is that maybe they aren't passengers at all, just people taking a stroll.

I run up the gangway, looking left and right for a crew member to direct me to the purser's office. No-one tries to stop me. I enter the first unlocked door I come across and find myself in a narrow passage leading to the foredeck.

The man I took for Arne is standing there with his hands in his pockets and his foot propped on a winch, talking to a sailor. The sailor's jersey has horizontal stripes that ripple when he slips his hand beneath it to scratch his chest.

The man does not look in the least like Arne. Nor would he if he stopped screwing up his eyes against the sun. The midnight sun, for all I know.

I leave the ship without having spoken to anyone.

It is still too early for bed, so I keep walking. After a bit I'm back on the square with the statue of Amundsen.

True, he had the advantage of those inside-out animals skins, but he didn't have Sherpas: loyal, tea-serving, sahib-venerating Sherpas for whom loads of thirty kilos are the norm and loads of sixty no exception. How heavy was that crate again? – the one the young Sherpa carried two hundred metres uphill? A hundred kilos? A hundred and fifty?

The stuff they print in the newspapers!

Sitting on the base of Amundsen's statue there are now three boys with their arms around three girls. The grass surround is dotted with crocuses, a sign of early spring at home. The air is filled with the cold screech of gulls.

I notice to my surprise that there is another monument on this square, which I evidently missed earlier on. It is not very big, hence easily overlooked, and headless. Just a rough chunk of red granite, with a bronze plaque fixed to the top.

I spell out the inscription. I am so intrigued that I write it down in my pocket diary:

Eidis Hansen labukt Balsfjord 1777–1870 bar denne steinen frå fjaera her og omlag hit. Steinen veg 371 kg.

Although I don't speak a word of Norwegian, the meaning is quite clear. I needn't have bothered to copy it out – I would have remembered anyway. Eidis Hansen. Carried 371 kilos. And he (possibly she?!) lived to the age of 93.

12

The weight of my assorted belongings adds up to just under thirty kilos.

This is confirmed when my suitcase and rucksack are weighed at the airport, which is just a small wooden building with a very long, narrow jetty protruding into the water. That is all.

There are six other passengers wandering about, idly helping themselves to leaflets from the counter and then putting them back. Two of them are men in waders carrying bundles of fishing rods. There is also a woman with three little girls, all of them wearing ski-pants. We wander in and out of the building.

The sky is bright, though sunless.

But then, just as the green seaplane touches down, the sun bursts forth, as if the aircraft had ripped open the lid of clouds. Walking to the end of the jetty, I suddenly think my trip is going to be a great success.

There are ten seats on the plane, five down each side, each with its own little porthole.

The net on the back of the seat in front of me contains the regulation sick bags as well as a route map mounted on cardboard showing the coast and the mountains in meticulous detail. A couple of post office sacks are tossed aboard, after which the hatch is slammed shut.

*

This is flying the way our great-grandparents must have dreamt of it. The wings of the aircraft extend from above the portholes, so my view is unobstructed.

The seaplane cruises at an altitude of roughly 300 metres. The coast and the mountains look like scale models. It is easy to recognise the map in the landscape: coastline, bays, islets, glaciers, rivers, barren heights. A pity we are not flying over the terrain I will be exploring for my thesis.

My thesis! I have been poring over the names on the cardboard map for some time, but now my concentration vanishes. My failure to obtain the aerial photographs washes over me like a wave of toothache. My imagination shifts into overdrive. Those photos nobody would give me – I wouldn't even need them if I could get hold of a helicopter . . . But how? . . . Maybe a sports plane, then . . . No, a helicopter might be better after all . . . An army helicopter? Or one belonging to the Topographical Service?

I'd be able to survey the terrain from any altitude I liked! I'd be able to take my own photographs! And the moment I spotted something interesting I'd bring the helicopter down to collect a sample. Is this the latter half of the twentieth century or what? What else are helicopters for? If I were studying medicine I wouldn't be deprived of X-rays or cardiograms, would I? It's like being a kid in craft class having to saw away with a little handsaw instead of a mechanical one. Or expecting an apprentice chef to prepare a cordon bleu meal on a wood fire or a single burner.

Nummedal, Oftedahl, Hvalbiff and the whole Geological Service – they can stuff their aerial photographs.

Snag is, I don't have a helicopter.

*

I remember vividly Sibbelee's reaction when it dawned on him that I would be needing aerial photographs.

Sibbelee displays certain symptoms when about to make a pronouncement he is unsure of. Bluffing is signalled by a thrust of his underdeveloped chin. But an underdeveloped chin does not lend itself to thrusting. What happens is merely that the skin is stretched taut from chin to Adam's apple while the head is thrown back.

'Aerial photographs,' he said, displaying all the said symptoms of bluffing, 'of course you need aerial photographs. They are a must in modern research. You can't get away from that.'

As if I had any intention of getting away from it!

'But how can I obtain them, Professor?'

'I shall send a note to Nummedal. Nummedal is an old friend of mine, so that should be no problem.'

My expression must have been one of relief, joy and admiration, because Sibbelee's usual self-congratulatory smile spread across his face as his bluff went uncalled. A smile which at first you take to mean: aren't I wonderful and famous and in the know, but which you realise later meant: managed to avoid dropping myself in it, thank God.

Either way, at the time I thought it was perfectly normal that Sibbelee should ask his old friend in Norway to supply me with aerial photographs.

And it *is* normal, surely. The fact that I still do not have them could easily be due simply to a succession of failed connections.

It must have slipped Nummedal's mind that I was coming. He's an old man, after all.

As for Hvalbiff, he knew he couldn't get me the photographs, because they were in transit from Oslo to Trondheim, but what could he have done about it? I had probably left already, and anyway Hvalbiff wouldn't have had my address, and so had no way of letting me know they were not in his possession.

And Oftedahl? Oftedahl had nothing to do with it, being the head of a different department. Still, he put himself out for me. I can't reproach him for anything, he was very obliging . . . as far as I know . . .

13

The seaplane tilts sideways at such a steep angle that my porthole is almost parallel to the ground. The same goes for me, with my face against the glass. Alta slides past under my eyes: small houses dotted along a huge bay. Trees in the low-lying areas, bald heights. As if the treeline were the result of a gigantic hand reaching down to sweep the vegetation off the slopes and batten it down in the valleys.

The plane rights itself again, the water now is very close. The floats seem poised to seize the surface, like the talons of a bird of prey.

Landing on water. I hadn't noticed how odd that sounds before. The engine stops. All the noise, the throbbing, dies away. Like waking from a dream: one moment you're flying, the next you find yourself floating on a vast expanse of water.

The pilot emerges from the cockpit and opens the hatch.

The silence gives way to the low chugging of a motor-boat. There's not even a jetty here in Alta, unlike in Tromsø. The boatman throws a rope to the pilot, who is waiting on one of the landing floats.

I step out of the cabin onto the float and from there into the motorboat. My rucksack and suitcase are passed down.

At this distance from the shore I can't see whether anyone has come to meet us. Arne?

Behind me the seaplane splutters to life again with a succession of loud bangs.

I look back and watch as the plane gathers speed, the floats generating great waves surging towards our motorboat. Tossing on this man-made swell, we head for the shore.

Arne? Yes, Arne. He is waving his hat. He looks like the man I mistook for him in Tromsø, except that he is waving his hat much more slowly than the other person did.

People in thinly populated countries favour the slow manner of greeting. I don't have a hat, so all I can wave is my hand.

The seaplane swerves and banks in an avalanche of noise. I follow it with my eyes until it disappears and then look back to the shore.

Some way up from the water's edge a road follows the contour of the bay.

The man is still waving his hat. He is not Arne. He stops waving. He is accompanied by a woman and three children, all wearing trousers and tall boots.

They move away without waiting for me to come ashore. They must have been mistaken, like me, thinking or hoping I was someone they knew. Or they just stopped out of curiosity.

I am harrowed with uncertainty. Was I right after all, yesterday in Tromsø, when I thought the person waving at me from the ship was Arne? Because it's quite possible that Arne had already left the ship by the time I got there, and that the person I saw later wasn't the one (i.e. Arne) who'd waved at me in the first place.

The motorboat pulls up to the beach, the engine is cut, the bottom scrapes over pebbles. I step ashore.

A sharp sting sets my left eyelid twitching. I clap my hand to my face and my fingers come away smeared with splattered mosquito. My head is wreathed in mosquitoes. They settle on my forehead, my nose, the backs of my hands. I have to take charge of my luggage, so am powerless to fend them off.

The boat is left behind, deserted.

So this is it. Where do I go from here? There is a wooden staircase leading up from the beach to the road, which has a low boundary wall of stones.

I load my rucksack, grab my suitcase and have just started climbing the stairs when I catch sight of someone on the road trotting in my direction. I can only see his top half. No hat of any kind. He vaults over the boundary wall and runs down the slope. I am struck by how thin his legs are, but also by his agility and sure-footedness. I stop and wait. All the time he looks straight at me, smiling, but not waving.

Arne is wearing tall boots and an anorak. The strings of his down-turned hood dangle on his chest.

'Hello!'

'Hello, Arne!'

Arne immediately takes hold of my suitcase and goes up the stairs ahead of me.

'The plane is usually an hour late,' he says when we are up on the road, walking side by side. 'I still had some shopping to do, I did not expect it to be on time today.'

He speaks a cautious form of English, picking his words carefully, keeping things simple.

'We will leave the suitcase at the house. You can change there. The bus leaves at three o'clock. Plenty of time. Okay?'

*

Arne is about a head taller than me. His hair is very fair and quite long. It is already thinning at the back and greying at the temples. Everything about him seems old, although he is only a year older than me: twenty-six. His clothes are decidedly old, with patches on his trousers as well as on the elbows of his anorak. I saw him glancing at his watch when he said the bus would be leaving at three. It is not a proper wristwatch but an old pocket watch mounted on a leather strap, the way they were sold ages ago when wristwatches first came into fashion.

'A long journey, isn't it, all the way from Amsterdam?'

The platitudes I offer in return (How is he? When did he arrive in Alta?) do nothing to convey my relief at our meeting having gone to plan.

It suddenly comes to me that I live in constant fear of having to survive in a world where everyone is out to fool everyone else. Intent aside, though, there's no reason why Arne couldn't have had an accident half an hour before my arrival. Run down by a car. Or a heart attack – how strange, the family would think, there didn't seem to be anything wrong with his heart. So young, too! Or he could have had a fall. Lost his footing on an apparently innocuous rise and come crashing down, possibly slamming his head against a crag.

I break out in a sweat, constantly brushing mosquitoes from my hands and face. Glancing at Arne, I see that his head is also under attack.

'I could have got here two days ago,' I tell him, 'if I had travelled straight here from Oslo. But I went to see Nummedal, and Nummedal said I should call at the Geological Survey in Trondheim on the way.'

'Who did you talk to over there? Was it [*unintelligible*]?'

'Hvalbiff wasn't there.'

'[*Unintelligible*] is Nummedal's sworn enemy.'

'So I gathered in Trondheim.'

'It's Nummedal's chauvinism that gets to everyone in the end.'

'Chauvinism? Nummedal did mention . . .'

'He talks about it to every foreigner he meets, and goes on and on about his fellow Norwegians' lack of patriotism.'

'I did meet some Norwegians who were somewhat apologetic, saying everything was much better in London than in Oslo. But the Dutch attitude to foreigners is the same. I was on a train once and there was this Dutchman showing a Spaniard the Dutch royal coat of arms on his passport. See this? he said. Dutch lion. Now only dog. This was in Spain, mind you. And it took the Dutch an Eighty Years War to get rid of Spanish rule.'

'Well,' Arne says, 'the longest spell of independence for Norway has been the last sixty years. First it was the Danes, then the Swedes. Our language is of no consequence in the rest of the world. Every student has to know English, French and German. Without them you can't complete a degree. Because of this our own language has sunk to the level of some sort of patois, a medium for apprentices. The most advanced studies are written in foreign languages. The great minds come to us in English by way of English textbooks – a language we can read quite easily, but which we can seldom speak or write without making mistakes. I notice it even now, as I am trying to explain this to you. If I were speaking Norwegian, I could be more subtle, more precise.'

'I understand you very well.'

'Still, having to speak a language that is not your own means having to step back, there is no doubt about that. Why do you reckon colonised peoples like Negroes, Indians, and so on have a reputation for being like children? Because they were forced to communicate with their masters in languages they did not know too well.'

'Don't any good books get translated into Norwegian?'

'Of course they do, there are plenty of translations. But you can't get away from the fact that you're not reading the real thing. Some people find that depressing.'

'Depressing? Why? It's only depressing if you think in terms of nations, and each of those nations wanting to be top dog. But the world is one big conglomerate. You know that.'

'Know?' Arne retorts. 'Yes, I know *here*' – slaps his forehead – 'but not *there*.' He stabs a finger at my chest. 'And do you know why that is?'

I tell him I have no idea.

'It's because deep inside everyone, however sensible, lurks a madman. A raving lunatic, a lunatic who may not be clinically insane but whose condition develops from the same source: from the child we were when we were one, two, three years old. That child, you see, learns only one language. The mother tongue.'

Arne says all these things quietly, not too fast, not too slow, in a clear, even voice. Which is remarkable given that we are going up a steep, sandy incline. No huffing and puffing from him, and yet he is climbing at the same steady pace as he was walking before.

'If you're a small country,' he says, 'where politics and fashion and films and cars and machines and practically everything else is imported from abroad, and if beyond that practically all essential books, that is to say the books that are right, books that contain the truth, books that are better than most local books, the "founding books" so to speak – if those books are all foreign, then the countries producing them will regard you the same way as colonial powers regard their colonies, and city folk regard the provinces. Colonies and provinces, they're on a similar plane – not up to date, unsophisticated, always getting the wrong end of the stick, ignorant, backward, and so on.'

We have now reached the top of the sandy rise, where we join another road, unmetalled, but nevertheless a main road. Modest timber bungalows stand among the trees on either side. There are no gates and no fenced-off properties.

A little girl on a tricycle rides alongside us for a time, not using the pedals but pushing herself along with her feet. She calls out to a boy launching a toy glider in the air with a catapult. The glider gets caught in the top of a spruce.

'What did she say?' I ask.

'She said "watch out!" But children don't listen to what other children tell them. Children are more likely to believe their fathers than someone their own age. We do the same, we're always more inclined to believe a foreigner than a Norwegian, even if the Norwegian knows what he's talking about. Whenever someone comes up with a new idea here in Norway, people say it can't be any good because it hasn't been written about in American books. But if an American makes some nonsensical claim and a Norwegian contradicts it, they say: What does he know? He's from the sticks! Let him go to America for a year! In a small country it's always the copycats who get the acclaim. That applies on all levels. Now that Ibsen and Strindberg are dead, everyone is convinced they were the greatest writers Scandinavia ever had. But not when they were alive! Any old woodcutter qualified for the Nobel prize . . . but Ibsen and Strindberg never got it!'

Arne halts.

'This is the house,' he says, 'mind you don't step on the grass. Grass is a rare plant as far north as this, so people are very careful with it.'

A screen door twangs shut behind us.

'The owners are away in Olso. They have lent me the house.'

Arne puts my suitcase down in the middle of the living room. I unload my rucksack and clap my hands to my cheeks, swatting the mosquitoes that followed us inside. Arne takes a spray can from the mantelpiece, and a mist released by the pressure of his index finger spreads a smell of camphor.

It is clear that Arne is using this place to camp in. This is no exaggeration: he has turned the living room into his first bivouac. The furniture has been pushed back to the wall. On the floor lie a tent, tent poles, a half-packed rucksack, a folding spade, boxes of knäckebröd, tinned food, a theodolite and a hefty wooden tripod with adjustable legs.

I stoop to pick something up.

'What's this?'

'A fishing net. To catch fish on the way. Otherwise we won't have enough to eat.'

'What about the horse? Did you have any luck hiring a horse to take our gear to the first camp?'

'Not yet. Maybe later. We'll see how we get on in Skoganvarre.'

The net is one metre wide by fifteen metres long, coarse-meshed and made of pale blue nylon. There are corks attached along one side, and little weights along the other.

'How is this used? Do you drag it through the water?'

'No, you just let it hang upright. The fishes get their gills caught in the mesh.'

I open my suitcase, take out a pair of corduroy trousers, thick woollen socks, a dark blue cotton shirt, my hiking shoes, a jumper and a windproof jacket with a zip.

I take off my tie, shoes, grey flannel trousers, nylon socks and shirt. I put on the other clothes. I slip a belt through the loops of the corduroy trousers and attach my compass case to the belt in such a way that it hangs to the right of my stomach. Into my pockets go cigarettes, matches, handker-chief, penknife and the measuring tape I remembered to buy in Tromsø. Before stowing it away I pull it out to arm's length; fine quality steel tape, two metres long, nice and flex-ible, white on the side with the markings. Well! Not every-thing has gone wrong, then! My meeting with Arne has gone exactly according to plan, and I didn't forget the measuring tape, either!

Fifteen minutes later we slip our arms through the straps of our rucksacks and set off.

A frayed string hangs round Arne's neck with the ends tucked into his right breast pocket. I am intrigued by what he's got in there. He doesn't seem to own anything that isn't old and worn. Take his camera – a case that's so scuffed the leather looks inside out, a badly cracked shoulder strap about to fall apart and a loose buckle which has been reattached with a bit of bent wire. Not only is his anorak patched, even his rucksack has been mended: with squares of canvas in different shades.

14

Before Arne shoulders his rucksack I furtively heft it to check how heavy it is: much heavier than mine.

When we are outside I say, more out of concern about not pulling my weight than out of politeness:

'Look here, you're carrying more than me. That's not really fair.'

'Don't worry, you'll make up for it later on, once we've stocked up on all the food.'

I gladly take his advice not to worry, in so far as the prospect of having to carry even heavier loads permits.

We make our way between the bungalows and spruces back to the main road. The ground is almost completely bare, and every single spruce around here is stunted. I am carrying the tripod, which is heavy, switching it from one shoulder to the other at intervals. Mosquitoes keep settling on my face and on the backs of my hands. Even cigarette smoke doesn't keep them away.

Arne points to the leather case hanging from my belt:

'What have you got in there?'

'A compass. Care to take a look?'

I open the case and hand him my compass.

'Jesus, what a beautiful instrument. Did you buy it specially for this trip?'

'No, I've had it since I started at university.'

'It looks brand new,' he says, with what I take to be a guarded look.

'My sister gave it to me seven years ago. She's always afraid I'll get lost.'

Feeling discomfited for some reason, as if I'm telling a lie, I return the compass to its case.

'So you have a sister?'

'Yes, six years younger than me. She's an odd girl. Pretty, but very dim. Because she's religious, you see, superstitious even. Were you brought up a believer?'

'Fortunately not.'

'We weren't either. I wasn't even baptised, nor was Eva. But she's considering having it done now.'

'There's a book called *The Face of God after Auschwitz*,' Arne says. 'A fine face that must have been . . .'

We both break into nervous laughter at the thought of what God saw when He pulled that face.

Can this be Alta's high street? At any rate the bus station is here, with the post office across the way.

We set down our luggage beside that of the other prospective passengers. Arne crosses to the post office, I stay behind.

Among the people waiting at the stop are several Lapps. I study them intently, comparing their clothing with the post-cards I have seen. No two are dressed alike. Standard European dress has crept up on them in fits and starts.

One old man still wears the home-made boots of soft rein-deer hide. Some of the women have changed to wearing ordinary shoes and flesh-coloured nylons, which clash horribly with the rest of their outfits: the bright blue blouse gathered at the waist with a belt, the red cap with ear flaps.

They sit huddled together on the edge of the pavement, talking in low voices, their faces wrinkled and waxy, wreathed in smiles. Their hands are blackened by ingrained dirt, which almost makes the skin gleam. Suspended from a strap over their shoulders they carry a sort of swag-bag encrusted with a variety of metal objects: medals, figurines, coins, I can't tell what all of them are. The men also have enormous knives hanging from their belts, in leather sheaths curved at the tip.

The sole inhabitants of the land I am heading towards. What would I ask them if I could speak their language? Whether they're happy? But that isn't something you'd ask someone whose language you do speak, either. Whether they feel their life is better than ours? Whether they ever wish they were ordinary Norwegians? They'd probably say they never stopped to think about it.

Arne emerges from the post office, waving a letter as he crosses the road to join me. A letter? Who from?

The letter is from my mother. I wish she'd get off my back. A letter already – she must have written it the moment I left or it wouldn't have got here so soon. I don't feel like reading what she's got to say just now, so I stuff the envelope in the breast pocket of my windproof jacket and trail after Arne.

He goes into the bicycle shop next to the bus station. The salesman and Arne exchange elaborate, formal greetings. Then the bicycle man smiles at me and says:

'How do you do, sir?'

Arne, it turns out, has decided we need cloth hats (American Army Surplus) with a flap of mosquito netting all round. I put mine on at once and tie the net under my chin. Another essential purchase is Finn-Oljen, an extra strong mosquito oil, which we promptly smear on every bit of exposed skin. FORSIKTIG! *Warning! Harmful to mucous membrane*, it says on the label.

We busy ourselves with the oil until the bus arrives.

The rucksacks are loaded on the roof. We board the bus, and just as the driver makes to shut the door a Lapp woman comes hurrying towards us, carrying a toddler with a leg in plaster. The driver rolls forward a short way towards her and stops to let her in.

'Tell me, Arne, are the Lapps discriminated against, on racial grounds, I mean?'

'They used to be treated a bit like second-class citizens, but not any more. We do all sorts of things for them. But it's difficult to get them to send their children to school.'

'Do the Lapps speak Norwegian?'

'Most of them do. They don't speak it among themselves.'

'Can a Lapp achieve any position in society he chooses?'

'I've never heard of a Lapp having that kind of ambition. All it takes is a change of clothing – once they take off their traditional costume they're as Norwegian as the rest of us.'

'So why don't they?'

'Because they feel different. I reckon the sense of difference is primarily connected with language. That alone is enough to make them think along different lines. Lapps probably think: Why bother, we will only be seen as fake Norwegians anyway. They would become estranged from all their relatives. And why should they want to do that? Being a Lapp is nothing to be ashamed of.'

'Hardly a comfortable lifestyle, though.'

'Most people get their self-respect from forgoing comforts of one kind or another.'

*

The bus rides over a long narrow bridge. There are no cars, and trees are becoming a rarity too. The road is of compacted earth, because there is no kind of surfacing material that can withstand the sub-zero temperatures.

Now and then we go past a bulldozer levelling a section of the road that has become rutted in the past winter. The bus rolls along at a steady, slow speed, most of the time in clouds of dust.

Arne and I sit with our maps spread out on our knees, making notes of such features as catch our attention. Hills, lakes, rapids, ravines. The sky is clouding over. The sun sparkles in the wide, shallow rivers as though celebrating the last of its victory over the rain.

When we're in the middle of an open plain covered in heathery shrubs in shades of dark green, pale green and red, the woman with the toddler tells the driver to stop. She gets off the bus into the driving rain; it's raining so hard the water coursing down the windows distorts the landscape. The woman heads into the wilderness carrying the child. Not a footpath or even a track to be seen.

'What happens when a Lapp falls ill?'

'They can go to Alta, or to Kautokeino, or Karasjok, whichever is nearest. But the majority of Lapps no longer lead a nomadic life in tents, they have jobs in fish factories and so on. The Lapps still keeping reindeer tend to be very rich, with herds running to several thousand animals. Plenty of children and plenty of reindeer, that's what they want. The way people cling to tradition sometimes makes me despair of rational arguments ever improving the lot of mankind.'

*

We have been going for about two hours when we arrive in Skaidi. There is a wooden stall selling lemonade, chocolate and hot sausages. The bus stops just long enough to allow the passengers to stretch their legs. This is the highest point in the region.

I go for a stroll, hands in pockets. All the passengers are wandering about, in different directions. The sky is now thick with dark clouds and it's as chilly as a cold winter's day in Holland. I look out over the rounded hills, some topped with large, smooth boulders. Pools and small lakes in the low-lying areas. Some distance away, by the largest of the lakes, I spot a tent made of reindeer hides wrapped tepee-style around poles.

An old Lapp emerges in full regalia, holding a pair of reindeer antlers in each hand. From his mouth hangs a curved pipe, and although he is unshaven you can tell by his sunken cheeks that he hasn't a tooth left in his mouth. He ambles along, doesn't come towards us and doesn't engage anybody in conversation.

The Lapps travelling with us ignore the old man, but another passenger, a youth in the traditional white student's cap, buys an antler from him.

The bus starts up again, makes another halt in Russenes, then continues its journey.

It is half past ten by the time Arne and I get off at Skoganvarre.

15

A stretch of calm water. A river widening into a lake. A few spruces, none of them tall. Dark slopes.

The driver clambers onto the roof of the bus to pass down our rucksacks, which we set at the side of the road. Lastly, he hands us the wooden tripod.

The bus departs, then silence. The rain has lifted, the clouds have dispersed, the sun is low but blazing in full force. At home, when the sun shines like this at the end of a summer's day, we know dusk will soon fall. As it is, it's going on for midnight, and this is as dark as it will get. I rest the tripod against my shoulder.

A wooden house designed like a villa with conservatory stands at some distance from the road. In front of the house, slightly to one side, is a green tent.

Arne says:

'Qvigstad may have gone to sleep already, or else he's gone off somewhere.'

The tent is zipped up all round. Arne goes up to it and I hear him call Qvigstad's name as well as some other words. Arne sinks onto his haunches. Straightens up again.

'Gone fishing, I suppose.'

To keep myself occupied, I take both our rucksacks, one in each hand, over to the garden.

'Mind the grass. It's even rarer here than in Alta.'

'What's next?'

We cover our faces and hands with mosquito oil, then we both have a cigarette.

'Since we've got to be off again in the morning there's not much point in pitching our tent.'

'So where will we sleep?'

'I'll ask if we can spend the night on the porch.'

He means the conservatory, which is admittedly little more than a glassed-in porch.

While he goes to ask permission, I retrace my steps, taking care to avoid the patches of grass. I cross the road and sit myself down by the lake.

Nothing grows in the water here, which is so clear you can see the rocks on the bottom. The larger ones rise up above the surface. Whether the very largest qualify as islands is a matter of opinion.

I try to imagine what it must be like to spend all your life in Skoganvarre. There have always been people here, who did nothing but eat, drink, sleep, hunt and fish. What about the winters? The first snow falls towards the end of September, as far as I know. Their winters are devoted to staving off calamities. They have to ensure they have sufficient food and fuel. They have constantly to be on their guard, to know immediately what to do when someone falls ill. Or when a woman goes into labour.

Plop. A fish leaps from the surface and drops back into the water.

Snow in winter and thick clouds of mosquitoes in summer. Concentric ripples fan out from the spot where the fish jumped. Should I take a look at my mother's letter? It can wait.

On the far side of the lake I catch sight of two men with

fishing rods walking on either side of a threesome — no, foursome — of little girls, all holding hands. Their high-pitched voices gain a faint echo by the time they reach me. I hear a cuckoo calling. And also, intermittently, a sound like hedging shears snapping open and shut. But there are no hedges here, no shears either. Arne appears at my side, holding something resembling a small aluminium pan without a lid.

'It's all right,' he says, 'we can use the conservatory.'

He carries the pan by a rod jammed between the sides. Coiled around the exterior is a long nylon fishing line with a shiny spoon and a hook attached to one end.

'Feeling sleepy yet?' he asks.

I stand up, shake my head and laugh.

'This far north,' Arne says, 'no-one feels like turning in when it's summer. It's impossible to get children to go to sleep. Anyone living here is exhausted after ten years. Too much sleep in winter, not enough in summer.'

The shears come closer.

'What's that sound?'

'I expect it's a fjelljo, but I don't know anything about birds.'

I listen again to the sound, which is now further away. The most amazing thing about birds is their ability to produce noises like machines.

Arne positions himself at the water's edge with one foot in front of the other. I take out the bottle of mosquito oil and sprinkle some drops on the backs of my hands. But the mosquitoes are also attacking my scalp behind my ears, right through my hair. I haven't got my hat with the head-net — left it back at the house. Wearing a hat is torture if you're not used to it.

Arne holds the pan in his left hand, using his right to unwind a few metres of line. Then he whirls the hook round and round and suddenly lets go. It describes a high arc in the air, trailing the line, which unwinds easily from the pan. The thin line, blown to one side by a breeze I can't feel, slices slowly through the water, dropping tangents on ever-fresh circles, each one bigger than the last. Arne starts rewinding straightaway. The spoon dances brightly among the rocks, then vanishes. The line tautens.

'The hook's got caught.'

Moving up and down the bank, Arne jiggles the line, slackening and tightening it by turns as he struggles to free the hook.

16

He has been at it a full three quarters of an hour. I get up and saunter about, without straying far from his side.

I don't dare sit down again, afraid it will look like leaving him in the lurch. After all, if he made a catch he would share it with me. But I don't know how to be of assistance. Now and then I mutter directions, offer advice I don't believe in myself.

I haven't been to the lavatory all day. Behind the house is a copse that would do very well, a hillock with a few trees. But I feel obliged to wait until the hook has come loose.

Finally Arne takes a running jump and lands on a big stone jutting out of the water. From there he can exert more upward pull. Bingo! He immediately casts back the line and lands a fish, but it is far too small.

The anglers and their offspring come past with the squelching sound of damp feet in rubber boots. The clouds thicken, but are still rimmed with pink. Our shadows dissolve. I am seized with an absurd craving for total darkness. Sleeping when it's still light seems to diminish each hour of sleep by half.

When Arne finally heads back to the house, I climb the hillock. Between the trees I loosen my trousers, slide them down along with my underpants and sink onto my haunches. The mosquitoes make for my calves, thighs, buttocks, balls.

I see Arne stepping onto the porch, while I frantically brush my hands along the parts of me that are exposed. It has to be a very quick business, as they say. My eyes are popping. Primal instincts stirring in man, as when a dog or cat marks territory far afield. I have to laugh as I wipe my backside with moss.

In the conservatory.

Arne has opened a box of knäckebröd, a packet of margarine and a tin of minced meat.

I roll out our sleeping bags on the floor.

The door is clad with wire mesh, in which rust has corroded several holes. Flies now enter as well, attracted by the margarine.

We sit on our sleeping bags munching our crackers, with our maps spread out on the floor.

'How kind of these people,' I say (no sign of them yet), 'to let us use their porch. Any chance they might be able to find us a horse, d'you think?'

'I doubt it. But perhaps Qvigstad has come up with some idea.'

'What if he hasn't?'

'In that case we'll just have to carry everything ourselves.'

'I haven't seen any horses around at all.'

'Not a horse for miles round.'

'Couldn't we get a helicopter to drop us supplies on the way?'

(I say this in a joking tone of voice, but why should it be just a joke?)

'Good idea,' Arne says, 'we'll ask the Rockefeller Foundation, shall we? By the way, have you got any aerial photographs?'

'No, have you?'

'I don't need them myself. But for the kind of research you're doing . . . If it had been me, I'd have made sure I had some.'

'I asked Nummedal for them. Before I left Amsterdam, Sibbelee said Nummedal would let me have them. But when I spoke to Nummedal he told me I should apply for them in Trondheim, from Direktør Hvalbiff. Hvalbiff wasn't there, but I told you all that already. They did have aerial photographs, but the catalogue hadn't been unpacked yet and might still have been back in Oslo. I didn't dare tell you at first, I feel a right idiot not having them.'

'You can always pick them up in Trondheim afterwards, on your way back. Then you can examine them at leisure when you get home. Reverse order,' he says with a chuckle.

Through my clothes I scratch my thighs, my buttocks. The mosquito bites make my balls feel as if they're stubbled with horsehair. Arne fishes the last scrap of meat out of the tin and brings it to his mouth on the tip of his knife.

Could I be right in thinking he has not entirely dismissed the aerial photographs from his mind? Why do I have the feeling he is still pondering the subject? Maybe I am imagining I can read his mind simply because my own is so preoccupied with the photographs. I really ought to have them with me now, to be able to compare pictures taken from a plane with what you see on the ground. Arne just said that to keep me happy. He licks the blade with the kind of discretion only found in those unaccustomed to using a knife in this manner. He puts it down and, keeping his eyes lowered, wipes his mouth with a paper handkerchief, or rather dabs at it gently.

Abruptly, he raises his eyes and fixes me.

'Tell me, Alfred, what's your main field of interest? What specifically, I mean.'

I trace a circle on one of the maps with my index finger.

'These holes . . . They are generally taken to be dead-ice holes, aren't they?'

Arne leans over for a closer look.

'Yes, well, there are claims nowadays that some of them could be pingos.'

'Ah, pingos, the last word in geology! But do you know what Sibbelee thinks? That they're meteor craters.'

'Meteor craters?'

Arne's jaw drops, making his face even longer than normal. His eyes, however, are steely.

'Yes,' I say, 'meteor craters – a new perspective, and one I find very appealing. Especially in a landscape like this . . .'

He is so astonished by what little I have said that he can't stop himself interrupting:

'But this landscape consists entirely of rocks and sand deposited by glaciers in the Ice Age. When the climate improved and the glaciers melted, this place turned into a mash of stones and sand and clay with the occasional wedge of ice. The ice-wedges thawed eventually as well, creating the holes we see now, which are usually filled with water. Such depressions are to be found wherever there was once land ice – northern Germany, say, or North America. What reason is there to think of meteors?'

'Surely not everything need be attributed to the ice?'

I sigh, but haven't finished yet:

'One of the striking things about those holes is that they're always more or less round.'

'Anything that melts becomes more or less round. Ice-wedges and meteors both become round.'

'You think so?'

'Why would a large meteorite be any rounder than a wedge of ice?'

Why indeed? After a pause I say:

'Still, it's a very interesting hypothesis. I'm going to do my utmost to prove that some of those holes are meteor craters. I get palpitations just thinking about it.'

'Better not think about it too much then.'

'I'm ambitious. I can't help it, even though I know where I got it from. My father was a promising botanist when he was killed in an accident, just before my seventh birthday. He fell into a crevasse, in Switzerland. A few days after we heard of his death, a letter arrived saying that my father had been given a professorship. The speakers at his funeral weren't sure whether to refer to him as Professor Issendorf or as Mr Issendorf. My mother brought me up to believe I was destined to make up for his broken career by being successful in my own. In other words, it would be truly sensational if I were able to prove that some of those holes are in fact impact craters. And also interesting for the layman, now that there's so much stuff being written about craters on the moon.'

'Yes.'

Arne gives me a tight-lipped smile, and then, while his eyes continue to smile more from pity than from derision, he opens his mouth the way people do when they are about to share a secret (this is a special way).

'Your professor, Professor Sibbelee, he's been advancing this idea for quite some time. Were you aware of that?'

'Of course. But how did you know?'

'I don't want to discourage you, but Sibbelee told Nummedal about that meteorite theory of his ages ago. Nummedal was in the habit of mentioning it during his lectures, when he thought the moment had come for a bit of comic relief.'

'Oh well, I suppose that's because Nummedal himself wrote a book on the subject, in which he interprets the holes as dead-ice formations. Nobody contradicted him for fifty years. So what good would it do Nummedal to take a different view in his old age? Why would he abandon his own life's work?'

'If that's how you see it, why bother to ask him for those photos in the first place?'

'Why not? Surely Nummedal wouldn't be so mean-spirited as to deliberately stand in the way of my research?'

'Perhaps . . . He probably saw you as a supporter of the meteorite hypothesis right from the start.'

'But I'm going all the way there to do proper research! If Nummedal turns out to be right, I wouldn't go and claim that he's not, now would I?'

'I'd be careful if I were you. It's Sibbelee you're writing your thesis for, not Nummedal. Sibbelee will be none too pleased if you don't come up with some shred of evidence for his theory.'

Arne strips down to his underwear and crawls into his sleeping bag.

'Most of the holes have never been explored,' he mutters. 'So you never know.'

I too get into my sleeping bag, and follow his example of using his rucksack for a pillow. Provided you position it so the buckles don't get in the way, a rucksack makes a fine pillow.

I shut my eyes, but keeping them shut takes an effort. The light of the midnight sun shines crimson through my lids. A last glance at my watch. One o'clock. The fjelljo shears its hedge, the cuckoo proclaims its triumph.

17

I yawn. I am tired, but unable to sleep. My down sleeping bag is much too hot, even though I have left the zipper undone.

Arne's asleep and snoring.

I am wide awake. And, yet, lying on the wooden floor without a mattress isn't as uncomfortable as I had feared. The trick is to maintain a position for as long as possible, it's just the shifting around that hurts.

The sweat pours from my limbs. I crawl out of the sleeping bag, whereupon scores of mosquitoes settle on my bare shins. I sit there with drawn-up knees, rubbing my legs, staring into space.

At the far end of the porch are two broken wicker chairs, one on top of the other, next to a sewing machine on an ornate cast-iron base. This is as good a time as any to ponder how they make those wooden covers that protect sewing machines from dust. An oak panel curved cylindrically against the grain. Extraordinary that the wood doesn't split or crack. Indestructible. Great craftsmanship.

The top half of the door to the rest of the house is glazed, and curtained off on the inside. I haven't set eyes on the occupants. Odd, considering they are putting me up. If you can call this putting up.

When I sit up straight my nose is level with the window

ledge. The panes are stippled with thousands of mosquitoes: cobwebby legs, slimy bodies. I stare at them while I scratch one mosquito bite at length, then press a sharp thumbnail into it crosswise. Itching submerged by pain.

No harm in another cigarette. I pull my jacket towards me, fumble in the pockets and come across my mother's letter. If I read it now I can write her back saying: I read your letter by the light of the midnight sun.

By the light of that heavenly body I read:

As we won't be able to send you any post for weeks and won't be hearing from you for a long time, which I'm dreading, I thought I might as well write to you now.

I'm so proud you got that grant, Alfred, and I'm sure you'll come up with a brilliant thesis. If only your father had lived to see this!

In his day it wasn't nearly as easy to obtain funds for research abroad.

Thinking of you, I'm often reminded of the career your father might have had if he hadn't died so young. To me it's like a vindication against Fate: that you will carry on where he left off. Oh goodness, I remember so clearly that when it happened you were going through a phase of asking everybody if they could get you a 'meteor'. We had no idea where you picked up that word, but you knew exactly what it meant! That's when Daddy knew you had a talent for science. It's such a comfort to me to think that when he passed away, he did so fully confident of your talents, dearest

Alfred. I'm so glad you have always set yourself the highest standards, because that's the only way to achieve anything. The more you look the more people you'll find who haven't stayed the course for one reason or another.

(Ignore these blotches – [*arrow*] – just a few tears shed by yours truly.)

Did I ever tell you about that time your father put an advertisement in the newspaper for a meteoric stone? For weeks he'd been racking his brains to find some way of getting hold of one. He was set on giving you a meteoric stone for your seventh birthday, but as you know he was no longer with us when the day arrived.

It's amazing, but now that you have done so well in your studies I have to admit that, sometimes at least, things do turn out the way one had always hoped they would. Shame is that things don't take a turn for the better until after they have taken a turn for the worse.

I'll stop wittering on now, I promise.

. . . .

There is a postscript from Eva at the bottom:

Mum stop wittering on? That'll be the day. You know, Alfred, if only she could let go a bit more she wouldn't be so nervous.

. . . Your loving sister

Let go a bit more!

It's a miracle she didn't say let go of what! And it's not true that my mother witters on. I'd sooner call her uncommunicative. Widowed mothers who talk about the past all the time can't keep secrets from their grown-up sons. As for my father putting a wanted ad in the paper for a meteoric stone to give me on my seventh birthday – this is the first I've heard of it. The same goes for my wish to possess one: I haven't the dimmest memory of any such thing. A meteorite! Imagine wishing that at six years of age. And still wishing it! If my father had lived I might never have wanted flute lessons. Not that I got my way. She probably refused me out of a sense of fear. Fear that I'd grow up to be a flautist instead of taking on my father's career and carrying on where he left off.

Three o'clock. I fold up the letter, blowing away some mosquitoes, squashing others. I crawl back into my sleeping bag, pull it tight around my neck. I am drenched in sweat, but set on keeping absolutely still. I am so hot I feel as if I have a raging fever. Maybe the heat has a narcotic effect. Time stops, and the next thing I know my head is thumping.

The ache is so bad that I heave myself into an upright position. My watch tells me it is a quarter to twelve, and Arne has gone. The sun lances into the porch, trapping the heat inside. There's a fetid smell of sweat and mould. Feeling bruised and battered, I reach for my socks and shoes. Arne's vacant sleeping bag gives shape to his absence.

My left eyelid, inflamed by a mosquito bite, will only open halfway. I lace up my shoes, get up and step outside.

The flap of the green tent is now open. On the ground nearby lie clothes, also sleeping bags turned inside out, but Qvigstad is nowhere to be seen.

Not one sleeping bag – two.

I just stand there. Light a cigarette, scratch my left arm with my right hand and my right arm with my left hand. Small black gadflies alight on my skin soundlessly and painlessly, but still leave fat drops of blood behind when I brush them off, even if I haven't killed them. The blood is my own.

'Alfred!'

Arne emerges from behind the house with two other people, one of whom is Qvigstad, although I barely recognise him. Qvigstad waves at me with his free hand; he is holding a long fishing rod with the other. The third figure is also equipped with a casting rod.

Qvigstad stops two metres short of me and makes a little bow.

'Doctor Livingstone, I presume?'

We laugh and shake hands. Qvigstad has sprouted a ginger beard since I last saw him. The beard combined with the thatch of ginger hair, the high forehead and the steely blue eyes, staring as if nothing will escape them, reminds me of someone. Who? Vincent van Gogh.

His companion is scruffy-looking and fair-haired. He is chewing on a straw. I have to ask him to repeat his name (it is Mikkelsen), after which he mumbles:

'I talk very bad English. Sorry.'

Standing with his legs apart, he angles his feet outward a couple of times. Then he spits out the straw and crawls into the green tent.

Qvigstad has spent a year in America on a grant, he speaks excellent English, much faster than Arne, but then that may just be the way he always speaks.

'Had a good journey?' he asks. 'Come by plane, did you? The benzin didn't run out then?'

I shake my head, wondering at his use of the Norwegian word for fuel.

'Anything's possible in Norway. You never can tell. People don't know the simplest things. For instance – do you know where the word benzin comes from?'

'Benzin? . . .'

'From Benz. Mercedes-Benz, don't you know. Let's get into the tent. Have some breakfast.'

The Livingstone quip is ancient, but I've never heard the one about benzin.

Their tent has an extra triangle of netting to close off the entrance. Once I am inside Qvigstad zips it up, after which Mikkelsen kills all the insects with a spray can.

Arne and Qvigstad begin chatting in Norwegian. Mikkelsen lights a primus stove in the middle of the tent and puts on a small pan of water to boil. There is nothing for me to do but listen to the mosquitoes and flies tapping against the canvas overhead. It sounds as if it's raining. It takes ages for the water to boil. Mikkelsen stirs in the powdered milk, oats, sugar and raisins. My ears are filled with the hiss of the primus and the patter of insects. It is a fine tent, fairly new, with aluminium poles. All their gear seems to me to be first-rate.

Arne and Qvigstad unfold a map, while Mikkelsen stirs the porridge. I wish there was something I could do, but what? Qvigstad takes a curvometer out of a flat case, measures something on the map, confers with Arne, then taps the map with the back of the instrument to emphasise his point.

Should I wash and shave? Nobody else seems to have bothered, nor does the idea appeal to me either.

*

Three Norwegians walking abreast on the road, with me at their side. The heat is oppressive, not a cloud in the sky and yet the atmosphere is hazy.

I am not sure what we will be doing today apart from the final preparations for the expedition, such as buying food. There has been no more talk of hiring a horse.

A small general goods store.

A grey woman hands over eight loaves of brown bread, a dozen eggs in a carton, honey in tubes, margarine, tins, a cheese with an orange rind, Sunmaid raisins and three packets of coffee beans. No ground coffee available. Now what?

The woman has the answer: she goes to the back and returns with a coffee grinder, of a kind I have never seen before: it looks like a tin music box painted red.

I almost snatch the utensil from her hands.

'Let me do the grinding!'

'Fine! You do it.'

Outside, sitting on a large stone, I proceed to grind the coffee.

The mill is not very good. It's as if the beans get crushed instead of ground, and it takes an inordinate number of turns of the handle to crush just a small quantity of beans. Fending off mosquitoes with one hand, I turn the handle with the other. I throw the crushed beans back into the mill, but that has no effect: they trickle down almost at once, as through a funnel.

Arne, Qvigstad and Mikkelsen have now come to sit with me. We take turns with the mill, each of us whizzing the handle round until our arms get tired. It takes an hour and a half to grind all three packets of coffee beans.

With the provisions in a box of corrugated cardboard (how many kilos?), we make our way back to the tent.

Mikkelsen boils some water in an aluminium kettle, to which he adds a spoonful of ground coffee. We eat bread with sardines and drink coffee, which tastes horribly bland. Sherpa Danu would not have served this to his sahibs.

'Sherpa Danu,' I say aloud, and I tell them what I read in the newspaper.

Qvigstad says:

'It's only the expeditions to Mount Everest you get to read about in the papers – never any others. People have no idea how many researchers are out there without it ever being reported in the press. They're nameless, and though their expeditions may be less spectacular, that's not to say they're less dangerous.'

'And no help from Sherpas,' Arne says. 'They have to carry all their own gear.'

In the late afternoon we set off along the lake until we come to the river, which we follow upstream until it is sufficiently narrow to cross by jumping from one stone to the next.

Arne, Qvigstad and Mikkelsen are wearing knee-high rubber boots, I am the only one with ordinary leather hiking shoes. Just one wrong move and my feet will be sopping wet for the rest of the day.

Without bothering with a run-up, I manage to land on the first stone. Made it! Concentrating hard I leap onto the next, and then to the others, pausing on each stone to get my breath back; when landing I can't help giving the occasional yelp as I struggle to keep my balance.

Arne, Qvigstad and Mikkelsen don't even jump, they just progress smoothly from one stone to the next as if the whole river didn't exist. At last I am on the other side, with dry feet. A prodigious achievement by my standards, and my heart pounds in my throat. I catch up with the others at a trot. The road peters out into a footpath leading to the lake. The path comes to an end at a lakeside hut made of sods of turf. To the side of the hut lie two wooden sleds which look very much like small boats, and moored to a post driven into the bank is a long boat like a dugout with an outboard motor.

Qvigstad, Arne and Mikkelsen come to a halt. So do I. Qvigstad calls to someone inside the hut. A swarthy little man emerges on bandy legs, wearing a red-and-green check shirt, corduroy trousers and rubber boots. His nose is flat, his eyes slant and his black hair sticks up like a clothes brush. Laughing the shy laugh typical of Lapps, he shakes his head by way of greeting. From his belt dangles the awesome knife in its sheath with the curved tip. Qvigstad says something to him. He goes back into the hut and reappears with an empty rucksack. They confer. Arne, Qvigstad and Mikkelsen seat themselves on the ground. I follow suit. The man squats down, facing us. He unsheathes his awesome knife, slices a twig off a bush and sets about whittling the tip into a point. Mosquitoes crawl familiarly over his ill-shaven cheeks, his eyelids, his lips. He says something from time to time, and when he listens his jaw sags. The twig in his left hand dwindles steadily.

And so we remain for a good half hour. When finally we say goodbye, the empty rucksack is swinging from Qvigstad's hand.

18

By seven, the green tent has been struck and packed up. All our possessions are now spread out in little piles around us.

Arne inspects the rucksack belonging to the swarthy little man.

'It's a small one,' he says, 'I wonder if that's deliberate.'

'Small rucksacks can take heavy loads,' Qvigstad offers.

'He says he is very, very strong,' Mikkelsen says.

We divide all our gear over the five rucksacks. Into the strong man's rucksack go the two tents, primus stove, theodolite, paraffin container and all the tinned food. We tie the eight loaves on top with a piece of string. We? In reality it is Arne and Qvigstad doing practically everything, leaving me idle. Each time I venture to help they beat me to it, or snatch away whatever I pick up.

The only contribution I get to make is lining up the rucksacks on the shore of the lake, as there are five of them. I take the rucksack intended for the strong man and can barely lift it with both hands.

'Arne, are you sure this isn't going to be too heavy?'

'That man's as strong as a Sherpa!'

'Hold on,' Qvigstad says. 'We'll give him the eggs as well. If he breaks them, I hope for his sake he's as strong as he thinks!'

'How long will he stay with us?'

'For the first twenty-five kilometres, then he'll go back. Otherwise there won't be enough food left for us.'

In other words: after the first twenty-five kilometres the contents of the five rucksacks will have to be divided over four, which we will have to carry the rest of the way ourselves.

If only I had done more sport! If only this wasn't my first visit to Norway, then I wouldn't be so worried about having to cross raging rivers using stepping stones, with thirty kilos on my back. Even in the Pyrenees last summer, with Diederik Geelhoed, there was the village for us to return to at night. We didn't do much carrying at all. Just sandwiches, and on the way home a couple of rock samples. I think back on the salted meat and runner beans with oil, our daily fare in Setcases.

The sun glitters crimson in the water, pushing light and heat towards us like a bulldozer. My head still aches and my eyes sting.

Each of us stands up in turn, positions his camera, cocks the self-timer and hurries back to pose with the others. Click. Arne is the only one to take a photo without himself in it, because he hasn't got a delayed-action timer.

'What's keeping the strong man?'

'I saw a monument for a strong man in Tromsø. Carried a stone weighing three hundred and seventy-one kilos, apparently.'

'A monument?' Qvigstad asks.

'Yes, the actual stone. It's still there, with a bronze plaque on top.'

'I expect they left it there because he didn't have the strength to take it away.'

Mikkelsen and I laugh. Arne stands up, peers through his fists binocular-wise and says:

'There he is.'

The V-shaped ripples drawn by the long boat with the outboard spread over the entire lake.

There's only room for Qvigstad on board, and we hand him all five rucksacks plus the tripod. The boat, which is no wider than a tree trunk, can't take more than two people. Arne, Mikkelsen and I are to walk around the lake and then some distance along a river, up to an agreed spot where Qvigstad and the strong man will be waiting. Then we will continue on foot, straight across the watershed. Over the Vaddasgaissa range and then to a lake. Lake Lievnasjaurre.

I follow Mikkelsen and Arne across the river as before, leaping from stone to stone. I wish I could stop having these sombre visions of what will happen if I lose my footing.

What if the moulded rubber soles of my hiking shoes lose their grip all of a sudden? In the meantime I am keeping count: it is six paces across the river, over five half-submerged stepping stones.

Made it, once again.

Now for the higher ground. The slope is studded with mounds of greensward harbouring a core of ice. My ankles buckle with every step.

We have left the last of the trees behind. Nothing but black crowberry, knee-high polar willows, and dwarf beeches no taller than heather, apart from which they are exactly like ordinary beeches: same trunks though no thicker than a twig, same leaves though no bigger than toenails. They could be scale models for a mock-up landscape.

It is now seven thirty, and marginally less hot than it has been all day; the wind has dropped.

I take a colour photograph now and then, just as a souvenir. Something to show my mother and Eva later on. What was that girlfriend of Eva's called, the one she brought home with her the day before I left? She confused me so much I didn't catch her name. She wasn't in the house more than ten minutes. Pretty young, eighteen I'd say. Oh well. I could show her the photos some time and tell her about my trip. Might even be someone I could marry, two years from now, say, when I've finished my thesis. We could get engaged on the day I receive my PhD. That would be a banal thing to do, in Diederik Geelhoed's opinion. But what do I care if hundreds or indeed thousands of other people have done it before – it's hardly the sort of occasion that calls for anything inventive.

Some people can be so boring about those things. Including Diederik Geelhoed. The kind who go around in sandals instead of shoes, just to be different. I think it's sad when people can't channel their energy into areas where being different really makes a difference. I wouldn't go around with Diederik if he weren't so easy to talk to. There's no-one I can open up to as much as to Diederik. Which is strange. Or is it? Maybe it's just the feeling that there are certain issues you can only raise with someone you think will know what you're talking about. But there are also things I wouldn't for the life of me share with Diederik. There's a limit to what you can give away about yourself to even the closest of friends. Everything beyond that limit is forbidden territory, and is best not even hinted at. Which is why you say: 'Right you are, Diederik, marry in haste repent at leisure. The faculty is a business venture run by comedians, and the professors wear black academic robes to disguise their intellectual conmanship. Enemies of the Working Class to a man!'

Never will I let on to Diederik there are only two or three things I want so desperately that failing to achieve them would mean my life was not worth living. One is finding a meteor crater, another obtaining a *cum laude* for my PhD thesis, and then there's marrying Eva's girlfriend, becoming a university professor . . .

Qvigstad and the strong man are waiting for us at the prearranged spot along the river, where the bank is steep and slippery. The boat is moored to a rock. The five rucksacks are lined up in readiness along with the wooden tripod.

Gnawing the hangnail on my thumb, I watch as the strong man sinks to his knees, slips his right arm through the corresponding strap of his rucksack, draws himself up with the load angled on his hip, then slips the other strap on. He smiles. He hooks his thumbs behind the straps and takes a few slow steps. Then, after a moment's pause, he stoops to pick up the tripod as well.

I wait for Arne, Mikkelsen and Qvigstad to take their pick of the remaining rucksacks. The last one will be for me. Protestations flit across my mind ('No need to leave the smallest one for me! Oh, come on, don't overdo the hospitality!'), but there doesn't seem to be a single English word left in my vocabulary, so I keep quiet.

I take up the burden assigned to me, aping their gestures. Damn, even heavier than I thought. Bowed down by my rucksack, I follow in their footsteps, initially sinking to my ankles in the mud, then placing my feet gingerly on the soggy slope. My camera and the pocket containing my map, both dangling from my neck, knock against my stomach with each step. Having to jerk my head up to look in the distance makes me feel like a mole or some other creature designed for keeping their eyes to the ground. I can feel the blood swelling in my temples and hammering on the ache in my skull. Having let down my head-net, I survey the landscape through a green haze of mosquito netting.

Twenty paces already. I am not lagging behind. They are walking as slowly as I am. Feeling the weight of their ruck-sacks, just like me. No-one speaks.

Two birds swoop across my path, strenuously flapping their wings as though intent on flustering me.

How stupid of me not to listen when that girl said her name. Her expression was a mix of levity and melancholy, a bit like certain sonatinas. It is not often I compare a girl to a piece of music, but when I do it is always a girl I am so dazzled by that even if I saw her every day it would be months before I dared to touch her. As if I had to study the music first.

She could be called Filippine, Renate or Francine. Or Dido – that would be good. My mother's name is Aglaia. How such an unusual name can sound so distasteful is beyond me. Yes, Dido would do very well.

I glance at my watch. I can look at my watch any time I want. The straps of the rucksack have rucked up my sleeves in my armpits, so my forearms are half exposed. Crawling with insects. The mosquito oil has long worn off, washed away by sweat.

It is five to nine. It was a quarter to when we met up with

Qvigstad and the strong man. That makes ten whole minutes of trekking. Each step feels as if it will be my last. My watch has a revolving second hand. So I can measure exactly how long it takes to put one foot before the other: two seconds. As for the distance covered – not more than sixty centimetres each time, is my guess. Per minute that is thirty times sixty centimetres. Which is eighteen metres. Sixty times eighteen is . . . is . . . nought, six eights are forty-eight, six plus four is ten, which is one-nought-eight-nought. Which is . . . *just over one kilometre per hour*!

We'll never get there at this rate. It'll take us a day and a night just to cover the first twenty-five kilometres.

I notice that Qvigstad, Arne, Mikkelsen and the strong man are now gradually getting ahead. I force my legs to go faster. I was panting before, now I am gasping. I push up the head-net to get more air, and with my next intake of breath a mosquito flies into my mouth. I can feel it at the back of my throat, on my epiglottis . . . I cough, splutter, try frantically to muster some saliva, gulp.

I have swallowed it.

19

As a famished prisoner prizes every potato, even a sliver of potato peel, for the nutrition it contains, so I now perceive distance as a precious commodity, gradually coming into my possession with each step I take.

Each step shortens the twenty-five kilometres stretching ahead. Each step is one in the right direction. My mouth and throat are paper-dry from all my panting.

Much as my head feels it is about to explode, much as I have to strain every muscle to keep my balance despite the load on my back, I am making headway. We all are. It will be some time before we reach our limits.

To think that people shunted megaliths weighing up to five tonnes over the moors, simply to build burial chambers! How they managed without horses, winches, wheels is a mystery. But it may have taken several generations to assemble twenty or thirty boulders in one place. Building cathedrals was to the Middle Ages what shunting megaliths was to the Stone Age. Levering them forward with the aid of tree trunks, half a metre a day. Which is one hundred and fifty metres a year. One point five kilometres in a decade. How many boulders of a size they considered large enough would there have been lying around the countryside? How big was the radius within which they collected them? Ten kilometres? Twenty? Surely not more. It was a feasible, if lengthy, process. Anything is feasible, provided people aren't in a hurry, provided they have faith in their children and grandchildren and great-grandchildren and don't doubt the necessity of the task at hand – such as building barrows for the dead.

Cathedrals took even longer to build, and they were just as useless. Barrows are the Stone Age version of cathedrals. What is my cathedral? I am bulding a cathedral of unknown proportions, and by the time it is finished I will be long dead and no-one will ever know of my contribution.

The slope becomes less soggy as we climb. It also becomes less steep, and after a while there is no gradient at all.

We unload our rucksacks onto some big rocks. We have been hard at it for twenty minutes. Qvigstad strolls around, swinging a colossal hammer with a handle half a metre long. He steps up to a sugar-white rock and knocks off a corner.

'I've chipped one of Mother Earth's teeth!' he roars.

Arne opens his battered camera case and takes out his old Leica. Handling it as if it were a piece of antique porcelain, he raises it to eye level. The camera itself is battered, too, with glints of brass showing through cracks in the black enamel.

Arne presses the shutter, then says, with a rueful shake of the head:

'Perhaps . . .'

From here it looks as if the Vaddasgaissa range begins just over the next hill, but according to the map we have at least another fifteen kilometres to go.

The celluloid window in my map pocket is too scratched to be of any use in this light. The transparency of these windows never lasts beyond the first trip. I pull out the map and study the route with my magnifying glass.

I try to count how many rivers we have yet to cross. There seem to be ten of them, all big. Small ones are not marked on the map. Nor are the rises and falls indicated in any detail: variations of less than thirty metres are ignored. Which is to be expected. One centimetre on the map represents one kilometre in reality.

As I fold away my map, I see Mikkelsen offering Qvigstad a drink of water. Qvigstad takes a swig and passes the bottle to Arne. Arne drinks and passes it to me. My mouth and throat feel like pumice as I gulp the water down. We dig little graves for our cigarettes with our heels, then hoist our rucksacks. We are off again, downhill this time.

Going downhill brings fears about my knees giving way, but they are proving remarkably trustworthy. The complexity of the human knee! With each step the combined weight of torso, rucksack and thighs slams on the bundle of slithery ligaments and cartilage at the head of the tibia known as the knee joint. No tearing, no dislocation. Imagine if a grain of sand got in! Even the tiniest particle would cause havoc. Where did I hear about rock-hard crystals of ureum forming in the joints of people with arthritis, or was it rheumatism? Oh, Father, what agony! This pain is so excruciating that it attacks the very organ we use to overcome it!

Going downhill means gearing the entire body to shock absorption. The resilience of the meniscal cartilage. The strength of the tendons: beyond belief if you know how easy it is to bend a wire until it breaks. What a piece of work is man! But what an ordeal to put your own piece of work to this test!

If you tip your chair back often enough the legs will break. I even managed to break a metal chair that way once.

Isn't the sheer, incomprehensible toughness of the human body enough to make you despair of this torture ever coming to an end?

Downhill. Responding willingly to the pull of gravity, but it's hardly a question of willing, because I can't stop.

The carpet of moss thickens, then come the dwarf beeches with their dark green leathery leaves, and later still the polar willows with their asses' ears of pale green felt. The branches set about untying my shoelaces.

A stretch of spongy peat, which I sink into. Better to step on stones, but they are all round. Pools of black water, with nothing growing in it. Bigger and bigger pools, with black earth in between.

The river. Shallow. Hardly any current. Mikkelsen, Qvigstad and Arne stop to scoop water into their plastic cups. I haven't got my cup to hand. Should I take off the rucksack to hunt for it? My mouth is so parched that I can't shut it any more – what, already? Arne turns round and passes me his plastic cup.

I go up on my toes where the water is less shallow, but by the time I reach the far side both my feet are wet and cold.

Far side . . . pools, marshes. More of those grass-covered hummocks with a core of ice which are known by the Icelandic name of *thufur*. More polar willows, then a stretch of dwarf beeches petering out into just moss and stones. The slope steepens. Insects patter on my canvas hat like hailstones. The low sun sets alight the clouds of mosquitoes circling the heads of my four companions.

We have done fifteen minutes of climbing. How much

more of this slope is there? How steep is it? Steep enough for it to be impossible for me to stand up straight without the weight of my rucksack pulling me over backwards.

I plod on, putting one foot ahead of the other. Each step counts. A miracle, wouldn't you say? One step. Just one step and the distance to the top is less than it was before. Step, step, merely lifting the foot and bringing it down slightly further on. Couldn't be simpler. Hardly more strenuous than standing still, what with the heavy load on my back. Step. Between the stones there is moss. Also bare ground. Sand and pale grit, an occasional bleached bone or vertebra. No sign of anyone having been here before. But then we too have been covering our tracks.

My watch tells me it's nine thirty-five. We've been going for nearly an hour. An hour already! And I can easily keep it up for another hour, two hours, three, as long as I like. It's bad, but it's not getting worse. Where's my headache? Gone, since I haven't given it a thought.

The top.

When we take a rest the strong man doesn't even bother to take off his rucksack. He looks round for a stone of exactly the right height for his rucksack to fit on top, and then leans back, holding the collapsed tripod like a spear in his crossed arms.

I spread my map on the ground and take out my compass. I try to align the map along a north–south axis, using the compass. But the ground is uneven, and the compass needs to be horizontal for the needle to rotate freely. My hand is trembling too much for me to keep the instrument steady on my palm. Holding the map with the other hand doesn't help.

The sharp stones dig into my knees as I lean forward.

'What are you looking for? North?'

Arne squats down beside me. He repositions the map.

'There you are,' he says.

Now I can see what is on the end of the frayed cord round his neck. It's a plastic boy-scout compass. He holds it in his left hand. As it is a fluid compass, it always points roughly north, whichever way it is held.

'This is where we are now, isn't it?' I ask, indicating a spot on the map.

'Oh no,' Arne says. 'Not there. We're only here.'

He stabs a chewed yellow pencil stub at a point three centimetres further down. Three whole kilometres.

I focus on the map and the landscape by turns, trying to match the one with the other. I raise one knee, but that only increases the weight bearing down on the other and hence the pain. I sit down, but find I can't bend over far enough to read the map. Damn! I'm not in good shape today. What will they think? I don't want to be a laughing stock. I WILL NOT BE LAUGHED AT.

They must speak highly of me when my back is turned! I must be just as capable as they are, regardless of my in-experience – more capable, in fact.

20

Black shadows of the Vaddasgaissa streak southwards across the plain. Beyond the shadows the ground is pale green, grass green, bottle green, British racing green, brown. Small lakes and winding streams reflect the blues and pinks of the sky in shades of anodised aluminium.

All the pools and lakes are linked by streams. Not a single hole remotely suggestive of a meteor crater. I have never actually seen a meteor crater, just pictures in books. If I came across one I might not even recognise it.

But the man who first thought of attributing a hole in the earth's crust to the impact of a sizeable meteor? Who was he? When and where did he make his discovery? What was his name?

A deep loathing of textbooks engulfs me. Don't textbooks describe everything as if everyone has always known that that's the way they were? Where does that leave all the human effort, doubt and despair that had to be endured before a particular conclusion could be reached? Ninety-nine out of a hundred discoveries are seen as foregone conclusions, or else as the work of legendary figures, nameless supermen to whom the failures or semi-failures of their predecessors simply did not matter. There is no glory in geology. Just think: all those writers getting their names and photographs in the paper thanks to my mother's weekly articles, whereas I can't come up with the name of a single expert on meteor craters. Yet there must have been hundreds. It's not just me who's so ignorant, not even Sibbelee would be able to give you names. Nobody can, apart from a few scholars specialising in the history of science. Nobody reads what they write either, except for the tiny number of people who happen to have taken an interest in the history of science instead of in umpteen other subjects that are no less fascinating. But the information never runs to more than a name or two, possibly a few dates, and that's it. Rarely if ever do scientists spend their days in the company of people who could write their biographies.

How happy I would be to find just one little stone of cosmic provenance. A meteorite. I vow that no detail of the wildernesses roamed by me will escape my notice. But these mountains offer nothing but rubble.

I am falling behind again. Not by much, but I am finding it harder and harder to keep my head up. Almost doubled over now, I try to make my legs go faster.

What if she were called Dido. Where did I get that name from? Dido, Queen of Carthage, fell in love with Aeneas, the hero who fled, carrying his father on his back. A sight heavier than my rucksack.

Her name certainly isn't Dido. But I can call her that anyway. I don't know her address, not even her surname. Too late to ask Eva. I won't be writing to anyone at all during the next couple of weeks.

My purpose here is to find something. Something that will cause a sensation. The rest is irrelevant. Any fool of a tourist can send postcards. I have other priorities. Still, there are plenty of things everyone else is capable of doing. But not me. Not me . . .

Yet another river. A wide one. It gets wider and wider as I approach. The strong man is already on the other side, gesturing, calling out. Arne, Qvigstad and Mikkelsen are perched on different stones in the rushing water, laughing. They look as if they're playing tag, ducking this way and that as they spring from one stepping stone to the next.

The river foams like a waterfall. The bank is so soggy that I am almost knee-deep in mud. I stand still.

The stone closest to me is occupied by Arne. How did he get there? It is quite pointed, and one-and-a-half metres out from the riverbank. He can't just have stepped onto it, he must have taken a running jump. But how, on such muddy ground?

Looking further away I see Mikkelsen flexing his knees. He gives a shout, flies through the air flailing his arms and lands on the stone already occupied by Qvigstad. They grab hold of each other, teeter, regain their balance. Then, one after the other, they stride across the remaining stepping stones as if they're wearing seven-league boots. They catch up with the strong man, who has already started walking.

I am still at the water's edge, scanning the river upstream and down, but can't see any stones closer to the bank.

Arne reaches out to me.

'Jump,' he says. 'Draw up your knees as much as possible.'

Jump! My feet are sinking deeper and deeper in the mud. Bracing for push-off will only make me shoot into the ground like a bomb. Arne's hand is too far away for me to catch hold of it. I can't very well keep him waiting, though. False step, losing my balance, being fished out of the water soaking wet, watch ruined, camera full of water, rucksack with food – not just my own food! – sopping wet, down sleeping bag waterlogged. I can't remain standing here and I can't walk away either. What a nuisance it'll be for the others if I arrive at the other side soaked to the skin. Not that they'll laugh at me, they're too polite.

I am unafraid. There is nothing to be afraid of for someone who has no choice, someone with only one thing left to do: the impossible! I lunge forward, grope for Arne's hand – miss it, fall flat onto the stone he's standing on, face smashed, waist-deep in water, ankle fractured. I jump. It's as if Arne and I exchange a fleeting handshake. My right foot touches down, the rubber sole has excellent grip, the left foot follows, I draw myself up and there I am, standing next to Arne on a pedestal in the rushing water. He bends over. Scoops water with his cup, then offers it to me.

'Let me take your camera and that map pocket.'

'Why? They're not heavy.'

'Just let me take them, then they won't get wet in case you slip.'

He lifts the straps off my neck and passes them over his head. Then, taking a big stride, he brings his foot down on the next stone and swings the other leg right over to the stone after that and so on to the other side. Next thing I know I am doing the same. Seven huge strides across the frothing current.

Made it. I am standing beside Arne. He lifts my camera and map pocket by the straps and hangs them round my neck as if they were medals of office.

21

When I get home at about five and have nothing to do while Eva makes tea, I often take out the hefty MALLINCKRODT MEMORIAL VOLUME OFFERED BY HIS STUDENTS from the cabinet it shares with my father's other books.

It invariably falls open at the page with the big pasted-in photograph, which unfolds to twice the width of the book.

The picture shows the participants of the Botanical Conference at Lausanne in July 1947.

They are ranged in five rows. The ones in the front, mostly women, are sitting on chairs, those in the second row are standing, with the heads of the third and subsequent rows hovering above them. How this was achieved is unclear; presumably they stood on chairs.

My father's head is in the last row, almost in the middle, and he is one of the few participants not looking into the lens. He is shown in three-quarter profile, as if he's saying something – or otherwise listening – to a very old man with a beard diagonally in front of him. Such a mistake! The bearded professor (Von Karbinski, Cracow) isn't talking to him at all.

How do I know his name is Von Karbinski?

Very simple.

On the facing page is a diagram of the group. It is quite small, and very schematic. All it shows, really, is the pattern in which the heads are arranged. Each head is rendered in outline, and each has a number. The numbers correspond with a list of names. So it's easy to see who the participants are and where they're from. That's how I know that the old man diagonally in front of my father is Von Karbinski from Cracow.

However, there are two heads without numbers, and consequently without names. One belongs to a girl in the far left of the front row. Some secretary, no doubt, who happened to be there when the portrait was taken. But the other head belongs to my father. Not yet famous enough, I suppose, when he accompanied the great Professor Mallinckrodt to the conference in Lausanne in 1947.

A century from now, or two or three, when my mother, sister and I are long dead, anyone who cares to will be able to find out who attended the conference in Lausanne by consulting the MALLINCKRODT MEMORIAL VOLUME. Von Karbinski from Cracow, Stahl from Göttingen, Pelletier (Lyon), James (Oxford) . . . but when their gaze stops at my father's face they won't know who he is.

My mother, Eva and I are the only possessors of the memorial book who know him: one of the youngest men in the picture, black quiff, no spectacles, no old-fashioned wing collar either, no, his attire seems scarcely outdated.

Alfred the First (my grandfather's name was Paul, my great-grandfather's Jurriaan, but my most illustrious ancestor was Hendrik, Lutheran dominee at Purmerend and author of *Parnassus: A Collection of Peerless Poesy*, published in 1735. No-one reads it any more. We don't even have a copy).

Alfred the First, I mutter, sliding the book in amongst the others on the shelf. Usually I glance in the mirror after that.

Died young. Before he had the chance fully to develop his talents.

What is odd is that I do this quite often, several times a week in fact, and it has been going on for years: opening the book while waiting for tea, taking a look at my father, noting the absence of a number in his head, muttering 'Alfred the First', and so on.

Not so odd, though, that this ritual should come to mind now. Arne and Qvigstad might well become very famous (Mikkelsen strikes me as too dim). One of the pictures we took in Skoganvarre will be published in a book, duly furnished with names and date. My name has got to be there along with the others. It must be.

22

We have been following this river for quite some time. Flat terrain, I mean no rise and fall. But now our route takes a different turn, and up another slope we trudge.

There is a constant alternation between plains and rises, stony ground and mosses, rock formations and peat. Difficult becomes easier, then easy becomes more difficult. My forebear the Lutheran dominee would have said it was the other way round. The rivers are my main worry – how many more are there? Eight? Nine? And they won't all be shallow either.

Tough becomes tougher, but there is an upper limit. Climbing brings elevation, steep becomes steeper, but in the end it always eases off again.

The bare stretches are strewn with small stones, not one of which merits pocketing. Here and there a tussocky shrub is covered in tiny pink flowers. I don't know the first thing about plants, can barely tell the difference between bilberry and bell heather. The *Dryas Octopetala* with its yellow-and-white flowers is the only one I recognise, thanks to the geological period named after it.

Knowing a bit more about the flora would give me something to do in the absence of interesting types of stone. But plants have never interested me. Maybe I was put off by my father having died in pursuit of them. A victim of science

— my mother seldom refers to him otherwise at solemn moments.

We are now surrounded by mountains on all sides. It's like walking on the bottom of a serving dish covered by a lid of black cloud, except that the lid is slightly off centre, creating a slit through which the brassy sunshine pours in.

Arne has been adjusting his pace to mine.

'Aren't you hungry?' he asks.

'Are you?'

'Ravenous. Cold, too. We must have something to eat soon.'

We each have a piece of dry knäckebröd and a handful of raisins the next time we stop for a rest.

Descending to a stream, scooping water, knocking back four cups in a row while the sweat turns icy on your skin, wading through wetlands, more polar willows, dwarf birches. The ground is no longer cushioned. I need so much air that I barely get the chance to close my mouth and roll my tongue to work up some saliva.

I have to cautiously worm my hand under my head-net to wipe the sweat from my eyebrows. The stink of mosquito oil assaults my eyes. Maybe I have rubbed some into my mucous membranes, despite the dire warning in the instructions.

The terrain becomes ever harder, no more dwarf birches, just scattered rocks with no level ground between them. Tortured muscles form iron cuffs around my ankles, and lugging my rucksack feels like dragging a cartload of flour.

This slope is very long. Longer than the last one?

Arne is the first to reach the top, where he makes a halt, leaning his rump against a rock. He is joined by Mikkelsen and the strong man, both of whom lean back in the same way. Qvigstad, who is just ahead of me, looks round for another conveniently sized rock to lean against. The two of us lean back. He offers me a cigarette. I flip up my head-net to have a smoke. My face is instantly covered in mosquitoes. Once the cigarette is alight I lower the net again, but have to keep it away from my face to avoid burning holes in it. The smoke is trapped underneath and I seize up, coughing. My ears throb and I have never known my heart to make such a deafening noise. My torso feels like plate iron enclosing a gleaming, high-powered engine relentlessly propelling me forward in life.

Qvigstad says something, which I don't catch.

'What did you say?'

He raises his voice to a shout:

'Anna Bella Grey! A beauty with two heads and three tits!'

I want to say who's she when she's at home, but decide it is too silly. He doesn't need encouragement anyway.

'I saw a picture of her naked,' Qvigstad roars. 'Unbelievable. Completely normal from the waist down. See the potential? A tit for each hand and another for your mouth. And that's not the end of it. What she can do with her two heads, or rather her two mouths . . . it's mind-boggling.'

Silence. Then he adds, dropping his voice:

'I can only get it off with black women, you know.'

'Oh?'

'Ever since I went to America. Once a negress always a negress. A tiger that has tasted human flesh . . .'

'Is it the same, then?'

'I reckon. My inborn puritanical nature. Psychiatrists maintain it's because my mother couldn't possibly have been a negress. You kid yourself that it's about the beauty of black skin — finer and softer, no blemishes, pimples, blackheads, nervous rashes, no hair in the wrong places. Perfect skin for people who don't wear clothes. But subconsciously you see the image of your mother in every white woman, and being with your mother makes you impotent, precisely because you started out wanting her and her alone.'

He blows out smoke.

'Maybe they make too much of it in psychiatry. Personally I think it's because I was born in Norway, where there aren't any negresses. So when I was a kid and other kids told me their smutty stories about snogging, I never thought of negresses.'

He flicks his cigarette away, grinds it into the ground with his heel until every trace of it has vanished and walks on without further comment.

I lean forward, and in so doing lift the rucksack off the ledge of rock. I set off, lurching and staggering at first. Even smacking my lips fails to get the saliva running now. Trickles of salt-saturated sweat run down either side of my nose, stinging my cracked lips. Aeneas walked all the way from Troy to Rome carrying his father on his back.

The shadows cast by the Vaddasgaissa reach to the bottom of the slope. It is half past three, and as I step out from the shade the sun feels slightly warmer than when we first arrived in the mountains. I squat down by a stream and slurp three cups of water. Where are we?

Mikkelsen is out of sight. Over the next, slightly lower hill. Arne vanishes next. Qvigstad, too, is well ahead of me. But I will catch up. It is not as if I'm dawdling. Now it's Qvigstad going over the hill, but he doesn't vanish completely. He's going up again, getting taller! Two or three more steps and I can see him full length once more. I catch sight of Arne again, too, far away, on yet another slope.

Mikkelsen? Same goes for him. He was just hidden from view by an outcrop. The only one still missing is the strong man. Where is he?

23

The strong man is down on his knees blowing a fire. He has improvised a little stove with some stones to prop up a frying pan. The flames crackle. For the rest silence all round. Arne, Qvigstad and Mikkelsen are huddled on the other side of the fire. The smoke billows slowly towards me, so to them I am probably looming up from a dense fog. When I am close enough to make out their voices, I hear they are speaking Norwegian.

I unload my rucksack and lie down on my stomach next to Arne.

'Is this where we'll be staying?'

'No, but it's very near here.'

I drag out my map. Arne points to our current position before I have even started looking. Lake Lievnasjaurre is four centimetres away. Four kilometres.

We eat bread with fried eggs and drink a lot of coffee.

The conversation is mostly in Norwegian, for the strong man's benefit. There is nothing for me to do but rest. The strong man puts out the fire, cleans the frying pan, packs away all the items he has used, fetches drinking water. If only we could keep him with us! Not enough food? What about Sherpas – don't they have to eat? Or do they survive on moss and stones? I'll have to ask Brandel how they manage in the Himalayas. No, needn't bother, the solution couldn't be simpler. The ratio is a hundred Sherpas to four sahibs, and twenty-five Sherpas can easily carry all the food they need, plus provisions for one sahib. Just one strong man, however strong, is not enough for the four of us.

I run down the slope towards the next river. That I have got this far with a rucksack heavier than I have ever carried before proves I have nothing to fear. It's just that I'm out of practice. I'm obviously strong enough. Yes I'm weary, but this weariness is like a headache, a temporary hardship that has nothing to do with lack of energy.

The river I am now approaching is not wide, but the current is fast. Plenty of stepping stones. The secret is not to wait about. No furtive casting around for a stone even closer to the bank, just forging ahead with a step, stride, and jump without thinking what you're doing any more than when you dash down a flight of stairs.

First step . . . second . . . don't look at the water, keep your eyes on the next stone and your foot will land there automatically . . .

Oh!

Damn! Damn! Damn!

My right foot is up on the stone, my left in mid-stream! My trousers are about to split at the crotch. Cold water seeps up to my groin. Arne looks round, then turns back to help me. Qvigstad, Mikkelsen and the strong man press on; thank God they're too far away to notice what's happened.

'It's nothing! It's nothing!' I yell, shifting my entire weight onto my right leg, but in doing so my foot slides off the stone and I pitch forward onto my knees.

Nothing matters any more. Splashing more than necessary, I wade the rest of the way.

'My rucksack is still dry. It's nothing, really.'

'No, you can't go on in this state. You must change into dry socks or you'll get sores on your feet.'

Arne lowers his rucksack to the ground and takes out a pair of grey socks rolled up in a ball. I sit down meekly and untie my shoes, breaking a nail on the wet laces. There is blood trickling down my shins. I pull up my trouser legs, dab my knees with a handkerchief. Grazed, that's all, but the pain bites to the marrow.

Arne passes me a towel. I have to accept his help. If I don't I'll only cause more delay. I am no match for him, I have no practice, I don't belong in this country the way he does.

'Sorry,' I mutter, 'I'm so clumsy, I've always been very clumsy. I'm doing the best I can, but it doesn't always work. I'm sorry.'

24

Flat-topped mountains with steep, rugged flanks. Like shards of broken pottery magnified to gigantic proportions. This is what an ant sees when making its way between the jagged edges of a broken tile. This is how I see the mountains, but I only lift my head briefly now and then, just to check which way the others are going. The rucksack puts such a strain on my neck that if it weren't for my shoulder blades my back would be wrapped around my spine, in which case the straps would slide right down my arms . . . nothing to hold them up . . . Crazy imaginings. Dark stains spread along the straps, my sweat having seeped through layers of clothing. That much is true. As if the moisture is being squeezed from my body by the leather straps.

Am I tired? I don't care. Would I prefer to stop right here and call it a day? Not at all. But it does come to me that there is an immense disproportion between the physical and the intellectual exertions demanded of me. I'm like the man who invented the electric motor a hundred and fifty years ago, in the days when insulated copper wire didn't exist, when it wasn't on sale all over the place as it is now, in any shop selling light bulbs. He couldn't afford raw silk, so he was reduced to tearing up his wife's wedding dress to have something to insulate the copper wire with. For months he did nothing but the most mind-numbing labour imaginable: winding shreds of silk around lengths of fine copper wire. Compared to the time he spent doing that, the actual invention was achieved in a flash.

Ah! Never in all my years at university have I been required to get down to such basic activities as now – and no-one will ever notice. When my thesis is finished there won't be any mention of blistered shoulders, grazed knees, splitting headaches, or of mosquitoes and carnivorous flies. I wouldn't dream of telling anyone about those things. Not about those things nor about what lies ahead . . . perhaps.

My thoughts turn to all those geologists, thousands of them who, like me, never breathe a word about such annoyances as being in debt, going without food, suffering sunstroke, undertaking long expeditions to no purpose, people working against you, underhand behaviour.

I feel an irresistible urge to conjure up the worst possible scenario: that all my effort will have been wasted. Think of those occasional boulders you see on the moors in eastern Holland – who's to say they weren't dragged there by some primitive man, slaving away year in year out to advance half a metre a day, sleeping beside his boulder at night . . .

No horses in those days. Let's hope primitive man was aware of the possibility of using tree trunks as levers. He grew old. People aged much more rapidly in those days. My barrow-builder, grizzled by the age of thirty! Fell ill and had to give up long before his boulder was close enough to another one for us, his descendants, to think: Hey! A barrow for the dead!

There is no trace of anyone having devoted his entire life

to getting that particular boulder to budge. It looks no different from the others dotted about the moors, and no archaeologist would give it a second thought. It's pathetic, and what's even worse is that when we do recognise a boulder as being part of a barrow, we still have no idea who the architects were, let alone what they were called. Their names will never be known. There's no-one in the whole universe who knows. And if, a thousand years from now, they find some way of tracing those identities it won't make any difference to me. I'll die without ever knowing the answer, like Christiaan Huygens, who died not knowing that one day people would be sitting in The Hague watching gunfights between rebels and soldiers in San Domingo, or Julius Caesar, who died unaware of the existence of America. The Aztecs performed human sacrifices on a nightly basis, to ensure that the sun would rise in the morning. They had done so since time immemorial, the way we wind up our clocks before going to bed. Not a murmur from anyone, not a soul who dared suggest it might be worth finding out what would happen if they skipped the ceremony for once.

Was there ever an Aztec who raised his voice to protest: 'What we're doing is insane!'

In a world where so many sacrifices have already been made without any effect at all, how can anyone believe there are still sacrifices worth making?

My eye is caught by a stone that looks slightly different from the others. I stoop. The rucksack pitches forward against the nape of my neck. I flail my left arm to keep my balance. I pick up the stone.

Not particularly heavy. A piece of gneiss, scattered here

by the million. Having taken the trouble to pick it up, I slip it in my pocket.

The slope I am now going down is thinly blanketed with mist, as if the ground is simmering. A stretch of water glistens in the deep, beneath the mist. A lake, larger than the other lakes: Lievnasjaurre!

Arne is way ahead, in the distance. Where will he stop, when will I see him shed his rucksack?

I glance at my watch: four o'clock.

It is half past five when Arne halts on a flat-topped rise near the lake and unloads his rucksack. The strong man is next, he too sets his rucksack on the ground, along with the tripod he's been carrying. But Qvigstad and Mikkelsen just stand there facing each other, talking, their thumbs hooked behind their shoulder straps. In no hurry to get their breath back, apparently.

They are still standing talking when I turn up a quarter of an hour later. I ease one of the straps off my shoulder and lower the rucksack carefully to the ground. Qvigstad takes out a packet of cigarettes. Interrupting his Norwegian exchange with Mikkelsen, he offers me one, saying:

'Maggots are just as happy to feast on the carcass of a hyena as on a dead bird of paradise. Ever thought about that? Mikkelsen hasn't.'

Then he moves away to offer the strong man a cigarette.

Arne says, in English:

'Fifty kroner will do.'

We all draw out our wallets to contribute. Mikkelsen has already unpacked the strong man's rucksack. We let him keep a tin of sardines and a box of knäckebröd for the journey home. Without having sat down even for a moment, he shakes hands with us all and heads off, back where he came from.

'He was very strong man indeed,' Mikkelsen says.

A peculiar kind of vivacity takes hold of us, as if the sun, reappearing now higher in the sky, is bearing us along to its own rhythm, blotting out all thought of sleep. I feel as fully awake as if I had just got out of bed. Arne asks me to get the fishing net out of my rucksack.

All four of us walk to the shore of the lake with the net that is supposed to hang in the water like a curtain so the fish get their gills caught in the mesh.

A breeze is rising. As we unfold the net it flutters and catches on the bushes at the waterside. Just as well there are four of us, or it would be impossible to untangle the thin nylon strands from the swaying stalks.

Finding wood for a fire is no picnic either. The polar willows are too wet and the dwarf birches too tough to snap off. There is a type of resinous shrub that can serve as firewood, but it's not plentiful around here. The flames keep going out, in spite of our taking turns to crouch down to blow on the embers.

'Lapps,' Arne says, 'always travel with some birch bark under their shirts, for kindling.'

Qvigstad puts an end to this challenge of the great outdoors with a dash of paraffin. Coffee is brewed in the small kettle while we work our way through thick slices of bread with tinned meat. The meat is called Lordagsrull. Viking Brand. How apt.

Slowly chewing my food I take in the view. At the far side of the lake rises a lone mountain, almost perfectly conical in shape. The type of mountain that people who have never seen mountains imagine them to be like, the type of mountain Dutch children put in their drawings. Its name is Vuorje (pronounced: Voor-ye). The low sun floods the peak with crimson, and at the dark base lies an expanse of snow.

25

Qvigstad and Mikkelsen have disappeared into their pale green tent with the double-fabric top and sewn-in ground-sheet. A cabin of canvas, closed at the front with a triangle of mesh. Insect-proof. Before bedding down they will have used their spray to dispose of any intruders. In other words, they will be shielded from the plague as long as they remain in the tent. A pause in the battle that rages twenty-four hours a day.

I lie next to Arne, who's snoring, so I don't get a wink of sleep. I wonder if I will ever sleep again. Arne's tent is shaped like a pyramid propped up in the centre with a broken broom handle wound round with copper wire to join the two pieces together.

This tent does not run to a sewn-in groundsheet. A pair of loose rectangles of plastic is all we have to stop the damp rising into our sleeping bags.

The white canvas sides are heavily patched, like Arne's clothing, and are pegged to the ground at the corners only. We have weighed down the edges with stones to keep out the worst of the wind, but there's no way of keeping out the mosquitoes. So they congregate at the apex of the pyramid, which, since I am on my back, is in my direct line of vision. From there they sally forth to feast on our hands and faces.

*

This cannot go on. Not getting any sleep at night is going to do me in, sooner or later. I push down my sleeping bag and sit up. Out with the mosquito oil, then, for another lavish application. After that I put on the hat with the head-net and tie the flap securely under my chin. Finally I crawl back into my sleeping bag, pull up the zips, wriggle my arms inside and try to remain absolutely still. My eyelids are red curtains. The sun is already so high and so harsh that even from inside the tent it hurts to look at the side it is beaming on.

Arne snoring. The fjelljo trimming its hedge. Birds in general twittering, screeching, circling overhead with beating wings. The sweat starting out on my legs collects into drops which trickle down, causing an itchy sensation. Mosquitoes and flies raise and lower the pitch of their buzzing in full accord with the Doppler effect. Oh, you can tell exactly where they are simply by ear. Over the past day I have developed a successful technique of killing them by means of slaps to the head, my hands being guided by sound not sight. The sonar-driven *coup de grâce*. In my current position slapping is impossible, and besides it shouldn't be necessary. The head-net should offer full protection. But a pinprick sensation on my nose makes me suspicious. I open my eyes. Settled on the mesh just above my right eye is a mosquito. The net is in contact with the tip of my nose. So I may not have imagined the pinprick at all, the insect could easily have attacked me through the mesh. By blowing hard I manage to shift the net a few centimetres away from my nose, and, as the fabric is fairly stiff, it stays like that. Provided I keep my head perfectly still.

The mosquito that bit me returns to the big top in triumph, boasting of its heroic exploit. Several dozen of its siblings swarm down to see if it's telling the truth. They alight.

Ascertain at a glance that I'm unattainable.

A glance is all it takes! Whereas my own eyes ache from trying to focus on the pests at such close quarters.

I close my eyes, the better to eavesdrop on a debate in the insect world.

'He's lying,' one mosquito says, 'he didn't bite, he just had a sniff round.'

'Yes, I bet that's what he did,' another chimes in. 'Because the smell around here is mouth-watering.'

'Mouth-watering, you say?' a younger sibling asks.

'Precisely. Mouth-watering. You're not old enough yet, you haven't learnt to appreciate the smell of mosquito oil.'

'Like a kid who's too young to appreciate a dab of mustard on his beef.'

Then mama mosquito pipes up with the explanation:

'No, it isn't that. The mosquito oil manufacturers have invented a new product. The stuff they make nowadays makes people smell much better than before.'

What drivel, I think to myself, but how else am I to conserve what little humour I have left? A sense of humour is a precious asset in precarious circumstances.

In due course several mosquitoes discover that my filter is not hermetically sealed. Treading with caution, no doubt mindful of the memoirs of the world's leading speleologists, they are in the process of insinuating themselves into the bowels of my sleeping bag. This is intolerable.

I tug furiously to open the zips and sit up. It's as if a wave of hot steam discharges from the sleeping bag when I peel it down to inspect my legs. Drops of blood here and there. This can't be the work of mosquitoes. Horseflies, more like. The mosquitoes, observing my uncovered state, descend on me to celebrate the capitulation. I have to keep my hands flapping madly from my groin to my toes to fend them off. Some of them seem to think the hairs on my shins provide excellent cover, a wonderful camouflage designed expressly for their benefit. A misapprehension savagely avenged by the thunderclap of my hand. But what can my hand do against thousands upon thousands of mosquitoes? About as much as God's lightning can do to strike down sinners: fascists, communists, capitalists, Christians, Moslems, Buddhists, animists, the Ku Klux Klan, Negroes, Jews, Arab refugees, the Chinese, the Japanese, the Russians, the Germans, the Dutch in Indonesia, the Americans in Vietnam, the English in Ireland, the Irish in England, Flemings, Walloons, Turks, Greeks and any other miscreants I may have overlooked.

I light a cigarette, crawl out of the tent. Ouch, my grazed knees.

My trousers are hanging out to dry on some shrubs. They're still wet, but I drag the clammy fabric up my legs anyway. The same goes for the socks.

I go back inside and lie down on top of my sleeping bag, fully dressed. I can't protect my hands. Too bad.

The point now is to start feeling drowsy. I try merely relaxing, eyes closed, hands loosely folded on stomach. That's better. I relax some more, yes, I think I've got it, I am getting drowsy, my jaw sags, could that be the onset of a yawn? I think it is, because my eyes are watering. Oh what bliss to be asleep now . . . I yawn, and it appears to be a genuine yawn, I mean when your mouth remains agape longer than expected and then closes of its own accord. Time I got to sleep. Not sleeping night after night – how will I ever get the brilliant research done to fulfil my father's legacy? . . . I must sleep, but how? Sleeping while the light is getting stronger all the time . . . is like . . . now what would be a good comparison? Shedding woollies at the onset of winter. Or . . . damn! It was bad enough with Arne's snores making a din like a wooden craft being splintered on the rocks, but now my hand is itching like mad, too. I can feel my heart racing with anger, and the next thing I know I've opened my eyes to inspect the back of my hand. Five bumps and three mosquitoes, their ringed posteriors tilted up scorpion-like. I slap them with my other hand, shake off the moist remains, sit up and scratch the bumps with slow deliberation.

Arne stops snoring. I turn my head to look: his eyes are open.

'Maybe we'll pay heavily in the afterworld,' he says.

'As if we're not paying enough in this one. Some creation this is – billions of creatures having to depending for their survival on the blood of others! I'm thirsty.'

'Me too.'

Wriggling halfway out of his sleeping bag, he reaches for his water bottle and a carton of Sunmaid raisins.

We help ourselves to a handful, which we chew slowly with a drink of water.

Arne says: 'I often wonder whether people realise that they might be completely mistaken about their place in the scheme of things. Remember that stuff about the first being last, the last first? Who's to say we won't be welcomed into the afterlife by a host of mosquitoes? Wielding the sceptre up on the big throne could be a virus – the foot-and-mouth virus, say.'

He pauses, then gives a laugh.

'Hell, I'm beginning to sound like Qvigstad. You should

ask him, he'll tell you. Qvigstad's a metaphysics buff. He knows all there is to know about things like the afterworld, the future a thousand years from now, life after nuclear war, test-tube babies.'

26

Qvigstad puts his arm out sideways, holding one end of a branch between forefinger and thumb. The branch hangs perpendicular to the ground, with a large fish impaled by the gills on a snapped-off side shoot.

'See this? Red belly!'

'Freeze!'

I raise my camera to my right eye.

'Could you lift it up a bit?'

The fish, in sharp focus, fills the centre of the frame along with the branch and the hand holding it. Beyond the hand Qvigstad's arm arcs back towards his head, which will probably be blurred, but still recognizable. I use a wide aperture. Mount Vuorje in the background and the dark clouds against the blue sky will be dimly visible.

'With that hat and beard you look like a highwayman — except there aren't any highways here.'

Clutching my camera like a priest his prayer book, I move closer.

'This is lake trout,' he says, pointing to the fish, 'red belly. Much bigger than the other sort.'

I would like to prolong our conversation, but can't think of anything more to say. Qvigstad is one of those people you feel like asking: What do you really think of me? (but who'd ever ask such a question?), to which he'd say:

Nothing at all (but who'd ever give such an answer?).

We are joined by Mikkelsen, after which the three of us walk back to the tents. Mikkelsen takes the stick with the fish from Qvigstad, saying:

'It is not surprising that the founders of great religions were mostly fishermen.'

'Is that so?' I ask, to humour him.

'Of all the things going on in the world, life under water is the least visible to man. Nothing is further removed from us than the world under water. That's why the water world is the most powerful symbol of the afterlife. Heaven is reflected in water. Fishermen know more about the water world than anybody else. They take out creatures never seen before, they sink to the bottom in a shipwreck. That's why all the great prophets are fishermen.'

'And they drown, too,' Qvigstad says. 'A most intelligent interpretation – had it been you writing history.'

Back at the tents he squats down and starts gutting the fish with a knife as big as the ones Lapps wear on their belts.

Arne is busy folding the net into zigzag pleats. Mikkelsen goes off to cook porridge on the primus. I have nothing to do. It is probably wiser not to help my companions at all than to hinder them. They have been on dozens of these expeditions before. They know exactly how things should be done, or in any case how they want them to be done. If I offered to help they'd be too polite to say no, but what they'd be thinking is: it takes ages to explain exactly what he's supposed to do, and as he's so inexperienced we can do everything in half the time.

Still, I am thankful no-one has mentioned my mishap in the river yesterday. Not that they have any reason to complain. I didn't cause a delay. I managed to keep the contents of the rucksack dry, and not a peep from me about the pain in my knees. So as not to stand around idle I go over to Arne's tent and get out my notebook. I reread what I wrote yesterday, adding a comment here and there. My entries up to now don't promise much in the way of new perspectives. Nor have I observed anything to support Sibbelee's bold hypothesis. This queasiness in my stomach – could it just be that I'm hungry, or is it the smell of paraffin, burnt porridge and fried fish? In the meantime I ponder the definition of scientific practice. Does hunting for something no-one has found yet and then not finding it count as practising science, or as bad luck? Or is it a sign of insufficient talent? Who's to say? A terrible fear wells up in me: having to go home empty-handed. Nothing to show for myself but a pack of nice colour snapshots, just the thing for handing round during family gatherings. Nothing that might impress either Sibbelee or Nummedal.

'Breakfast ready!' Mikkelsen shouts.

I go over to them and sit down.

It is beginning to dawn on me that Qvigstad seizes every opportunity of putting one over on Mikkelsen.

I have never seen Mikkelsen laugh, anyway his face is totally unsuited to expressions of amusement. And his skin, pale and dingy with yellowish down, is at pains to hold his lumpy frame together. His arms are thick and flabby like the arms of a female harpist. Were it not for his sturdy boots, shabby head gear (no head-net) and stained work shirt, you wouldn't think he was up to much. But he is – he can carry the heaviest of loads and take the most perilous of leaps without difficulty.

If you saw him in a pavement café, smartly dressed (navy

blue blazer, grey flannels), you would probably take him for some milksop who spent his allowance on flowers for darling Mummy. The type who gets to be called 'Buddy' by everyone after two days in military service . . . unless he's taking a swipe at his fellow conscripts, that is. That'll be another thing Mikkelsen's good at, I don't doubt – not a sound, not a flicker of emotion crossing his pasty face.

Naturally Qvigstad never says anything that might provoke Mikkelsen into demonstrating what he is capable of. All he does is take issue with practically everything Mikkelsen says, not that he says much.

'But still,' Mikkelsen says, 'no-one can deny there must have been a god who made everything.'

'The number of suppositions no-one can deny is infinite,' Qvigstad says. 'Just as infinite as the ways in which you cannot split an atom. That doesn't get us anywhere.'

I eat fish with a grubby fork from a grubby plate. The fish tastes so delicious I would gladly launch into a panegyric! For the first time in my life it dawns on me what all those back-to-nature philosophers are on about. I am happy. I am eating a fish of such noble taste and freshness as is not else-where to be had for love nor money. Take away the fishing net, frying pan, margarine, matches to light the fire, and you're left with food that owes nothing to civilisation. Now I know why Negroes and Indians didn't bother to invent blenders or refrigerators, and never again will I laugh at the cranks who dismiss civilisation as a form of collective insanity. Oh for a Lapp to appear at my side! I would press him to my heart, now that I know what riches he personi-fies.

'But anyway,' Mikkelsen flounders on in his broken

English, 'anyway God must have created the universe, it is what people believe all over the world.'

'So what does that prove?'

'That people need an explanation.'

'Oh, come on. All it proves is that people content themselves with an explanation that doesn't explain anything.'

Arne tugs at my sleeve, saying:

'Hark the great Qvigstad! In his element, he is.'

'Listen here, my boy,' Qvigstad says. 'The one problem all those so-called gods never tackle is the origin of matter. Take the Edda, or whatever you like. Snorre Sturlason maintains that it started out with the creation of Niflheim and Muspelheim. Out of what, may I ask? The Edda doesn't tell us, nor does Snorre. Between Niflheim and Muspelheim lay the yawning void called Ginnungagap, in which the streams coming from Niflheim froze solid. Sparks from Muspelheim fell on the ice, and the resulting pairing of heat and cold gave rise to a hermaphrodite giant by the name of Ymir. Fascinating I grant you, but that is not the point. The point is that you never get to hear where it all came from. Ymir fell asleep and sweated profusely. Then a man and a woman grew under his left arm.'

'That's it, then,' I say. 'Once you've got a man and a woman the rest is history.'

'Don't be so sure. One of Ymir's feet had intercourse with the other, and Bor was the result. Bor, remember, the one who fathered three sons with Bestla the female giant: Odin, Vili and Ve.'

'Anyway,' Mikkelsen says, 'all those myths may be ridiculous, but that doesn't mean to say that there wasn't a god who created the universe. God is a great mathematician, Einstein said so himself.'

'Einstein said: a mathematician, Snorre Sturlason said: sweaty feet. This just goes to prove that people can only talk about things they have personal knowledge of. Explaining the origin of matter is something not even a dervish would have the nerve to attempt. What doesn't take any nerve is making up stories about what some god or other did with the stuff once it existed.'

Arne says:

'Some of those stories aren't as far-fetched as you think. Try substituting Niflheim with Scandinavia eight thousand years ago, and Muspelheim with the Mediterranean world, from where word of Vesuvius or Etna could have spread northwards. Looking at it that way, mythology isn't all that different from geology.'

'Hear that, Mikkelsen? Good point!' Qvigstad says. 'All those folk tales of yours can, if push comes to shove, be justified on rational grounds.'

'I am not talking about seven centuries ago, when Snorre Sturlason wrote all that stuff down, not about eight thousand years ago either. I am talking about the beginning. No-one can stop me believing there was a god at the start of it all.'

'Why a god? Why complicate things with a being no-one has ever laid eyes on? God's just a word, it means nothing.'

'It means: he who created everything.'

'Do me a favour! It's so much simpler to assume that man created everything, if only because we know what the word "man" stands for. That still leaves us with the question of who created man, but that doesn't matter, because the question of who created god remains unanswered: even the greatest theologians don't know. So it's simpler and less bogus if we skip the whole god routine and say that everything is man-made. Proof of this will come in due course. The signs are hopeful: all mythologies, after all, operate between two opposite poles. One is the beginning, the creation, and the other is total ruin: Ragnarok, the Twilight of the Gods, the Apocalypse. Well, the end of the world is at our fingertips as we speak. So why not creation, too? Einstein seeing God as a maths teacher! Think of it! God as an omniscient mathematician, physicist, chemist, biologist! Hardly anyone seems to have noticed how appalling the implications are. Because what kind of god would this be? A god who one day thinks up a set of complicated problems, much as a schoolmaster. The sum of these problems is the cosmos. Into this cosmos he introduces a being called man, who is ignorant. Then he settles down at his lectern to see how his pupils progress. Well! They refuse point-blank to do any homework! They go to bed with each other without realising that children will be the result, they club each other to death and eat each other up. It takes them thousands of years to come up with a language, and several more to develop a script. Then God becomes wary, and quickly brings out a book containing all the wrong answers. He sits back and watches as a generation is devastated by infectious diseases, for which the subsequent generation discovers a remedy. Ether had been in existence for three centuries before its anaesthetic properties were discovered – something God omitted to reveal in his Bible. Moreover, until then, if your leg got blown off in battle, the stump would be dipped in boiling oil. God sniffed up the stink of burning flesh without batting an eyelid. He didn't care when a few million old women were burnt at the stake as witches, he just smiled. He let cholera, typhoid and the plague wipe out entire cities before permitting the microscope to be invented and consequently the germs of disease to be unmasked. In short, man is *der ewig Betrogene des Universums*, as they say in German. The eternal loser in the Universe! It's a favourite expression of mine. Not a day goes by without me thinking of it. Because at that school run by the creator even the best pupils fail their exams. God gives very low marks. A weird notion of God, that is. A notion we can clearly do without. God may have had some meaning for primitive peoples who believed things would always remain the same. But for us, who are continually changing the world, each new discovery offers further proof of our creative potential. The sun is a huge thermonuclear reactor and the brain a computer miniaturised to the extreme. What will this add up to in the long run? To the conclusion that we ourselves are the creators of the universe.'

'But then it is strange that not one of those creators left behind an autobiography, no?' Mikkelsen says.

'Even if it isn't historically accurate we'll be able to prove it eventually, and that's what counts. Dinosaurs didn't write autobiographies either, but we have geologists to tell us how they lived. There may have been races of humans in the past who were technologically more advanced than we are – but our descendants will catch up with them in a few million years. You mark my words! Rocks, organisms, the sun, all man-made in gigantic laboratories.'

'So where did the laboratories come from?'

'I know it's hard to prove I'm right, but it's even harder to prove I'm wrong. Look. Time is not a constraint. It may not be billions of years since it happened, but billions raised to the billionth power. As long ago as you like. It is impossible to conceive of time having a starting point. Claims to the contrary are by definition nonsensical. If infinite numbers can go on for ever, so can time. *Everything* could have happened before, and I mean literally *everything*. All this stuff I've been saying about men making things in laboratories is nothing compared to all the other things that must have been going on without our knowing anything about it, at least not yet.'

Mikkelsen says: 'But if that is how you see it, there must be people living on other planets, in other galaxies even.'

'Why shouldn't there be?'

'Well, if such people existed, or still exist, they would have made far more progress in space travel than we have.'

'Yes. So what?'

'Don't you think it a bit strange, then, that no geological stratum predating the Tertiary has been found to contain a trace of human existence, not a single arrowhead, not an axe, never mind a rocket fuselage or a transistor belonging to a UFO commander?'

'Aren't you listening? I'm talking about *everything* being made by man – radiolariae, brachiopods, archeopteryx, tree ferns, the lot.'

'But they are almost identical to the plants we have nowadays, and we know for a fact that we did not make them.'

Qvigstad draws his heels under himself, holds out his arms and stands up in one fluid movement.

'Siamese twins,' he says, 'have babies with two navels. Did you know that?'

Arne and I break into laughter. Mikkelsen gives a look as if he is filing this away in his mind along with all the other wisdom he has been hearing.

27

Curious as to why all Arne's possessions look so shabby, I asked him last night if he gets on well with his father.

My question puzzled him:

'Don't you?'

'My father died when I was seven.'

'You hardly knew him, then.'

'No, but I suppose I loved him dearly. Sometimes I think I'm still trying to get into his good books.'

'Who knows.'

'I don't believe in life after death, but sometimes I feel as if I'm doing things in the subconscious hope that my father is looking on. Perhaps it's just that I don't care to admit I'm doing them with an eye to my mother, who's still alive.'

'You are very introspective,' he said.

'But it's so simple. If I hadn't known who my father was, if I'd been a foundling, I might have done exactly the same things I'm doing now, but I'd believe my motives were completely different. So you are on good terms with your father, are you?'

'Too good maybe. My father is rather a rich man, you see. He has always been very successful. I am his only son. That complicates things. 'Night.'

*

A sunny morning. Each one of us sets off on his own. My skin is smooth, dry and brown – whether tanned or impregnated with grime and mosquito oil is hard to say. None of us has bothered to wash, let alone shave. Heating water is too much trouble and a cold shave too painful, especially with all those mosquito bites. Not shaving makes the cheeks itchy, but the stubble serves as protection.

I even tried going without my head-net for a bit: less stuffy. Mikkelsen and Qvigstad aren't wearing head-nets. No doubt Qvigstad's thick beard is better protection against insects than mine, and Mikkelsen himself is probably too repellent to attract them.

I have been roaming around all day without coming across one iota of support for my sensational hypothesis. The notes I have made until now don't add up to more than half a page.

At six, on my way back to the tents, I catch sight of Arne. With much ado, he is preparing to take a photograph of a sizeable outcrop of glacial rock, for which purpose he has climbed onto another outcrop with a sheer drop of several metres on one side.

Arne is doing some kind of gymnastics. Flexing his knees, moving his head forwards and backwards with the Leica pressed to his eye. I charge up the side of his outcrop and join him at the top. Pressing the shutter, he mutters:

'Perhaps . . .'

'Why do you say "perhaps" every time you take a picture?'

'My photographs don't usually turn out very well.'

'You can't be serious! Anyone can use a camera nowadays. Plenty of teach-yourself books.'

'It isn't that. Look, the lens is loose in the collar – that's the problem.'

'Buy a new camera. Ask your father to get you one.'

'Oh, him. Every time I see him he asks sarcastically whether I've taken any pictures lately. The moment I show them to him he offers me a new Leica.'

'Well then.'

'I don't dare.'

'What's daring got to do with it? What's so bad about your father buying you a new camera?'

'I'd feel I'm not worthy of it.'

'But you'd be using the camera for work, not amusement.'

'Makes no difference. Anything new, anything costing money makes me uncomfortable. As if I don't really deserve it. I've always had that feeling. People think I'm tight-fisted sometimes. If I were I'd be saving money, and I'm not. Remember we were talking about your father last night?'

'Yes. Why?'

'In my case it's got nothing to do with my father – feeling unworthy, I mean. It's just another example of taking things into account which I don't believe in.'

'What don't you believe in?'

Arne rubs his neck and pats his hair with his free hand; he's holding the Leica with the other.

'I know it's none of my business,' I mumble awkwardly. 'I hope you don't mind my asking.'

'No, I don't mind, I even told someone on a train once, and I had never met that person before. I believe, or rather I seem to believe – because I don't – that denying myself things will bring me some wonderful reward one day.'

'Such as?'

'Such as making a major discovery.'

'And you reckon a faulty camera will help?'

Arne laughs as he puts his camera back into the battered case. I am not telling him anything he hasn't heard before from all and sundry, including himself. But he is not about to give up just yet; maybe he wants to see if he can argue me into a corner.

'Columbus discovered America with a rowing boat,' he says.

'There were no better ships in those days.'

'But he got there in the end.'

'That was a one-off. There's no point in discovering America twice over. Your countryman Thor Heyerdahl sailed to Hawaii on a raft, but Hawaii had been discovered ages ago.'

'He wanted to prove you could get there on a raft.'

'And I suppose you want to prove you can use your old Leica to . . .'

'I know what you're getting at. But I could never stand setting out with a brand new tent, top-of-the-range instruments, the most expensive camera, the lot, and having nothing to show for it at the end.'

Was it to change the subject that I stepped into the void? What is happening to me?

The world flashes past, I let out a scream as I plummet down, feet first. The pain in my skull is so bad that I don't dare open my eyes. I am sprawled at the base of the rock. I can sense grit under the palms of my hands, but can't see anything. Arne stands over me, seizes me under my arms and drags me upright. I try taking a step forward, but my right leg won't move. There's blood running down into my right eye. Pushing Arne away with my left hand, I hear myself protesting:

'I'm all right! I'm all right!'

But he won't let go. The world floats back into my mind as seen through the bottom of a beer glass. When I wipe my eye my hand comes away covered in blood, and there's also blood on my right trouser leg. How did it get there?

I am lying by a large fire, stripped to my underpants; Mikkelsen is busy frying half a dozen trout. Now and then the smoke billows over me.

The wind is variable.

My left hand keeps brushing up and down my left leg to chase the mosquitoes away. My right leg has been cleaned and bandaged. There's a gash from knee to ankle. A big wad of cotton wool taped to my forehead shades my eyes from the sun.

I smoke a cigarette, but the taste is vile – it always is in the vicinity of sizzling margarine. My leather compass case has become scratched in the fall. My precious compass! I snap it open and peer in the little mirror. It looks as if there's a snowball with a core of ice lodged in my forehead. My beard, too, catches my attention. It's a shade lighter than the hair on my head, something I wasn't aware of before. Funny how much there is to discover about a face you've known for so many years. For the first time I realise the potential for camouflage offered by a man's beard.

'Satisfied with your beard, are you?'

Qvigstad comes over to sit with me. I snap the compass shut and put it back in its case.

'Shaving,' muses Qvigstad. 'Can't imagine why they invented it. For thousands of years men have been obliged to go around like defoliated trees summer and winter – why?

Nobody knows. On the other hand, you'd think great men with beards like Moses, Socrates or Marx must have had their reasons for disguising their faces.'

He puts a cigarette between his lips and holds out his hand. I pass him my matches.

'Thanks. Heard this one yet? Two colonials are called up for medical examination. The doctor notices that one of them has a tattoo on his shrunken dong – some word, apparently, of which he can only make out the first and last letters, an *s* and an *e*. What does it say? he asks. Well, Doctor, on lonely nights in the jungle you can sometimes read it quite clearly, and then it says *Simone*. Simone? Yes. You see, doctor, it's my wife's name, and her name alone is enough to lead me not into temptation. Right. Then the doctor turns to the other colonial and discovers a similar tattoo with an *s* and an *e*. Another Simone? No, Doctor. What then? Well, Doctor, it says *souvenir d'une nuit chaude passée en Afrique Occidentale Française*.'

Spreading his arms wide, crucifix-style, Qvigstad roars: 'Soooo long! Dirty bugger, eh?'

Afterwards we all eat knäckebröd, fried fish and cheese. Arne brews coffee and Mikkelsen produces a bottle of brandy, which we use to lace the coffee.

Arne has washed the blood off the leg of my trousers. He passes them to me, saying:

'You could have been dead.'

I could have been dead. But I am not. I survived. I am not even seriously injured.

Thinking of my father, I pull the trousers up over my aching knees, squashing insects in the process.

What exactly caused his death when he fell? Did he land on his head? Or was he hit by a stone that rolled down after him? Why didn't he get away with a knee injury? If he had, I might never have come to Finnmark. I might have become a flautist.

I am not superstitious, but why should all these notions be entering my head just now? Why do I have this sense of having gained a reprieve, temporarily at least? My fall is a replica of the fall that killed my father. The same evil spirit that pushed him off the precipice has been urging me to undertake the same kinds of adventures as my father, so I'll die the same kind of death. But it hasn't worked. I've paid my dues. I've survived. I'm not dead, and my injuries are minor. I've put the evil spirit in its place, it won't bother me again.

If I'm not superstitious, why is it these ideas keep floating into my mind?

I slip my belt through the loops on my trousers and re-attach the compass case. It still looks seldom used, and yet I've had it for years. It looks new, and the knock it took a while back has left an equally new-looking mark on the leather. It doesn't signal wear; on the contrary, the case looks newer than ever.

At what point does damage stop and wear begin?

'Alfred, look! Over there!'

Arne, Qvigstad and Mikkelsen are standing shoulder to shoulder, staring intently at the far side of the lake. Mikkelsen is holding a pair of binoculars. I stand up, stare, see nothing, then suddenly realise what they're looking at.

The flanks of Mount Vuorje appear to be shifting, as if the ground, the vegetation and the patches of snow have grown legs.

Steeling myself, I stagger towards Arne.

'Listen! Listen carefully!'

I listen, open-mouthed. The air is filled with rumour, a sound that is hard to describe. The low rumblings of some immense horizontal creature overlying the entire mountainside.

Peering through the binoculars it's as if you can hear the animals grazing. Most of them are fawn or brown in colour, but a lot of them are white with tan markings. We take turns with the binoculars to scan the slope for someone herding the animals, but he could be miles away. Gradually the herd bears down on the river.

'The wind is blowing this way,' Mikkelsen says. 'So we can get much closer to them if we want.'

'They're almost as shy as animals in the wild,' Arne says. 'The moment they catch our scent they'll be off.'

Reindeer. Fabled creatures of Christmas calendars and picture postcards. Deer with felt-lined antlers. Exotic, and reduced to a cliché by a surfeit of celebrity. Not that I've ever heard of reindeer producing a constant hum, never read about it in books, wouldn't have guessed it either.

I struggle on after the others to get as close to the animals as possible. The low sun casts my shadow ahead of me, elongated tenfold. The terrain now is greatly varied: moss, shrubs, stones, all making different sounds on impact. No other noise but the rush of water. It's only when I stand still that I can hear the reindeer, the way you only hear your own heartbeat when you're lying quietly in bed. The animals in the front line are already stepping into the water, and still our presence doesn't alarm them.

We can now hear the bells worn by some of the bucks. But even that sound doesn't transport us back to civilisation.

Low clouds, so low as to touch the ground, roll across the water towards us. Swathes of white mist give us a striped appearance. We straggle back to the tents.

It is one thirty a.m. The clouds are moving faster than we are, blotting out the sunshine. The temperature drops sharply in the space of minutes. We sit down by the dying fire to drink the last of our coffee, after which we all turn in for the night. Reaching his tent Qvigstad twists round to deliver a parting shot:

'Hey! A young naked negress – not talking, just smiling!'

Arne and I are in our sleeping bags, which we have pulled up to our chins. Things aren't so bad now, thanks to the coolness brought on by the clouds. But the bugs obviously want to shelter from the coming shower and the top of the pyramid is so thick with them that you can destroy scores at once just by reaching up and clapping your hands.

We eat raisins, drink some water, smoke another cigarette.

Arne waxes philosophical.

'Do you remember what we were talking about just before you had your little encounter with the force of gravity?'

'Yes?'

'It's strange that nobody really does anything for its own sake. Being thrifty is my way of placating Fate, and then there's you, thinking your father's watching you.'

'My father is no more real than your fate, the fate you hope will reward you for your austerity.'

'What about your mother?' he asks. 'Your mother is still alive, isn't she?'

'Yes.'

'It can't have been easy for her to bring up two small children on her own.'

'No, not easy, but not as hard as you might imagine.' His remark has struck a chord. Here goes, I think to myself.

'My mother,' I say, 'is Holland's foremost essayist. She became successful not long after my father died, and she kept it up for years. Night after night she'd sit at the table in the living room pounding on a big office typewriter. Which she still does. Starts at eight sharp. Makes coffee at ten, then takes a break until a quarter past. Sometimes she pours me and my sister a cup too, she even did that when we were quite young, after which we were sent to bed. We'd be wide awake, of course, hearing our mother's typewriter until midnight. Every week she writes two articles for magazines plus half a page for the Saturday supplement of a national daily, and she also contributes to a monthly cultural magazine. Her subject is foreign literature. A total of thirteen articles each month, in which she reviews some thirty books. And she travels all over the country to give talks. She's an undisputed expert. Hemingway, Faulkner, Graham Greene, Somerset Maugham, Sartre, Robbe-Grillet, Beckett, Ionesco, Françoise Sagan, Mickey Spillane or Ian Fleming – anyone wanting to appear cultured simply reads what my mother has written about them and then parrots her opinion without mentioning where they got it from. She's been awarded the Legion of Honour and an honorary doctorate from the smallest university in Northern Ireland, the name of which escapes me. As you can imagine, there are over thirty books each month for her to write about, sometimes as many as fifty.'

'And does she read them all?'

'Not a single one. She doesn't even open them, to avoid damaging the spine. What she does is copy the titles and the authors' names onto little cards. Most critics don't even do that. A second-hand dealer comes round from time to time to collect the brand-new books for a quarter of the retail price.'

'So how can your mother write all those articles?'

'We have subscriptions to the *Observer*, the *Times Literary Supplement* and the *Figaro Littéraire*. My mother only bothers with books that have already been reviewed in those papers. Oh, quite openly, mind you! She even quotes them verbatim at times, complete with credits to the *Observer* or the *Figaro*, especially on off days when she can't come up with anything. "Just a quickie this time," she'll say. She's not alone in this, plenty of reviewers make even less of an effort. But my mother's a very conscientious person. Busy from morning till night, even works on Sundays. She compiles dossiers on all the authors whose books she reviews. In the living room back home we've got a big oak cupboard crammed with folders. She cuts out all the relevant items in the foreign press and files them away. Naturally, it can happen that there's something on the back of an article that she needs as well. So she has to choose which one to cut up and which to save. Then she goes and makes a neat typewritten copy of the one she cut up.'

Arne smiles faintly.

'Oh well,' I say. 'Maybe you'll meet her some day. She's thin and quite short, dark eyes, thin lips, nicotine-stained index and middle fingers. Smokes three packets a day. Goes to bed at two in the morning and gets up at seven, has done for years. My sister and I had a comfortable childhood thanks to her hard work. If my father hadn't died we wouldn't have spent as much as we did, because my mother isn't at all good with money. Always buying us new clothes, you know, nothing was mended because she didn't have the time. In the time it took her to darn a pair of socks she could make enough money to buy five new pairs, she used to say. We went to restaurants several times a week, because cooking was another waste of time as far as she was concerned. I feel sorry for her sometimes. I stay away from books myself. Whether or not she writes a load of rubbish isn't my concern. She churns out pretty much the same stuff every time. If the author's English she'll say his technique is masterly, that he has a fine sense of humour, that the characters are convincing and the plot well structured. If it's a French book the author will be intelligent, lucid, erudite, possibly a touch frivolous, and his engagement with the subject will be either impressive or slight. Dear old Mum! I wouldn't dare ask her whether she herself thinks her reviews amount to anything.'

'But even if she doesn't, she can still say: I did it for the sake of my children.'

'So can a burglar.'

'Who can honestly say they have always made a living off their own wits? Take Sauerbruch, the famous surgeon. Lost it completely when he got old, but that didn't stop people from flocking to his door. Everyone wanted to be operated on by the celebrated Sauerbruch, even though he was no better than a quack by then. His assistants had their own reasons for keeping quiet. That's how we all end up in the long run: party to some deception or other. Bakers sell inferior bread to raise their profits, the motor industry makes sure your car breaks down in five years, garages charge you for repairs they never made, clockmakers charge fifty kroner for cleaning your watch by blowing into the casework. Daylight robbery all round.

'I often think about the people who write those books my mother reviews. People who don't feel loved enough by their friends to be able to confide their innermost thoughts in them, so they think: Why don't I write a book instead? Thousands of copies will get printed and with any luck there'll be one or two readers who love me. So they spend two or three years writing, and then what do they get? They get the kind of ready-made drivel produced by my mother and her colleagues. Unless they get insulted, which happens a lot in their line of business. It's almost the norm, even.'

'What about all those people getting paid for writing stuff anyone could think up? That's stealing, too. Like when they write a thousand pages on a subject they could cover in a hundred?'

'All the same, it must be a great feeling if you can say: Here I am, I've achieved success and it's all my own work, I didn't have to lie or cheat to get there.'

'In a world where everyone's forever cheating everyone else? A world where practically nothing is known for certain? Don't give me that.'

'But that's my point. Not cheating is one thing, being first is another.'

'Who's to say? No-one knows how many cheats honestly believe they've always been straight.'

'In a way I hate my mother and everything she stands for. It's as if she sets a terrible example, forever saying: Look at me! As long as you get your share of awards, honorary doctorates and special funding, you'll have nothing to reproach yourself for. Whenever I'm with her I feel I'm making things far more complicated than they need to be.

Like insisting on paying with gold in a country of paper currency.'

'We are all under pressure from those around us – family, friends, acquaintances, people at work. They're the only people to whom we mean anything, let's face it. If you want that to change you need to become world famous, and who gets to be world famous?'

'If my mother were genuinely talented she'd be setting a better example, putting a different kind of pressure on me.'

'Do you really think children are better off with a genius for a parent? It's always the same old story: they take to drink, get thrown into prison, commit suicide. Why? Because the son of a genius seldom turns out to be a genius himself – for the simple reason that not enough of them are born. So what can he do? Becoming a genius like his father is not on, whereas that's all that counts in his world. So the children of geniuses often opt out in the end. They vanish.'

'I know it's difficult. If you want to keep your integrity and your independence, you need to think of something worth making sacrifices for.'

'But then there's no way of keeping your integrity unless you discover something new – unless you count the integrity of Don Quixote, that is.'

'And then there's Galileo, the enviable ease with which he confessed he was wrong when he knew he was right. In the face of incontrovertible truth, personal integrity is just a bagatelle.'

'Precisely, and don't you forget it. That's why scientists are on the whole such an unprincipled lot. And for the most part their discoveries can't hold a candle to Galileo's truth, either.'

28

Flying insects patter against the canvas, inside and out. Arne snores. At least the sun doesn't shine. All four planes of the pyramid are dingy in equal measure, and shutting my eyes actually keeps out most of the light. I must get some sleep. I am not suffocating in my sleeping bag, my legs hardly hurt provided I keep still, the hardness of the ground doesn't bother me, and although my head is throbbing I haven't got a headache. The wad of cotton wool is very hot, though. Must get rid of it in the morning. Treat the flies to some dried blood. The theory is that the wounds of animals heal quickly because they're kept clean by flies – clean flies, of course, flies that don't transmit dirt. There is no dirt around here to speak of, so the flies are presumably clean.

The pattering grows louder and also faster and more regular. Could be rain. A cold drop falls on my face. Have I been asleep? I prop myself up on my elbows and cast my eyes in every direction. The tent is leaking all over. Arne carries on snoring. There's water dripping onto my sleeping bag, making dark stains on the pale yellow silk.

Puddles are forming on the sheets of plastic we're lying on. What can I do? It is not a major problem, of course, just a little water. But in the care instructions of my down sleeping bag it says that contact with water 'can cause irreversible damage to the insulation capacity'. As if being stuck without aerial photographs and falling off that rock weren't bad enough.

I give Arne's arm a shake. He opens his eyes, mumbles. I crawl out of my sleeping bag. Arne motions me to get off my plastic sheet. I roll up my bag and retreat to a corner of the tent. Cold water trickles down my back. Arne tips the water off the sheet and turns it over before replacing it on the ground. Even his boots and my shoes are full of water. I turn them over. Then we stow all the gear that mustn't get wet into our rucksacks, put our clothes on and lie down in our macs under a drum roll of rain.

Arne proffers the carton of raisins.

'Poor us,' he says. 'Poor, poor us. Creative labour is perceived by some philosophers to be on a higher, more interesting plane than the drudgery of bus conductors, char-women, factory workers and navvies. And yet the contributions made by creative minds, completely free of charge, aren't even mentioned by cultural historians.'

'Creative minds never get much of a mention. It's warlords, politicians and other confidence tricksters who get talked about all the time, not people with creative minds.'

'Not to mention the creative minds that fizzle out,' he says. 'Because how much difference is there really between a factory worker and an intellectual? I have always hated the idea of becoming a teacher. Going over the same ground year after year for half a century. Wishing you could tell them something new, yet having nothing to say.'

'And it can be worse,' I say. 'What about being stuck in a rut where there isn't anything left to discover? Even more ghastly is having a talent that no-one really has any use for. Like a talent for Greek. In a grammar school with five hundred pupils you won't come across more than one with a genuine interest in learning ancient Greek, and perhaps two or three others who'll be grateful later on for having had a stab at it. The rest of them leave school barely able to make sense of Homer because they did as little studying as they could. Through no fault of his own, the classics teacher is faced with educating generation upon generation to a poor level of Greek. To learn it properly takes time, and there is no time because no-one really needs ancient Greek. How can he keep his self-respect in those circumstances?'

'By doing his duty, the incomprehensible duty imposed on him by his incomprehensible existence in an incomprehensible world. The same goes for the rest of us.'

'That's the penalty for being incapable of doing truly creative work.'

'You're an optimist! Do you think the difference is really that big? Every intellectual profession consists for the most part in making laborious preparations to carry out operations that are quintessentially simple. Like frying an egg on top of Mount Everest.'

'You reckon? The telescope was invented by someone who looked through two magnifying glasses, one held to his eye and the other at arm's length. And it was a spectacular invention!'

'But in those days you couldn't go out and buy a magnifying glass from the local optician. You had to begin by grinding your own lenses. There's the rub.'

There's the rub indeed, and I help myself to another handful of raisins.

*

'Being a student,' Arne says, 'means labouring under a gross delusion. You feel you're making progress. Read one book after another. Sit for exams. Obtain diplomas. Intellectual advance, you think. The certificates are there for you to take home and show around. Parties are thrown to celebrate your success. Everything and everyone tells you you're making progress as long as you pass exams. I knew a student once who framed his certificates and hung them on the wall. And then what do you do? Once you've got the degree? It's back to doing your own lens-grinding. Or lugging a forty-kilo rucksack around for days on end. Or sleeping on wet ground in wet clothes. I'm sorry about that. It's all my fault. I should have bought a new tent. Qvigstad and Mikkelsen are high and dry, no leaks in their tent. But, believe me, setting out with a brand new tent and then returning without a major discovery – I don't think I could stand it. I do apologise. It's not fair on you. Just a silly notion of mine. All the same, if it all turns out to have been for nothing, if you don't find what you're looking for, at least you'll be able to say: I made the effort, I did my best, it isn't as if I didn't try. Forgive me. I'm terribly sorry.'

He mutters 'terribly sorry' a few more times, lies back with his arm under his head and begins to snore again.

It's as if he hasn't been fully awake. An instance of sleep-walking, or rather sleep-talking. But now he is undeniably sound asleep.

I wish I could sleep too.

Instead, I'm wide awake with fear. Imagine going home at the end of the summer having achieved nothing! Nothing but the satisfaction of having made the effort and done my best.

What could Arne have meant by what he said just now?

With the rain pouring down and him talking in his sleep, didn't it sound as if he was telling my future, complete with offers of consolation, absolution even?

Bad omen? Arne's the only one I feel at all close to. It would have been worse coming from Qvigstad.

Qvigstad bites into the world with big white teeth. Swings his hammer like a god. Leaps across rivers unhampered by the heaviest of loads. When he stops to take in the views all around it's as if he's surveying his own property. Fish rise to the bait the moment he casts his line. I have yet to see Arne catch an edible fish with his aluminium saucepan wrapped round with nylon fishing line.

He's no less tough than Qvigstad, though. Maybe tougher. Maybe Qvigstad wouldn't be up to hiking in derelict boots or sharing leaky tents with swarms of mosquitoes. Maybe Qvigstad wouldn't get any sleep at all in those circumstances, whereas Arne is well away and snoring. When the water drips onto his face his eyelid merely twitches.

The drumming of the rain drowns in the howling wind. It is so dusky in the tent that it's impossible to tell how far we are into the day.

29

The rain persists, and there is no sign of it lifting.

The four of us sit together in Qvigstad and Mikkelsen's tent, in the centre of which the primus stove is burning. Arne and I hold our sleeping bags aloft in the vain hope of getting them dry, manoeuvring awkwardly to avoid singeing. To think that Arne insisted I change into dry socks after I slipped in the river the first day. Now both of us are soaked to the skin, and our clothes won't dry until we get a few days of continuous sunshine. Sopping wet socks and shoes. Sopping wet sleeping bags with the down clotted into lumps of putty. Mikkelsen has a thermometer. He says it's three degrees Celsius outside.

Patches of moisture begin to spread around where Arne and I are sitting. Qvigstad and Mikkelsen regard us with dismay, as if we're a pair of cats rescued from a well. Their belongings are arranged in meticulous order. Their boots have been placed outside the tent in protective plastic bags, under the projecting eave of the double roof. Their feet are shod in Lapp slippers of soft leather to spare the groundsheet. Stray insects are dispatched with spray the moment they appear, after which their corpses are neatly swept into little heaps.

We take turns going outside armed with six sheets of toilet paper and the folding spade. It's the only way.

With my mac over my head, and the sides held out wide to avoid soiling, I take a shit in the pouring rain – standing. My injured leg is too stiff for me to squat. The surface of the lake looks like beaten pewter. Last night's reindeer are nowhere to be seen. I listen carefully, but can only make out the sound of the wind and the rain. Where can the animals have gone? There's nowhere for them to shelter. They'll be soaked to the skin like me, and I'll have to be stoical like them. The mosquitoes attack my buttocks, my thighs. I pull the cotton wool off my forehead and bury it with the rest under sodden moss. When I've pulled up my trousers I find I can wring streams of water from my shirt tails. Warm water, heated up by my body.

Naturally the primus can't be kept going for ever. Especially not now, because unless the rain lets up soon we're going to have to do all our cooking with paraffin. Where would we get paraffin once we've used up what little we have?

Moreover: even if the weather improves, how long will it be before the dwarf spruces are dry enough to use for fire-wood?

For all I know it could rain like this for a week, or a fort-night. I don't dare ask Qvigstad how much fuel we have left, but it won't be very much. If we can't make fires we'll have to exist on bread, knäckebröd and tinned food. We won't even be able to make coffee. And how long is our supply of bread supposed to last?

All these things go through my mind without panic, more with amusement. My only worry is that we might be forced to go all the way back to Skoganvarre to wait for better weather. But that hasn't even been hinted at. Qvigstad gets to his feet and Mikkelsen turns off the primus. They put on their rain-proof clothes, hang their map pockets round their necks, kneel down, unfasten the tent flap, reach for their boots, take them out of their plastic bags, put the dripping bags outside again, and so forth. Everything they do is methodical. Clouds of insects rush in as the pair of them leave. Arne closes the flap behind them. I expect him to reach for the mosquito spray, but the idea doesn't seem even to enter his head.

'I don't fancy spending all day in here,' I say. 'There's no point.'

'No, there isn't.'

Several mosquitoes have burrowed into my hair and are stinging my scalp.

'Come on, then,' I say.

'Do you mind if I take a look at your leg?'

'Oh no, please don't. It's fine.'

I roll over onto my stomach and crawl outside dragging my bad leg behind me, which I do with some difficulty.

By six in the evening I have covered a distance of at least ten kilometres in the rain. You end up not noticing the rain any more than you notice how wet you are when you're swimming. The intensity varies, as does the gradient of the terrain, as does everything else. Sometimes it's as good as dry for periods lasting up to twenty minutes.

I explored eight small round lakes today. Walked around each one, inspecting the margins for any ridges or ramparts. Most meteor craters are encircled by a low bank of matter thrown up by the stone's impact. Didn't see anything note-worthy. Slowing down to a snail's pace, I became increasingly aware of the raindrops impacting on the water, making it squirt up thickly like ripe tomato juice.

That is all I saw.

Picked up a few rocks on the way, though.

Returning to the tents I catch sight of Arne, who appears to be sketching. Before reaching him – before he has even noticed me, I hope – I discard the rocks. Afraid of him asking: What did you collect those for? I wouldn't know what to tell him.

As it is, Arne gives no sign of having seen me. He is sketching. One knee resting on the stony ground and the other raised at right angles, like a chair sliced down the middle. The seat of the chair serves as a prop for his notebook, which is shielded from the rain by a piece of clear plastic. He is drawing with his hand under the plastic.

Far be it from me to wish to disturb him. Ah! The wonderful solitude of nature study in the Arctic wilderness! How impressive is his dedication! This sounds a bit over the top, I know, but it doesn't mean to say I think he is ridiculous in any way. On the contrary, I find myself bowing my head as I advance.

Arne's eyes go back and forth between his notebook and the view confronting him. He is drawing with a stub of yellow pencil, but the point is perfectly sharpened and on the end is a metal cap. Cheap, but efficient.

I am now just behind him, a little to one side.

He sketches with short deft strokes, to very good effect. I couldn't produce anything half as good as this. I don't even enjoy drawing, really. More's the pity.

Arne uses the right-hand pages of his notebook for illustrations and the left for his notes, which I can't read because they're in Norwegian. But they look very neat and self-assured. Nothing crossed out, no smudges. Clearly numbered, well spaced. Not the kind of illegible jottings that can only be deciphered by the person who made them. These will keep their value even if Arne loses the notebook and it isn't found again for fifty years. Even if he drops dead.

Notes befitting a true scientist, travel notes inspired by immediacy: here I am, now. I must observe everything there is to observe, NOW. I must record all my observations in unambiguous terms comprehensible to all, mindful of the fact that any detail I miss or neglect to write down will be lost for ever, because going back for a second look is an impractical luxury.

'Hello,' I say. 'You make me jealous, being so good at drawing.'

'Really?'

He doesn't look up. His drawing looks like a plate in a textbook.

'Keeping notes is not my forte,' I flounder on. 'Fountain pens vanish into thin air, biros dry up the moment I get out in the open. And the points of my pencils keep breaking off, too.'

'You should get one of these,' he says, indicating the protective cap stuck on the end of his pencil stub. 'Dirt cheap, and it's got a little ring you can slide over it to keep it in place.'

He demonstrates how the ring slides up and down.

'Don't they have them in Holland?'

'No,' I lie. 'Never seen one before.'

'Biros,' Arne says. 'Another newfangled idea. Invented purely to make people pay more for a complicated version of something that's served everyone perfectly well for hundreds of years.'

I agree with him. But even with pocketfuls of sharp pencils to hand I wouldn't be able to draw as well as he does.

I wander off and sit myself down on a stone at some distance away, to let him get on with it.

When Qvigstad classifies his rock samples, he takes a small notepad and puts a number at the top of the sheet followed by the date of collection and the find-spot. Next he examines the sample through his magnifying glass to establish the geological type, writes that down too and tears off the sheet, which goes into a water-resistant paper bag along with the sample. Some days he comes back with as many as ten samples, each weighing two hundred grams or more. Obviously, he's accumulating an extra two kilos daily. This doesn't seem to worry him in the slightest. In fact his rucksack appears to expand by the day to accommodate fresh supplies of stones. I have never heard him grumble, either.

Then there is Mikkelsen. Mikkelsen collects grit and sand in little bags, but isn't above picking up the odd stone – quite big ones occasionally – which he then takes back and displays on top of the clothes in his rucksack as souvenirs.

I watch them coming over the hill towards me in single file, fishing rods over their shoulders.

Qvigstad has made another catch. The fish is very big this time; he can't remember what it's called in English, but naturally knows the Norwegian name: *Harr*.

Harr. I enter the name in my notebook. They check to see if I've got the spelling right.

We go inside the green tent and Mikkelsen lights the primus.

Arne joins us a moment later.

'Starving,' he says.

'Starving,' Qvigstad echoes. 'That reminds me, I ran into [*unintelligible*] the other day. Just back from India, for some United Nations welfare programme, I believe. He said that seeing the effects of famine over there doesn't stop European travellers from going to the local Hilton hotel for dinner. I said to him: If you really were cast from a different mould than Hitler or Himmler, you wouldn't have been capable of doing that. You had your eight thousand kroner or thereabouts for travel expenses. You could have shared out that money among four thousand starving people. It could have been used to fill the stomachs of four thousand people. A drop in the ocean, true, but for people who've gone hungry most of their lives getting enough to eat for once must be an unforgettable feast. That done, you'd have to make for the nearest airport, of course, on foot or with money borrowed from some consul. Not much fun, that bit, I grant you. Tail between your legs. But how bad is that compared to the suffering of four thousand starving people?'

'What did [*unintelligible*] say to that?'

'He said: Of course I'd have been glad to do as you suggest. But I wasn't supplied with funds so that I could give them away. I was supposed to write a report about the Social Science Relief Programme.'

'We all have duties to fulfil.'

'The guards at Auschwitz had families to feed, and crocodiles can't go without food either. Christ, what a smell in here.'

The tent is filled with blue smoke, but the fish tastes good. The bread we eat with it is soggy. Whose fault is that? Not mine!

'Nuclear disarmament under international supervision,'

Qvigstad says. 'D'you know what that means? It's a bit like having a wound on the back of your left hand and using the same hand to stick a plaster on it.'

He glances at Mikkelsen, who strikes me as someone who'd be familiar with this type of problem, but Mikkelsen doesn't respond.

'I wouldn't mind being an inventor,' Qvigstad goes on, 'of the cancan, say. It would be great to have invented the cancan, but it's been done already. I can't think of any other invention I'd care to take credit for.'

Arne says something to him in Norwegian. The conversation continues in Norwegian for a spell, at the end of which all three put on their waterproof clothing. I follow suit. Qvigstad and Mikkelsen are going fishing again, I take it, and it's probably time Arne and I headed back to our tent, since this one is too small for the four of us to sleep in.

Not until I am outside does it dawn on me that we are striking camp.

I don't ask any questions. I retrieve my rucksack and help Arne to dismantle the dripping tent and fold it up.

'Very bad for the tent,' he mutters. 'Folding it up when it is wet is very bad.'

No, not good for his precious tent, I can see that.

What is worse, though, is that the tent weighs a great deal more when wet. How much more? Three kilos? Four?

Add to that the water absorbed by the sleeping bag . . . I could try wringing it out (the ruin of even the finest down sleeping bag, according to the instructions), but it would still hold litres of water

I am past caring; it's too late to do anything about it anyway. I keep telling myself I'm a soggy reindeer, or a swimmer.

*

Arne and I finish our packing before Qvigstad and Mikkelsen. The rain is lifting again, turning first into drizzle, then into wet vapour.

I load the rucksack onto my wet back. How much heavier has it got since the day before yesterday? Hard to tell. I'm glad it's my turn to carry the wooden theodolite, it gives me a sense of security.

We walk in line towards the Lievnasjokka river, which flows from Lievnasjaurre lake. The river is a good hundred metres across, and fairly deep too, it seems. There are several jutting rocks, but none close enough together to serve as stepping stones. We walk along the riverbank for some time without coming across any rocks suitably spaced for getting to the other side.

This does not surprise Arne, Qvigstad and Mikkelsen. Qvigstad points to a section of the river without any stones at all, and Mikkelsen and Arne nod their heads in agreement.

They sit down and pull off their boots. We are going to wade across.

'Better keep your socks on,' Arne says, 'they'll stop you from slipping on the bottom.'

The entire riverbed consists of rounded stones.

I tie my laces together and hang my shoes around my neck. I plant the tripod in front of me in the river, then cling to it for support while trying to step firmly on the stones, not in the cracks. The cold bores into my feet like a dentist's drill.

The tripod isn't much use. Having to pull it out and then plant it further ahead means standing still for too long. The pain in the soles of my feet is unbearable, and my ankles ache from the sheer effort of keeping my balance. So I tuck the tripod under my arm and forge ahead, eyes popping from the strain of looking where to put my feet amid the splashes and foam.

Missed! My right foot slides out of control, I keel over and break my fall with my right hand, thereby briefly forming a triangle with my right arm submerged up to the elbow and the icy water lapping my groin. My left arm is raised to keep my wristwatch dry, my map pocket is dangling in the water. The tripod floats away, but thankfully gets caught on something almost at once. A sense of slow, obdurate calm comes over me. Taking my time, I drag my splayed right leg back into position, and with my feet together I finally manage to stand upright.

Qvigstad and Mikkelsen are on the far bank, watching my antics. Arne has turned back and is now wading towards me. I make a lunge for the tripod and seize it just before Arne gets there. My confidence restored, I take a plastic cup from my trouser pocket, scoop up some water and gulp it down.

Qvigstad and Mikkelsen turn and walk away, the way people walk away from a quayside incident after watching a skipper rescue his youngest offspring from drowning with his boathook.

30

The terrain now is fairly flat, and so stony that there is no vegetation to speak of and consequently no sogginess, despite the persistent rain. The topsoil is composed of yellow schistose debris. Anyone unfamiliar with the term will have to look it up in the dictionary, or take it on trust. One of the reasons why the range of subjects dealt with in novels is so limited is that authors want everybody to be able to follow exactly what is going on. Technical terms put readers off. Entire classes of trades and professions never make it into novels simply because it would be impossible to describe the reality without the use of technical jargon. Such occupations as do occur – policeman, doctor, cowboy, sailor, spy – are no more than caricatures in response to the delusional expectations of the intended lay readership.

In this open plain we come across several holes filled with water, which is so clear as to look almost black. Their sizes vary, but most of them are indeed circular in shape, or at least oval. Dead-ice holes? No tell-tale ridges thrown up by the impact of a meteorite. I pick up random samples of rock, and drop them again, disappointed. Who will ever know how much effort it takes to bend over in my dripping, leaden clothing, with forty kilos on my back, camera and map pocket swinging from my neck and a bulky wooden tripod in one hand? Even if I do find a meteorite – the prize, the great prize – all I will be able to say about it in my thesis is where and when I made my discovery, the find-spot being marked with a cross on a small map of the area. No-one will know what I went through. In the unlikely event that my data would move anyone to consider the human effort involved, they would merely think: this person spent an interesting summer trekking in the High North; while he was there his eye was caught by an unusual stone, and in picking it up he made a momentous discovery.

He picked up stones and had to drop them again.

Mount Vuorje, which is near the lake we have left behind, is still clearly visible thanks to the rapidly dispersing clouds. It is the only high mountain in the region.

Our new camp is midway between two smallish lakes fringed with green marshland.

The green is streaked with watercourses, sometimes at right angles to each other like ditches dug for peat. The sky is black, deep blue and dark red, swirls of pigment running together without blending. The sun comes out periodically, spreading some warmth when it does.

I let my eyes wander over this uncluttered landscape, without the seclusion of trees and yet secretive. Bare, but by no means bleak thanks to the subtle shades of the scrubby plants and mosses, the boulders and stretches of soil in between. Not a soul within a huge radius, and none likely to turn up, yet this is not what you'd call a lonely place. Why not? I can't say. I fall into a strange fantasy: staying right here, not leaving until the snow overtakes me a few months from now, causing me to freeze to death, painlessly.

Talk of pain. My injured right leg is swollen from ankle to knee, and the skin is so tight that the slightest touch feels like a pin being buried in the flesh as far as it will go.

Eyes smarting, ears burning, head swimming, I feel more exhausted than I can ever imagine feeling again as long as I live, but never have I felt wider awake. There's no knowing how much you can take until you've tried everything.

We pitch the tents and take off most of our drenched clothes to spread them out to dry. Mikkelsen found a reindeer antler earlier on, and hangs on to it like some silly tourist. First he tied it on top of his rucksack so it appeared to be sprouting from his head. Now he sticks the antler in the ground in front of his tent to dry his socks on. Come winter and it'll hang over his bed in his student lodgings, I've no doubt.

Qvigstad and Arne move towards the water with the fishing net.

I take my sleeping bag and try to separate the lumps in the down through the fabric. Perhaps it won't be ruined after all.

While I'm busy doing this, my eye falls on Mikkelsen. He is lying stomach down in front of their tent . . . doing what? Peering through a stereoscope. Laid out on a sheet of plastic before him is a batch of photographs, which he studies two at a time through the instrument. What is in those photos? I can make out pale blotches in the black borders, could be the imprint of drawing pins. But they could also be part of the image – that is, the faces of clocks and altimeters. Aerial photographs!

I drop my sleeping bag and go over to him.

My heart leaps into my mouth, almost as if it wants to get out.

'Hey, have you got aerial photographs?'

Stupid question, I must admit.

'Okay,' Mikkelsen says, still peering through his stereo-scope. I am standing right in front of him, in full view of the top of his skull, which appears to have plumes of greyish dust growing on it instead of hair.

'Have you got photographs of the whole area?' I persist.

He lifts his head at last and rolls over onto his side. Leaning on his elbow, he looks up at me.

'Yes. I have pictures of all the places I have to go to.'

He gestures towards the map lying beside him. It's the same map I have, the small-scale one, too small for any detail, but there are no better ones.

I crouch down for a closer look.

'Without these you can't get anywhere,' Mikkelsen says. 'Not in this place. I am very glad I have these air pictures.'

'Aerial photographs,' I reiterate, by way of correction. This sounds patronising, of course, but I have to get back at him somehow.

'Where did you get them?'

'Nummedal gave them to me.'

'Did Nummedal have any others besides these? More copies, I mean?'

'I don't know. These are from Hvalbiff's institute. Nummedal borrowed them from Hvalbiff.'

'When was that?'

'I don't know.'

'Do try and remember.'

He rolls back onto his stomach without comment, slides two fresh photographs under the stereoscope and then, before falling to, gathers the rest into a pile which he turns over face down.

At this point my hatred of Mikkelsen is so intense that I can hardly breathe. The notion of a monstrous conspiracy ranged against me takes hold.

It could have gone like this: Sibbelee sent Nummedal a letter telling him about the research I planned to do, at which Nummedal thought: Aha! Now's my chance to get back at Sibbelee for having contradicted me at that important conference all those years ago.

Sibbelee needs a favour from Nummedal. It would obviously be bad form for a professor flatly to turn down the request of a colleague, but Nummedal is too crafty for that anyway. More devious. He summons his pupil Mikkelsen and proposes an interesting little research project for him to undertake – *my research*.

Which is just fine with Mikkelsen. Why wouldn't it be? Nummedal gets Hvalbiff to supply him with all the photographs that *I* might be needing. Then Nummedal sends off his letter to Sibbelee – the very letter I have in my wallet still, saying *I wish your pupil a good journey to Oslo*, followed by his signature.

The Dutch pupil has a good journey to Oslo and calls at the appointed hour. In the meantime Nummedal has issued instructions. There won't have been many – none at all, in fact. He just doesn't tell the porter he's expecting a visitor. What could be simpler. Despite the porter's not being informed of my visit, I get into the building. Nummedal hears me coming up the stairs. He ensconces himself behind his desk. Acts the innocent. Aerial photographs? Of course we have photographs here! And all along he knows exactly which photographs I'll be needing and also exactly where they are. All those hours of pontificating back in Oslo, acting the Great Master imparting knowledge that was useless to me – he knew full well that I was wasting my time.

The mould-infested hulk lying at my feet has got hold of my aerial photographs. The hulk has no English, so I can't explain to him what's in my head. Loathsome runt. Strange, when I address a few words to him my own English comes out sounding runty. Murder comes to mind . . . I look around me, no sign of Arne and Qvigstad. At the same time I know I'm not really going to kick Mikkelsen's head in. I walk around him, panting. Nothing escapes me now. I know that going round him in circles acts as a surrogate for kicking him to death, which I could easily do.

Is there anything worse than being obsessed with a plan you know you'll never carry out, the kind of plan that would only succeed in a dream-world in which you're omnipotent? Such as kicking Mikkelsen to death, not even touching him with my hands, no, not even with my left foot. Just kicking and kicking my right foot into his face. No resistance from him except that he goes into spasms, letting out a hoarse grunt with each fresh blow. Then he chokes, after which he stops moving altogether save for the jolts caused by the final thrusts of my shoe.

I leave him lying there, stuff the photographs in my map pocket and stride away, indefatigable, straddling rivers on winged feet, knowing exactly where to go – because I spotted half a dozen or more meteor craters on those photographs of Mikkelsen's. Seven small ones and a large one in the middle. What is that I see? My attention is caught by a couple of shiny, glazed potatoes lying on the ground. I pick one up and am struck by its weight: seven times that of an ordinary potato, three times that of a normal stone of that size.

They are meteorites.

31

'Training for the hop, skip and jump, are we?'

Starting awake from my reverie, I notice Qvigstad and Arne standing by my side. Arne grins at me.

'How d' you mean?' I ask, and hear with shame an edge of hostility to my voice.

'You seem to have made a good recovery.'

I am racked with pain. My left calf muscle is seized with cramp, I can scarcely stay upright. I feel as if knitting needles are being poked through the marrow of my bones.

'He's got the aerial photographs,' I mutter.

'I didn't hear, what did you say?'

'He's got my aerial photographs,' I repeat, hardly raising my voice.

'Your aerial photographs? What do you mean?'

'I spent an extra day in Oslo,' I say, with my eyes fixed on Qvigstad, 'for the sole purpose of collecting the aerial photographs Nummedal had promised me. But when I got there Nummedal said he knew nothing about them. He told me I should go to Trondheim and apply to Direktør Hvalbiff. So I went to Trondheim. No luck there either, because the Trondheim people had long ago passed the photographs to Nummedal. Nummedal was just pretending. He knew perfectly well that Mikkelsen had those aerial photographs.'

*

I have never seen Qvigstad look at me with so much interest. Arne is standing just behind him, a little to one side.

'Arne,' I say, 'remember what I told you when you asked me if I had any aerial photographs?'

'Did I ask you that?'

'Yes, you did. You know, those aerial photographs that were impossible to get hold of. Searched the whole Institute in Trondheim, with the help of Direktør Oftedahl.'

'Oftedhal? I don't remember. And the director's name was Hvalbiff, you say? Strange, that is not a Norwegian name.'

'Yes, Hvalbiff. But Hvalbiff wasn't there.'

'Shame you missed him,' Qvigstad says. 'He sounds good enough to eat.'

'Oh,' I say dully. 'I didn't know Mr Qvigstad went in for cannibal humour. But that's what the name sounded like to me.'

'Hvalbiff means whale meat,' Arne explains.

'Tastes exactly like beef, but much more tender,' Qvigstad continues. 'And the funny thing is that there isn't a trace of fat, which is not what you'd expect from a whale.'

'Hvalbiff, or however you pronounce it, wasn't there,' I tell them. 'I ran into a geophysicist by the name of Oftedahl. He knew nothing about the photographs, but he did know who I meant when I said I was looking for Direktør Hvalbiff.'

'Oh, come on now,' Qvigstad says. 'But let's sit down, shall we?'

He sounds concerned. What is the matter with me? They're treating me like a frustrated child, but my eyes are pricking from dryness, not tears.

'All right,' I say. 'Let's sit down.'

*

197

Arne sits down and so do I. Qvigstad goes over to his tent and comes back with the brandy bottle.

The three of us sit in a row.

'The thing is,' I say, 'that Mikkelsen's got the photographs, the same ones I was supposed to pick up in Oslo. Nummedal must have known Mikkelsen had them. An application was put in for them long ago. Nummedal could have replied saying he didn't have them. Or he could have ordered extra copies. But no, he did neither. He made me go all the way to Oslo for nothing, then sent me on a wild goose chase to Trondheim.'

'Easy now,' Arne says. 'Aren't you jumping to conclusions? It's just come back to me that you did mention this. But it's perfectly reasonable to assume that Nummedal believed you could get them in Trondheim.'

'Right,' Qvigstad says. 'Unless of course it slipped Nummedal's mind, what with him being pretty old, and practically blind too. He's always been a bit of a crackpot, anyway. Does he still have the deaf and dumb porter?'

'The porter – deaf and dumb? Blind, you mean.'

'The blind scientist with the blind porter! How about that!'

Qvigstad lays his hand on my shoulder and pours a generous shot of brandy into my plastic cup.

I take a sip, then say slowly:

'The porter was blind.'

'How did you know he was blind?'

'He was disfigured and wore dark glasses . . .'

'In that vestibule where the sun never shines?'

'. . . and he ran his fingers over the dial of his wristwatch to tell the time.'

'A watch for the blind,' Arne says.

'Braille watches,' Qvigstad says. 'There's a brisk trade in

them after every war. People never learn, do they? Blind! And yet none the wiser!'

He stands up and goes over to the green tent, where Mikkelsen is still poring over his stereoscope.

He returns a moment later with Mikkelsen in tow, holding the instrument in one hand and the batch of photographs in the other.

'Of course,' says Mikkelsen, 'you may look at ze pictures if you like. Eet ees my pleasure.'

He deposits the stereoscope and the photographs on the ground beside me and moves away.

I lie down on my stomach the way Mikkelsen was lying a moment ago, position the stereoscope beneath my face and reach for the photographs. Did Mikkelsen leave them in the wrong order on purpose? Because they belong in pairs, with partially overlapping views. Without my asking, Arne helps me to match them up. Soon he is doing practically all the work: being so much more familiar with the terrain than I am, he can identify the pictures at a glance and show me the corresponding locations on the map without any trouble.

I look.

It is not the locations I am interested in. It is the holes. Pools or lakes that could possibly be meteor craters. Possibly?

My eyes sweep across the images systematically from left to right, top to bottom, as if they're using a soft paintbrush. The brush has to pick up on any holes partially encircled by a low ridge, like the imprint of a horse's hoof in a sandy track. See for yourself: throw a ball or a stone into dry sand. The missile will make a dent and the sand from the dent will throw up a ridge.

Big meteorites fall in a similar way. The matter they

consist of breaks up into fragments which become deeply embedded in the ground – but not always. Sometimes they bounce up and land a little way off with no more impact than if they had been dropped by a human hand. Those are the kind of meteoric stones people collect. Sometimes the meteor dissipates completely during an enormous explosion, due to the heat generated on impact. In such cases the only evidence of our planet having been enriched by a chip of some long-gone other planet is a hole with a circular ridge.

The photographs are ten thousand times smaller than the landscape they portray. Seen through the stereoscope they become three-dimensional. The mountains look higher than they are in reality, and the difference between plant cover and bare ground is clearly visible. Streams, rivers and lakes are recognisable by their inky blackness. Thus water is the most distinctive feature, and all the holes are filled with it. I scrutinise each hole, each lake, trying to gauge the circumference and the gradient of the sides. Lying flat on my stomach like this feels rather like lying on the floor of an aeroplane, gazing through a telescope at a world of black and grey.

Arne intones a string of names, but I am barely listening. Now and then I raise my head from the stereoscope in a show of interest in the details he points out on the map.

I can never concentrate when people start explaining things to me. My feeling is that if it's something I really want to know I can do my own explaining. I don't need anyone's help. Not even Arne's.

Dear, oh dear, how very sad. He doesn't hold with Sibbelee's theory. And there's no reason why he should, considering he's a student of Nummedal's. I can't expect any help from him in satisfying my only need: a meteor crater.

I have inspected all the photos. Plenty of black areas indicating pools and lakes, but they all look very similar. There is nothing in the pictures to raise my hopes of making my major discovery. I might as well call it a day.

Arne is his good-natured, obliging self, still busy sorting the photographs, pointing out discrepancies between the images and the corresponding locations on the map, and so on. I want to leap to my feet and shout: Oh just leave it! There's no need! I've seen enough! I'm not going to find a single thing here that will earn me any credit whatsoever, nothing to vindicate my father's accident! I'm going back! I'm wasting my time! I'm not cut out for this kind of monkish labour, I'm not some sort of bookkeeper in the field, I don't want to report, I want to discover! Everything you can find here has already been found and reported on elsewhere in the world. I'm not interested in lists, I'm not an archivist like ninety-nine out of a hundred researchers! I want to find something spectacular! But there's nothing here that hasn't been found before!

I don't say a word. I am putting up a front, playing for time like a schoolboy being bullied. What else can I do?

Not finding a meteor crater doesn't mean to say that I won't have found anything at all, even if what I do find has nothing to do with geology, or even remotely with earth science or cosmology. Not with any science at all, for that matter. This reminds me of a case described by Wittgenstein, in which the process whereby someone achieves understanding becomes subsumed into that understanding. Like saying: I understood after I'd had some black coffee. But the coffee had nothing to do with it.

Because it's beginning to dawn on me how the world works – my world, at any rate, the world in which I have a huge task to fulfil, the world in which I must succeed.

I realise now – and it is inconceivably stupid of me not to have thought of it before – that I should have got hold of the aerial photographs before I came here. Long before. I should have had them back in Amsterdam. I should have told Sibbelee: there's no point in going up north without seeing the aerial photographs first.

But this isn't the most important thing I've realised.

Even more important is that I'm having serious doubts about Sibbelee. After all, he's the one with experience in these matters.

I'm thirty years younger and still only a student, really, and off I went on a trip just because my mentor advised it. An ill-considered action maybe, but an excusable one. Because it's up to Sibbelee to decide whether or not I'm a brilliant student, and whether or not I'll succeed in my career. I couldn't afford to get on the wrong side of him.

Excusable or not, what I find incomprehensible is that Sibbelee let me go off without the photographs in the first place. What he should have said is: I've written to Nummedal requesting those aerial surveys you need, but he's not responding. So I would advise you to choose another subject for your research. Aerial photography is such a highly efficient, modern instrument of orientation that it would be absurd to take pot luck and rush off into the wilds without photographs. As absurd as putting out to sea in a modern liner without a compass, radio or radar.

Sibbelee is no fool. It is inconceivable that these considerations did not enter his mind. *But he kept his mouth shut.*

He let me go. Why?

Why? With the stereoscope in one hand and the batch of photographs in the other, I hobble over to Mikkelsen. Reaching him, I say:

'Thank you very much for letting me see the photographs.'

'Already ready?' he asks.

'Yes, ready.'

'Please, put zem before my tent, will you?'

I oblige, setting his possessions down on the sheet of plastic in front of their tent.

Why did Sibbelee let me go? It must have had something to do with Nummedal's hostility towards him. What's in it for Sibbelee? If anything, that I'll discover something that puts Nummedal in the wrong.

Another complicating factor. It wasn't until I got to Oslo that I found out that Nummedal was no friend of Sibbelee's. How could I have foreseen that? Sibbelee never said anything about him and the celebrated Professor Nummedal not seeing eye to eye. Of course not! Sibbelee wouldn't dream of telling his students: By the way, the great Nummedal doesn't think very highly of me.

Sunk in thought, I limp down the slope, away from the tents. It is not until I am at the water's edge that I become aware of my surroundings. The sun has been released from its cover of clouds and the ripples on the lake turn into threads of molten copper. Nothing to be seen, nothing to be heard, except for the mosquitoes circling round my head.

'This is,' I say aloud, in a solemn voice, 'what you might call a defining moment in the life of an inexperienced young man.'

I'm in a situation where I have no alternative but to carry on with what I'm doing even though I fear it's a mistake. Like knowing you're going in the wrong direction, but it's too late to turn back, or realising halfway through the race you've bet on the wrong horse. Is Alfred going to the races today? No, he is not. Because if I take all the possibilities going through my mind to their logical conclusion, the best thing for me now is clearly to go straight back to Holland and tell Sibbelee: I'm sorry, Professor, but it's no go, the research you recommended is not going to yield the results that either of us was hoping for. Good day, sir.

And then what? I'll be back where I started, knowing that I must achieve some great feat, but not knowing how to go about it. How will I ever find out?

My mother won't understand when I tell her I gave up because I realised there was no point in what I was doing. She'll think I'm ill. Sibbelee won't understand. No-one will.

What am I to do?

I cast my eyes over the lake, the sloping banks where nothing stirs. Few people have ever set foot here. Surely there is something worth finding. Something that has never been found before. There are so few places left in the world where no-one has been.

'Alfred! Where are you?'

*

I am being called to supper. This is like being a lodger. It's them taking all the decisions. They treat me as their guest. I'm sure Qvigstad was only being polite when he asked Mikkelsen to let me see his photographs.

Making my way back to the camp, where the three of them are sitting around the primus, it comes to me that Arne may well have been thinking: if there really were any meteor craters around here, we'd discover them ourselves – no need for some student to come all the way from Holland to find them.

An uncharitable thought, but most likely that was what was going through Arne's mind, for all that he's my friend and the one I know best. Because I find it very hard to believe that Arne was in the dark about Mikkelsen having the photographs.

Downcast, suspicious even, afraid they have been laughing at me behind my back, I sit myself down. The porridge is ready. As Mikkelsen starts dishing up he inadvertently jolts the pan, making the contents slop over the side and onto the burner, which goes out, hissing and fuming.

We all jump up, swear in various languages, laugh.

Arne pours the remaining porridge onto three plates, then scrapes the bottom of the pan with his spoon for himself. Making fresh porridge is not an option. We're low on paraffin as it is.

We finish our meal with two pieces of knäckebröd each. One with a slice of cheese, which is getting mouldier by the day in its greasy wrapper, and one with honey from a tube.

'Maybe,' Qvigstad says, 'it won't be long before they're capable of constructing computers that are cleverer than the cleverest human beings. Those computers can then be programmed to design new computers that are even more intelligent. Once we've got a computer capable of devising problems that are so complex that they couldn't possibly arise in the brain of a human being – and once we've got other computers to work out the solutions – that'll be the end of science as we know it. Science will become something like sport. Like archery contests at folkloric festivals, or rowing, or speed walking.'

'Or chess,' Arne says.

'Oh no, not chess, because we'll have unbeatable computers. Or it'll be possible to look up every single chess move in some kind of computerised logarithm table. Everything will have been calculated by then. Winning at chess will be a question of memory. No, chess won't be played any more. Makes you wonder what people will do for entertainment.'

Arne: 'Same as now: poker games, gossip, fishing, football and a daily fare of the same old newspapers and the same old shows on TV.'

Qvigstad: 'Well, yes. But what about the people who are special? There will be a whole lot of unused talent floating around. What an idea! To think: yes I have this talent, but everything I could have done with it has already been done. There's a machine with more talent than me.'

'Poor us,' Arne says, 'because science will become more anonymous than ever. No fame, no personal triumphs. Individual scientists will be swallowed up by their own discoveries. In due course everything about nature will have been discovered, and nobody will care a hoot who did the discovering.'

'Yes, anonymous,' Qvigstad says. 'Like the people who discovered fire and invented things like wheels and spinning tops. That won't stop the universities from giving out academic robes, degrees and honorary doctorates, though.'

'But by then,' Mikkelsen says, 'that kind of thing will be a matter of chance. Like now, with people becoming famous for nothing in particular. For instance: there are a hundred thousand girls with nice figures that no-one's ever heard of, but only one of them will become Miss Universe and get her picture in the paper.'

'Having nice boobs,' Qvigstad says, 'is different. There's a whole lot of girls having a whole lot of fun thanks to their boobs. Without it getting in the papers, I mean, just on the home front. Don't you think?'

'On the home front there won't be much call for mathematical genius, I gather, nor for the explorer's spirit of adventure, what with machines being better at everything and there being nothing left to discover.'

'Anyone aiming to be a famous scientist must be out of his mind,' Qvigstad says.

Yes, that is what he said. I wonder what he is thinking. Is he trying to make me feel better?

'Just as the iguanodon became extinct due to its size,' he concludes, 'so will the human race die out from sheer redundancy.'

32

My sleeping bag is still too wet. Better do without, then, and try sleeping in my clothes.

It is four o'clock. I have been checking my watch every half hour. Arne's snoring and a gale is rising, making the tent flap like mad. Good: mosquitoes don't like the wind. On the other hand, several bloodthirsty flies have sought shelter inside and are even now crawling under my shirt and into my sleeves. They don't hurt, but they leave fat drops of blood in their wake. They don't even try to escape their just deserts. I squash them with the tip of my index finger. Small black flies, smaller than the flies descending on the jam back home.

Raising myself on my elbow, I stare at Arne. He is lying on his side with his face turned to me and his hands under his cheek. His mouth is open, and I can see the full complement of his yellow, decaying teeth. The teeth of an old man. His whole face is timeworn. He looks as if he's already outlived the lifespan of his body. I can see the whites of his eyes through his half-closed lids. The dense stubble on his jaws makes him appear ancient, but also decrepit and shabby. A giant tramp, a dim-witted troll whose only means of communication is grunting and snoring. The noise keeps me awake, as on previous nights. Nevertheless, I do drift off now and then, because I wake up the moment the snoring stops. Each time it means Arne has gone outside. I stare at the apex of the pyramid, the mosquitoes' favourite rallying ground. I heave myself into a sitting position, a vile taste in my mouth. I take a long swig from the water bottle and light a cigarette. Keeping the insects at bay with waves of the hands combined with jets of smoke, I sit there for ten minutes or so, musing. When I reach the end of my cigarette I stick my hand out of the tent, make a hole in the ground with my finger and bury the stub.

I discover that I can't raise my right knee. The leg is swollen and weirdly discoloured. But I can still walk on it, presumably. Walking will be a sight easier than getting a wet sock over the foot. To do that requires contortions painfully similar to indoor gymnastics, which is something I never went in for, even when I was a boy and such exertions did not hurt. Lunging forward over my stiff leg I finally succeed in getting the open end of the sock over my upturned toes. The other sock is not a problem. I get to my feet, step into my shoes and crawl outside. It's half past ten.

Harsh sunshine.

The coffee pot, hooked from the end of a stick planted at an angle, is positioned over a small fire. There is nothing else to be seen. The green tent belonging to Mikkelsen and Qvigstad has vanished. What's up now? I don't see Arne either. Hobbling up the slope, I catch sight of him at the lakeside folding up the blue fishing net.

Glancing back and forth between him and the kettle, I can't decide how I can best make myself useful: shall I go down to help Arne with the net or head back to tend the fire – but if I do that I won't find out where Qvigstad and Mikkelsen have gone until later. The thin stick supporting the kettle is catching fire while the flames underneath are going out.

I limp back as fast as I can. It would be better if the kettle were propped up by stones, but there don't seem to be any stones of the right size hereabouts, nor any stronger sticks. Getting a kettle of water to boil without a primus is a complicated business.

I go down on my knees to blow on the glowing embers, carefully slipping in bits of moss and twigs.

When Arne turns up with the net, the water is finally beginning to simmer. He hasn't caught any fish.

'Where are Qvigstad and Mikkelsen?'

'They left about two hours ago.'

'Oh, I was wondering where they'd got to. I expect they'll be waiting for us with fried trout when we join them tonight.'

'I'm afraid not.'

'Why not?'

'We're going somewhere else. I'll show you on the map.'

Arne goes off to fetch his map while I tip some ground coffee into the boiling water. Our meal will consist of knäckebröd with honey from a tube, because the powdered milk and the oats are in Qvigstad's and Mikkelsen's luggage.

Arne settles down with the map. I nerve myself to put the question foremost in my mind:

'Was there any special reason why they left so suddenly?'

'A special reason? How do you mean?'

'I didn't get a chance to say goodbye to them.'

'Oh, that. But you were still asleep.'

He unfolds the map and takes up his magnifying glass.

'Are we supposed to be meeting them somewhere later on?' I ask

'No, I don't think that will be possible.'

I sink down beside Arne. My moustache has grown long enough for me to draw the bristles in with my underlip, and I sit there chewing them while my thoughts drift vaguely from one gloomy consideration to the next.

Arne explains that it was something to do with Qvigstad's research that made him and Mikkelsen decide to head north, after which they plan to return to Skoganvarre by way of Mount Vuorje.

'For us, though, it's best if we go south – down to here . . .,' and he points to a thin dotted line which on an ordinary map would represent a road, but evidently not on this one.

Our route, he declares, means following a trail that is only ten centimetres wide and hardly visible in the terrain, although it's marked with stones. That's to say, any sizeable stone along the way has a smaller stone on top, left there by previous travellers. This way of marking a trail is widespread in Norway.

Messages used to be carried along this route in the old days. From each marker stone the next one can usually be seen some way off, indicating the direction to be followed. It is customary for everyone using the trail to replace any pebble that might be missing from a big stone for one reason or another: displaced by the wind, or by melting snow. Because not only on the map is it a dotted line – it is in reality, too. With gaps of several hundred metres at times, where the trail has been erased, washed away or overgrown.

He puts aside his magnifying glass to pour coffee into our cups and squeeze honey onto pieces of knäckebröd. I take another look at the map, wondering whether Arne's planned itinerary will be to my advantage. Once we hit the trail with the marker stones we go east until we arrive at a place called

Ravnastua. It's marked on the map, but isn't really a village or even a hamlet. Arne says there's just one main house inhabited by Lapps and some annexes that serve as guest quarters. Hardly anyone goes there, of course, even in the summer. The place is maintained by the state as a refuge in the inhospitable wilderness. The nearest settlement is Karasjok, but the journey from there to Ravnastua is too long and too arduous to attract tourists, apparently. You might see the occasional eccentric angler, or a stray biologist or geologist, or a Lapp fallen on hard times. Arne has been to Ravnastua twice, and both times he was the only guest. Food and other necessities are delivered with caterpillar vehicles.

Arne's route, complete with detours and the old postal trail, means we have another hundred and fifty kilometres or so to go. At least by the end of it I'll have covered most of my research terrain. So Arne's route makes good sense.

But the question as to why Qvigstad and Mikkelsen decided to head north keeps nagging at me.

The sun bears down more fiercely than ever, promising oppressive heat for today. There are also clouds: massive ones, the size of twenty atom bombs exploding simultaneously. They look as if they're made of hot gas, not moisture.

I get to my feet, stamp out the remains of the fire, spread the embers around, empty the kettle and hobble to the lake to rinse out the dregs.

Norwegians, I have noticed on several occasions, approach one another with considerable reserve. There are about four million of them living in a country ten times the size of Holland, but Holland has three-and-a-half times as many inhabitants. Population density in Norway is eleven per square kilometre, not three hundred and sixty as it is where I come from. To a Norwegian, crossing the path of another member of the human race counts for something. They stop about three paces short of the other person, make a little bow, smile, think: might be a highwayman for all I know, shake hands and make discreet enquiries into health and happiness. I wonder if their farewells are any less formal.

I can't imagine that being the case. So why did Qvigstad and Mikkelsen make off without saying goodbye? At what unearthly hour can they have risen for them to have managed that? There was their tent to be taken down and their belongings to be packed, they had breakfast and talked to Arne. I must have been very sound alseep. But why the hurry?

Trekking in this harsh landscape is just a stroll in the park as far as they're concerned, I tell myself as I return slowly with the dripping kettle. They've been coming here for years, it's their home.

I am surprised by them in much the same way as other people are surprised by the Dutch, particularly the way we keep our balance on bicycles, dodging trams and cars in narrow streets and teetering along the edges of deep canals.

What am I doing here anyway, so far from home? Maximal results aren't necessarily achieved through maximal efforts alone, rather through the maximal efforts of whoever has the maximal advantage. The best shot isn't fired by the best marksman, but by the best marksman with the best range and the best rifle.

There have been no hints, no allusions of any kind to make me feel unwanted, but I can now barely stop myself from uttering the question out loud: Don't they regard me as wanting to beat the Norwegians at their own game? I bet that's how Nummedal saw me from the start – Oh by all means let him join the expedition, he must have thought, let him come a cropper.

Maybe I wouldn't feel so bad if I hadn't, on the whole, found the Norwegians I have met so likeable. Even Mikkelsen, all things considered.

Take Arne.

When I get back, he has already struck camp and packed. What is this? There's hardly anything left for me to put in my rucksack.

Until now we have divided the tent between us: I carried the canvas and he took the two segments of tent pole.

'Where's the canvas?'

'In my rucksack.'

'In your rucksack? Why?'

'It's better if you don't carry too much weight, with that swollen knee of yours.'

'But I hardly feel it any more.'

'That's not the point. It could get worse, so that walking becomes impossible. Then what would you do?'

'We'll see about that. Come on, give me the tent.'

'No, no, I'll take it. Tomorrow maybe.'

He starts walking. He has also claimed the hefty wooden tripod.

'Arne, give me that tripod!'

Without stopping, he says, over his shoulder: 'By all means, next time.'

I kneel and pack my rucksack. My load now consists of my personal belongings – sleeping bag, soap, toothbrush, underwear, various items I haven't even unpacked yet – and very little besides. Just two boxes of knäckebröd, seven tubes of honey, the kettle, a packet of salt and the aerated bundle of blue fishing net.

Limping along as fast as I can, I catch up with Arne, who, incidentally, slowed his pace when he saw me coming.

'Oh, come on now, Arne, this is not fair.'

I swear I said this without a trace of hypocrisy. I can even prove it. I am not so much relieved as worried about him carrying so much and me so little. Won't he get sick of taking on more than his share, in other words, won't he get sick of me?

In the meantime Arne explains to me that, strictly speaking, his load isn't heavy:

'You seem to have forgotten that I came here on my own in previous years. So I had to carry the whole tent then, didn't I? The whole lot, canvas, poles and the fishing net as well.'

I do my best to believe him. That there would be less food to carry if he were on his own doesn't count, really, given the diminished state of our supplies.

33

At three o'clock we are sitting on the brink of the deepest
ravine I have ever seen. It's as if an axe of cosmic dimensions had cleaved the earth's crust. The sides of the ravine
are almost vertical, with massive, jagged outcrops of rock.

A descent like this, it seems to me, is surely best left to
the expert mountaineer with ropes, crampons and a bevy of
Sherpas, the kind who will do anything for their sahib,
including carrying him on their backs. Or on a stretcher,
borne by a foursome of Sherpas. Four Sherpas . . . twenty
Sherpas . . . two hundred if needs be. Passing their sahib
from one to the other, like passing a bucket of water to
quench a haystack fire, leaving the sahib free to smoke his
pipe, write up his diary, peel a pineapple. Sahib gets his
picture in the paper, speeches, medals; Sherpas get a tip.

So far, my experience on this expedition is that things
don't always go from bad to worse. Ascent is invariably
followed by descent, the rain lifts periodically, marshland
gives way to dry ground, and even the stones I keep twisting
my ankles on are by no means a constant hazard. In short:
like everything else in life, the misery sort of evens out. But
I haven't seen anything like the sheer drop confronting us
now.

I glance at Arne, hoping he'll broach the subject, but all
he says is:

'Best to have a bite to eat here first.'

Best here? Hardly. We both get to our feet to hunt for dry twigs. It takes us a quarter of an hour to gather just a few handfuls of firewood.

I take three stones of roughly the same size and arrange them carefully into a hearth. Arne sets the frying pan on top, I lie on my stomach and light the first match. The twigs burn for a moment, then the flame goes out, leaving rapidly shrinking embers. Second match. I blow with all my might. Arne has opened a tin of meat and empties it out into the pan. I strike a third match.

'It was easier when we had the primus.'

'The paraffin had run out. Qvigstad and Mikkelsen are going to have to make fires, just like us.'

Fourth match. Even now, lying stomach down, I can see the yawning ravine. When I pause for a moment between bouts of blowing, my mouth won't keep still. It's not hunger making me gulp and swallow and scrape the inside of my lips with my teeth as if they need sharpening, nor is it appetite making my tongue writhe uncontrollably in the cavity it has known for the past twenty-five years.

Sweet Jesus, I'm scared. Even if I fell into the ravine and got killed, I'd still be mortified, albeit posthumously. Prat that I am, lunatic from the lowlands. Qvigstad and Mikkelsen have had enough of me. I'm a hindrance. Arne is too polite to show it, but what he's thinking is: I'd be better off on my own, make more headway, wouldn't be distracted from my work, nor would I have to carry all this stuff. Devil in hell! (this is the Norwegian equivalent of 'God damn').

Right now I can't imagine anyone being ashamed of anything once they're dead. Yet never have I felt so passionately that I do not want to die. The idea that my father could have been no more of a climber than me hits me like a blow to the jaw. Could he, too, have had a couple of falls prior to the one that killed him? Did his companions regard him as a liability, a hindrance, a slowcoach? His corpse certainly messed up their plans.

I sit bolt upright, my left hand clamped round my left calf and my right holding a slice of bread with a chunk of lukewarm meat on top, which I keep in position with my index finger. As I raise the bread to my mouth my attention is caught by the artery pulsating on the inside of my wrist. Monstrous – what a monstrous reminder of one's animal nature. Bestial. Doesn't my vein look remarkably like a worm? A worm wriggling to get out – there, there, you poor little thing, you'll be free sooner than you think, and it's going to be a huge disappointment. Because you can't do without me any more than a clam can do without its shell.

I bite into the bread and find myself grinning.

I have a sudden vision of pious little Eva consoling my mother: 'Don't cry, Mummy, Alfred's with Daddy now!'

She points skyward with a perfectly varnished fingernail. Then takes her compact from her handbag to repair the tear-smudged powder on her cheek. All her girlfriends lavish care on their nails, too. They're not very bright either, and they believe in God, like Eva. With me gone there won't be anyone left in the family to vindicate my father's death. It remains to be seen whether Eva will pass her exams next year, and there's clearly no hope of her ever contributing weekly pieces to seven Dutch publications with reports on what the *Observer* and the *Figaro Littéraire* have to say about twenty-odd foreign novels. Wittering on about God is what she's good at. I've stopped trying to un-convert her, and when I tell her she's obviously too dim to understand that the word 'God' is meaningless, she counters with: 'Let's see how far your brains will get you, shall we?'

I can scarcely swallow the food for helpless mirth. My ambition, anybody's ambition, is enough to make you choke with laughter, once you think in terms of having to prove to some silly girl that you're right and she's wrong. I'll show them how far my brains will get me! Because if I come to grief she'll just point a manicured finger to heaven saying: He's with Daddy now.

My mother might even believe her, who knows? She'd have the excuse of her age compounded by the shock of losing her son.

I get to my feet and the ravine yawns even deeper. The far side is dusty black, a sombre cliff where the sun never reaches. There's a smallish glacier on the cliff side. Streams of water run off it in deep gulleys, and yet the size isn't affected.

I hoist my rucksack and wait for Arne to take the lead. Where will he start his descent? Or will we walk along the precipice first for a bit, until we find somewhere less steep? I don't say a word. Arne kicks the hearth-stones away and stamps on the dying embers and half-burnt twigs. A fjelljo flies overhead, alights, becomes invisible thanks to its camouflage, gives three sharp cries: Morse code for the letter S, the first letter of SOS.

My situation is precarious for more reasons than I can keep track of, but it comes to me now that on top of everything else I feel trapped. I am afraid of what Eva will say if I fall to my death. On the other hand, if I reach the bottom alive, the terror I have experienced will be too laughable to relate to anyone, ever. And I can't very well ask Arne to consider taking another route – now that Qvigstad and Mikkelsen have decamped and my suspicions have been raised.

Never have I been so certain that what I'm going through is utterly futile and impossible to recount: me, following Arne down the side of the ravine with the depths rising up to engulf me like some invisible tidal wave in reverse: whatever I do, whatever happens to me, it will not be of my own volition.

A secret consciousness reveals itself.

The veil of mystery shrouding life in its entirety lifts momentarily and I know that at all times and in everything I do I am defenceless and powerless, as replaceable as an atom, and that all my resolve, hopes and fears are nothing but manifestations of the mechanism governing the movements of human molecules in the fathomless vapour of cosmic matter.

Arne's descent is nigh vertical as he slithers down a little way, perches on a rock, springs down to the next faster and faster, until he appears almost to be falling, with only his feet to slow him down. The drop becomes so sheer that it seems the only thing stopping him from plummeting to the bottom is an invisible parachute. I note that he keeps changing direction, zigzagging along an imaginary horizontal plane, scraping his shoulders against the cliff face.

In the deep lies the bright green bed of the ravine, threaded with lazy streams. The water looks as if it was spilt, but glitters like molten steel.

I focus all my attention on my feet, breathlessly picking my way while the blood pounds in my throat. I grab hold of the shrubs sprouting from cracks in the rock face, as if they could save me should I lose my footing. Ridiculous! Most of the time they come loose at the first touch. What if I slip . . . ? Will I crack my head against a jutting rock, or will I fall into a cleft and be wedged there with collapsed rib cage and broken bones? Sick with anxiety, I see that Arne has reached a wide tongue of loose shale, a fan of debris leading down to the bottom of the ravine like a gangway. An arrested avalanche of stone. Arne's feet are buried up to his ankles, but he's out of danger. Oh to be down there with him, for that is where my suffering ends!

With a surge of confidence I propel myself forward from crag to crag. No more hanging on to plants. My bruised knee is so painful I could scream, but my descent feels no less flowing and nimble than Arne's. Like flying down a staircase without thinking. I hardly look where I put my feet, while glimpses of the green depths alternate with the pale expanse of glacier across the way. My headlong flight is abruptly smothered in the spill of shale. I pitch forward, straighten up again, then run freely and fearlessly to the bottom.

My ears fill with the sound of water. The mosquitoes have stuck by me, and swarm around my head like electrons circling round an atom. Cold air wafts from the glacier towards me. I have to tilt my head back as far as it will go to catch a glimpse of sky: a blue serrated stripe. My shoes squelch through the green: peat and polar willows. I reach the water, bend down and drain two cups in quick succession. It is so shallow we have no need to go across barefoot. Anxiously scanning the cliff for the most suitable place to climb out of the ravine, I follow Arne in the assumption that he knows what he is doing. Are we to go across the glacier? No, that is a dead end: it abuts on a perpendicular amphitheatre of rock.

Reaching the other side of the stream I have a sense of sinking deeper into the moss with each step I take. The moss gives way to black mud. I am entrenched among polar willows that come to my waist. Arne's already climbing up the other side. How did he get there? My shoes fill up with water. I have to raise my legs higher and higher to make any headway in the bog, which is knee-deep. I can feel the seat of my trousers getting wet. But what can I do? My camera and map pocket, which I'm wearing round my neck, must not get wet so I hold them aloft, but then I have to drop them again as I need both arms to steady myself. I have to speed up, raise my legs even higher now, because staying in the same place for even a second means sinking an extra ten centimetres. My upper body is drenched too, not with water but with sweat. The mosquitoes attack my face, get into my eyes. I am panting so heavily that they get sucked into my mouth; I can feel them on my tongue, on my epiglottis. I don't shout for help because there isn't any. As a last resort I let myself flop forwards, across a thicket of willows. They bend under my weight, forming a web. Slowly I extract my left foot, manage to place it on three flattened willows, then pull the right foot loose and stand up straight.

Water pours from my rucksack, windproof jacket and trousers when I find myself on dry land again. Did Arne notice the difficulty I was in? I don't think so. Guided by luck or experience, he made his crossing in places where the peat was less thick or the ground-ice deeper down. He has no idea of what I'm going through. I start up the side of the ravine in an elongated zigzag, angling my feet against the gradient.

The glacier makes a rumbling noise like a hundred tubs

brimming over in a vast bath house. The ice has the dingy colour of sheets that haven't been laundered for months, and is so thickly encrusted with dust and grit that there's no white left. The shards of slate crackle underfoot like glass.

After descent, ascent comes as a relief. Going down is like falling in slow motion. Not like climbing. Sometimes, pausing halfway up a slope for a breather, you look down and are gripped with fear.

You'd like to turn back, but at the same time you know that turning back is just as risky as pressing on, so you press on.

34

I still can't believe I made it, didn't fall, hardly slipped even. Arne has given me one of his cigarettes. Mine are sopping wet. We are sitting side by side on a ledge of rock, right above the glacier. Arne hasn't commented on my wet clothes, he must have noticed how wretched such mishaps make me feel.

I take off my shoes, tip out the water.

Me:

'Isn't it strange, all those billions of things that have happened or are happening on earth, just vanishing without a trace?'

Him:

'It would be just as strange if records had been kept of everything.'

Me:

'Those records would have to cover every single thing going on in the world from one second to the next: a wave crashing against a pier, raindrops falling, everything three billion people do or think, every flower that blooms and wilts – complete with dimensions, geographical longitude, latitude, colour and weight.'

'Why only in our world? The exact history of the universe would have to be recorded, too. And an inventory of that magnitude would become a universe in its own right, a duplicate of ours.'

Me:

'Two universes wouldn't be enough. Because the history of record keeping would have to be recorded, too, in a third inventory: yet another universe. And so forth. An infinite number of universes, and there wouldn't be any point to them. They wouldn't explain anything.'

'No, they wouldn't. Wittgenstein said: Facts are internal to the question, not to the answer. The mystery is not how the world is constituted, but that the world is the case.'

'Ah! So you've read Wittgenstein?'

'He'll be read by more and more people as time goes on. Did you know he lived in Norway for several years?'

He props his notebook on his knee and starts sketching. I look over his shoulder. He draws the way other people write. Describes what he sees without using words. How I envy him!

I will get the hang of climbing rocks and crossing rivers eventually, I suppose, but not of drawing. I tried hard since early childhood, but it never amounted to anything. I could never stand all those psychologists theorising about the naive creative urge in the very young, claiming that kids draw cars with square wheels because they live *in a world of their own*!

The world I live in has never been a world of my own, it existed long before I came into it and I do not recall ever thinking cars had square wheels, not even when I was five and drawing them like that.

At five years of age I knew that my pictures were nothing like as good as the pictures in the newspaper, and after hours of scribbling I would tear up my drawing and burst into tears.

All things considered, I have not been overly blessed with

the kind of qualities that come in handy for a geologist. Poor memory, to the point of losing my way in places I know very well. Poor fitness, for lack of exercise. Illegible handwriting. Badly executed drawings.

What a mess! I go in for all this only because I set my mind to it, not because it is second nature. All I have is my ability to endure. That, and an ability quickly to distil meaning from books, which explains why I have always done well in exams.

Arne is better equipped for success than I am, and yet he begrudges himself all extravagance in case he fails to perform some great deed of science. Let's hope his defeatism won't rub off on me. My compass is better than his, and I'll show him I know how to use it.

Just sitting here idle is getting to me, and I fall to untying the cords of my rucksack. There is still water dripping from the bottom, inasmuch as the moisture hasn't been absorbed by my sleeping bag, which is turning from yellow to dark brown.

My notebook is soggy. I wave it gently in the air with my left hand in the hope of speeding up the drying process, meanwhile tapping my teeth with the pencil in my right hand.

Writing is out of the question. The pencil doesn't leave a trace on the damp paper, and pressing harder would only make holes in it.

This ravine is by far the most impressive phenomenon I've seen until now, but I'm incapable of making notes. What to do? Could take a couple of photographs, I suppose.

I take my camera out of its case, hold it up to eye level, press the shutter. That is one picture, but I need some more. I twist the knob to advance the film. It's stuck! Some water must have got in, dissolving the gelatine coating and jamming the mechanism. There's nothing I can do about it. I can't open the camera, as I'd lose the whole film. It's not going to get dark here for weeks, and if I don't open the camera I'll never get rid of the moisture.

Arne has finished his sketch. He shuts his notebook, takes a picture with his Leica, shakes his head.

'Perhaps . . .'

With a feeling that the utmost discretion is called for, I slip my camera back into its case. Then I pull my maps out of their pocket – likewise soaked. I spread them out on the warm ground and study the route we will be taking.

We are in the upland now. Hilly terrain. 'Bumpy' would be a better word. Like a mock-up of a dune landscape, with mounds of sand, loam and stones, and very little vegetation. It is ten kilometres south-west from here to the lake where we plan to pitch our tent. On the map it looks as if you can get there almost in a straight line, no obstacles of any significance.

I take out my compass to determine south-west.

Arne looks at his own map and stands up.

'That way!'

The direction he points in is ninety degrees off from mine.

'You're joking! It's over there!'

My turn to point. I am keeping my compass level on the palm of my left hand. There is no doubt in my mind, I am pointing in the right direction.

Arne's face contorts with suppressed laughter as he tugs at the frayed string attached to the plastic boy scout's compass in his breast pocket. He proffers his compass like a bar of chocolate, but I don't deign to look. I bend over, hoist my rucksack and start walking with my compass still balancing on my left palm. I can't have made a mistake! Arne will catch up with me later, when he realises he's the one who made a mistake.

The ground is dry and level. Hardly anything grows here. There are no steep gradients, so I can take big strides. A few hours from now my clothes – the ones I'm wearing, at any rate – will be dry. If the sun keeps shining like this I'll even get my maps dry, too. As for my notebook, I'll set it upright later on, with the covers forming a right angle and the pages teased apart so the air can get in between. That'll do the trick.

I don't pay much attention to my surroundings, engrossed as I am in comparing ways of getting my camera dry. If only it got dark here once in a while! Then I could crawl head first into my sleeping bag and open the camera without any light getting in, after which I could dry the interior with a clean handkerchief. Have I still got a clean handkerchief?

But it doesn't get dark here. Imagine having to live without darkness! I could try putting Arne's sleeping bag on top of mine for extra darkness before crawling in. What's keeping him?

I glance over my shoulder, but he's nowhere in sight. Surely he must have discovered his error by now?

It's childish and I hate to admit it, but the idea of Arne getting the wrong end of the stick for once is a bigger boost to my morale than I've had in a very long time.

'Arne! This way!' I yell. *In Dutch!*

It's the first time in weeks that a Dutch phrase has crossed my lips.

I climb to the top of a hill, no Arne. I go down the other side.

Going up a hill and then down again can easily confuse

one's sense of direction. As I am surrounded by hills on all sides, the contours of my horizon shift with each step I take. There aren't any prominent features for me to focus on. Just boulders. But there are too many of those to be of any use for orienteering. So I stop to take another bearing with my compass.

Something very odd has happened. The declination between the needle and the direction I plotted on the map is exactly ninety degrees less than last time. In other words, if my present reading is correct, so was Arne's, and I'm the one who's been heading in the wrong direction.

But I can't have been. My compass must have got wet earlier on, which is why the needle isn't turning properly. I move the little lever up and down a few times, making the needle jiggle on the pivot. I hold the compass in the sun, but there doesn't seem to be any moisture under the glass. I shake it a few times for good measure. Then I set it on the palm of my left hand once more and try to hold it in a horizontal position.

The needle persists in indicating an angle of ninety degrees off from the direction I've been taking. Idiot that I am. I must have got it all wrong. Misread my compass, and then pooh-poohed Arne's correct reading of his! Jesus Christ! I stare at the glass in shock, and soon my eyes are drawn to the little mirror. My face is fully attuned to my emotion: mouth agape in cavernous fear, sunken cheeks beneath thin stubble – like the son of God whose name I invoked – bump from mosquito bite on left eyelid, scabs of dried blood on right-hand side of forehead.

I am standing in the middle of a round hollow hemmed in by hills. The least I can do is climb one of them. I pick the highest one and charge up the slope at speed.

From the crest I see nothing but hills on all sides. I have completely lost track of where I came from.

'Arne!' I shout.

I shout Arne's name in all directions, but there is no reply, not even an echo.

Standing here shouting won't get me anywhere. He'll probably turn up any moment now, from behind one of the hills, and then he'll spot me here. Might as well take my bearings again, to be on the safe side.

I draw out my sodden map once more. Luckily there are three big rocks close by, about the size of piano crates. White, angular blocks of a sugary appearance with leprous patches of black lichen. Close set, as if they were once joined together. They come to my shoulder. The tops are fairly flat.

On one of them I spread out my map, which, given how wet it is, amounts to pasting it down. Now for another try with the compass. I take it out of its case, position it to the side of the map, stoop to pick up some rock chips and manoeuvre the chips until the bubble in the spirit level is centred.

My desk is so high that I have to read the compass in the flipped-up mirror.

Same angle as before: ninety degrees off from the direction I've been taking. My compass is fine and I'm a ninny. I still can't believe it. Before taking any decisions, I'd better get my map aligned exactly along a north-south axis. Gingerly I lift a corner of the map – it was already quite worn before, but now it's soaked through I'm afraid the paper will disintegrate. The map unsticks from the surface without mishaps. I spread it out again, but one of the corners is turned down. I smooth it out and in doing so brush against the compass with my sleeve.

The compass has vanished.

I come to my senses with my left thumbnail between my teeth, having received what feels like a stunning blow to the head. I begin walking around the perimeter of the blocks, trying to make out where the cracks between them are widest. I crouch down by each one to peer into the fissure, but can't see my compass anywhere.

In desperation I try climbing on top of the rocks – my knee! my knee! The sides are too straight. Should I try putting a smaller stone against the base for me to get up on? But for a stone to serve as a step it has to be quite big – too big for me to lift. I take a run-up and hurl myself at the lowest of the three blocks, slap my arms over the top, hook my fingers round the far edge and pull. Hanging on like this could make the whole thing topple backwards. Oh, to be crushed to death and be done with it all! No such luck – it must weigh at least three tons. I swing my left leg in search of purchase for my foot, but my toecap keeps scuffing downwards. Wriggling, yelping, frantically swinging my left leg, I miraculously succeed in getting my foot over the top. Now I can easily lever myself up. I stand up straight. First I look about me for any sign of Arne. I call his name two or three times. Then I sit down and peer into the fissures between the blocks. Pitch dark. Throwing down a burning match might help. My matches are soaked. Arne's got the extra box in his rucksack, all I have is this one box.

*

Hoping maybe to find the compass by touch, I reach into the fissures as far as my arm will go. It's such a tight fit that I have to roll up my sleeves first, and the sharp rock grazes my skin. I explore all three cracks, hoping, no, *willing* that the compass didn't fall all the way to the bottom, but is wedged within arm's reach.

I do not find it.

If I had a long rod, or a branch, then I could have another go . . . Blasted mosquitoes, why can't they leave me alone for once?

Not a single branch longer than fifty centimetres around here. It flashes across my mind that I could undertake a little expedition to some glen sheltered enough for proper birches to grow there, or spruces. But for one thing I wouldn't know where to go looking for the nearest sheltered glen, and for another I can't mark my current position on the map because I don't know it.

Retrieving my compass is impossible without another compass.

Any other options?

I slither down from the rocks and look in my rucksack, although I know there's nothing in there that could be of any use. I take out the fishing net anyway.

There are long cords attached to either end. I tie one of them around a fist-sized stone, which I can then lower into the deep by way of a dredging tool.

I dredge all three fissures, but all I turn up is black humus.

Some kind of stick is what I need, but I haven't got one. What's the time? Twenty to six. If Arne was so sure which way to go, he must have realised by now that I went off in the wrong direction. He must have realised that I genuinely made a mistake. Why hasn't he come looking for me?

'Arne!' I shout. Three more times I call his name.

Why didn't he find me ages ago?

I try lighting a cigarette by angling my magnifying glass to the sun, but the light is hazy and the rays are too weak. Besides, the cigarettes are damp.

Slipping the packet into my left breast pocket reminds me of the measuring tape in my other pocket.

I draw it out. Two metres. Good steel measuring tape. Springs back into its case when released. Flexible. I try probing the fissures with it. Whenever it finds something in its path I can feel it buckling. I try to prevent that by waving it like a whip and making it ripple, but it's too bendy. The sides of the fissures aren't smooth, of course. The tape keeps getting stuck, whereupon it crackles and twists. Damn! Damn! I feel nauseous. I pound my fist against the rock, bring my nose to the ground. All three fissures are explored in like fashion: get up, go over to the next slit, sink down on one knee while keeping the other one straight – ouch, ouch – lie stomach down with my nose to the slit, sniff the odour of rotting fungi. In goes my probe. I even try stuffing the full two metres of tape inside, no longer bothering to keep it straight. With any luck it'll bump against the compass and shunt it along until it comes out the other end.

Nothing works.

I roll over onto my back, prop my shoulder against one of the blocks. I draw the tape out to its full length and release it a couple of times, and each time it shoots back with a high-pitched whirr. What time is it now? My watch says twenty to six. Which is what it said last time I looked. It has evidently stopped. Must have got wet. Would be a miracle if it hadn't. Given to me by my mother when I started at university seven years ago. For someone like me, I told her at the time, a water resistant watch would have been more practical.

'Oh, Alfred! How can you be so horrid! After all the trouble I went to! I thought it was rather smart. Waterproof watches are so thick and ungainly. Don't you think this one's much nicer? It's the thinnest men's watch on the planet: two millimetres. Wonderful, isn't it?'

Yes, wonderful, but it's not working.

I prise the lid open with my penknife. Nothing to be seen, no water anyway. I blow into the casing, which is probably not very good for it, but what else can I do? Finally I wind it up as far as it will go, shake it a few times and hold it to my ear. It is ticking. I set the hands at seven o'clock. Just guessing.

After fifteen minutes it stops again.

A quarter past seven – that is, if my earlier guess of seven o'clock was right, because it could easily be quite a bit later. Either way, I have been here for at least an hour and a half, and Arne still hasn't found me.

The map is nearly dry when I finally decide not to hang around waiting for Arne to come and find me. I fold it up and slide it into its pocket. Then I walk around the blocks to check whether I have left anything behind, and also to make quite sure I haven't missed any clue that might lead to the discovery of my compass.

Nothing. Goodbye, compass. The case hanging from my

belt, the shiny leather case that still looks new, is empty. My left hand keeps opening and shutting the clasp.

All things considered, the most likely explanation is that Arne decided to walk back to the ravine where I went missing, and that he is waiting for me there.

But how am I to find my way to the ravine? I go round the three rocks one last time, hoping to recognise the direction I came from. But my eyes are irresistibly drawn to the fissures, as if there is still hope of sighting the compass.

I gaze at the rocks and the horizon by turns. A wavy line all around, not a tree or a bush to be seen, not a tree or a bush for me to recognise. And then, in the remote distance beyond the hills, rises the pyramid of Mount Vuorje. At least we were there before, even if it was some time ago. That is where we came from. If I head in that direction, I may find the ravine on my way. At least I can *see* the mountain, so I will be able to get there without a compass. I could even get there without a map.

35

My watch says eight thirty and it's not ticking. No idea when it stopped. An hour ago? Several hours? Not that I really need to know. When I'm worn out I'll just lie down for a bit.

No sign of the ravine. If only I could find it, then at least I'd be able to see roughly where I am on the map.

It's cold now, and the sun is very low. Could this be its lowest point? If so, it's the midnight sun, which would mean that it's midnight. In other words, the position of the sun indicates north.

I sit down, unfold the map and spread it out with the top facing in the direction of the sun. North, possibly. Looking about me, I try to see the map in the scenery. Looking at the map, I try to see where the hills are. I don't succeed, obviously. Impossible with a map drawn to such a small scale: 1 to 100,000. Besides, the sun may not yet have reached due north. If my watch hadn't stopped, if it were still working properly, I wouldn't need my compass – if the sun doesn't disappear, that is, and if I knew how much difference daylight saving time made . . . if . . .

What am I moaning for? As long as I keep Mount Vuorje in my sights I won't be completely lost. Better than Vuorje would be finding the ravine, where Arne's waiting for me. I'll offer a thousand apologies for causing a delay with my pig-headedness. *You know that, don't you, Arne? You can count on me.*

Can he really?

Truth is, my mood has lightened considerably now that I'm on my own. It's as if I've been under tutelage all this time, under the watchful, contemptuous gaze of my companions, who guessed my ambitious plans and who opposed them. Didn't believe in them either. As if their company prevented me from concentrating fully on my goal: finding meteor craters, collecting meteorites.

Now I'm alone I can, without embarrassment, give myself up to the illusion that an amazing discovery is just around the corner, justifying my hard labour. All the observations I've made until now are nothing but routine, anyone could have made them. The whole world and everything in it will at some point have been investigated, it's just a matter of time. If *I* deign to engage in this pursuit, it's purely for the purpose of making some astonishing discovery.

Astonishing?

A light flips on in my head. Did I look at those photographs of Mikkelsen's closely enough?

There could have been some detail he noticed and I didn't . . . That must be why he and Qvigstad split up from us! That's why they made off in such a hurry without saying goodbye! Maybe Mikkelsen didn't even show me all the photographs. Maybe he kept back the most important ones.

Where did they go? Back, of course, towards Mount Vuorje!

What luck that I happen to be heading in the same direction as they are!

My visionary imaginings reach further still. Nobody will be able to accuse me of deliberately misreading my compass, or of deliberately getting separated from Arne. My blunder wasn't too bad, after all. In fact, it's a blessing in disguise! Because going to Mount Vuorje suits me just fine. I wanted to go there anyway, to see what Mikkelsen's up to. I never wanted to let him out of my sight. If Mikkelsen were to find what I'm looking for – what could be worse?

The slope leads down to a green, marshy plain crossed by a slow-moving river branching out into three meandering streams. I am certain that I have never been here before. I can't think why I still haven't found the ravine. I must be going in the right direction, though: Mount Vuorje is straight ahead of me.

Nummedal's study. Enter: the professor and his pupil, Mikkelsen.

Nummedal: You must take care, Mikkelsen, for there is a spy in your group. Here, take the aerial photographs. Do not tell him you have them. If he finds out, think of some way of shaking him off. Throw him off the scent. Because here, at Mount Vuorje (Nummedal peers at the aerial photograph through a colossal magnifying glass, points with his pencil), there is a strange hole. Possibly the scene of some highly exceptional event. An event of the greatest scientific import, Mikkelsen! Take my advice, Mikkelsen!

Mikkelsen: Of course, Professor.

Nummedal: Don't rouse suspicions by hanging around on Mount Vuorje at the beginning. Keep Arne and the Dutchman company for a day or two, then you can turn back.

*

Mikkelsen all over! Made off as soon as I caught on to him having the photographs – the very photographs I went to all that trouble to get hold of!

He is not going to get away with it!

I sit down by the water and look at my map. Although I don't know my exact position, the mountain can't be more than four kilometres away. Four kilometres as the crow flies. On the ground that could amount to a five-hour hike, including periods of rest.

The sun is still shining, but has stopped giving warmth. My teeth are chattering now and I've got goose-flesh all over, as if my skin is trying frantically to keep my damp clothes from clinging to my body.

I see low shrubs studded with soft fleshy fruits resembling oversized, bright yellow raspberries. I pick one and put it in my mouth. It is full of seeds, yet the taste is slightly sour, like skimmed milk. Are they unripe or do they always taste like that?

There isn't much around here that is edible. Have I ever been on my own in a Dutch forest without any food? No, I have not. How would I survive? You can't eat beech nuts or acorns. Blueberries, brambles, mushrooms, that's all I can think of.

I extract one of the two sodden boxes of knäckebröd from my rucksack. The cardboard has split open in places. My health-giving crackers, so crisp and tasty, recommended by the world's leading doctors, also for anaemia, have turned into brown mush oozing from a disintegrating box.

Food is going to be the main problem, I think yet again as I cram the knäckebröd pulp into my mouth with my fingers, like a cook devouring the scrapings from a saucepan.

I stuff half the mash into a plastic bag, which I put back in my rucksack. Stupid of me not to slip a plastic bag over the box in the first place! I should have packed everything in plastic bags to be on the safe side, but I didn't, just because Arne, Qvigstad and Mikkelsen didn't either.

Next I take a tube of honey and squeeze the contents into my mouth until it's empty. Astronauts use tubes to eat from too, they have to squirt the food into their mouths because it's weightless. Imagine being an astronaut stuck in a spacecraft! I have all the space I could wish for! Me! Not them!

I can do whatever I please. Piss wherever I like, take a shit, scream at the top of my voice. And no-one will be any the wiser, unless I tell them myself.

A black-tailed godwit alights two metres away and struts around for a bit in the cotton grass, its slender bill curving upwards.

A rippling, fluffy blanket of pink is pulled across the sky by invisible hands. It doesn't keep me warm, in fact I feel very chilly, so I get up again.

I cross the three meandering streams without any trouble, after which I climb another slope. Reaching the top I cast around for a reasonably level spot to take a rest.

I spread out all my belongings around me. Sleeping bag – it would release streams of water if wrung, which I don't do for fear of compacting the down into a solid lump. Soggy knäckebröd. Six tubes of honey. Cigarettes, which are damp; matches, likewise damp. Notebook, damp. Packet of salt, damp, or, rather, rock hard. Fishing net.

I stuff everything back into my rucksack, as if I'm filling a rubbish bin. Finally I wrap myself in my plastic mac and lie down with my back to the sun, using my moist rucksack for a pillow. I feel truly spent now, and colder than ever.

Where will my body get the energy to withstand the freezing cold given off by my wet clothes? From half a box of knäcke-bröd and a tubeful of honey?

I will have to see about catching a fish with the net. Perhaps two fishes. How many could I catch in one go, if I'm lucky? A hundred? I am so tired that I may actually get some sleep. Not that the mosquitoes have given up, but then Arne isn't here to keep me awake with his snoring. No sleep, though. Sit up, cover face and hands with mosquito oil, lie back again. Fall.

Did I fall asleep?

The sun is in a completely different position now: beaming on my forehead. My legs are so stiff that I have trouble extricating myself from the plastic mac. I empty my rucksack again and spread out everything that's wet in the sunshine. Matches in a tidy row on a flat stone, which is already warm to the touch. The box itself has become unstuck, but I lay it out carefully to dry because the striking surfaces are indispensable.

All I can do now is wait. Go back to sleep, preferably. But I'm so hungry I can't resist finishing the remaining half of the knäckebröd. Having washed it all down with water, I lie down again and shut my eyes. I'm in a light summer suit strolling down a narrow quay, which doesn't seem to be open to the general public. Moored on either side are tall sailing ships, covered in rust because they've never been painted. It's like being in an alley lined with ships instead of houses. At the end of the quay there's a flight of steps leading to a lower level. I make my way between the rusty ships and go down the steps, expecting to find a urinal. I push the swing doors open. Not a urinal. A concert hall. Orchestra tuning up. Auditorium filled to capacity. Burst of applause. Not a single vacant seat. Yes, there is, just one – mine, bang in the centre of the auditorium. Tripping over people's feet, mumbling apologies, I squeeze between the rows towards my seat. I notice that the audience is quite elderly, no-one under fifty. The men are in dinner jackets and the women in evening dress, which means they're practically naked. Pale flesh, plump arms with a tracery of blue veins. All the women are wearing the same backless gown with décolleté plunging down to the navel and oddly shaped holes in the sides too, exposing further stretches of livid skin. Identical gowns? More than that: identical women. They don't look like anyone I know.

I sink into my seat and the lights go down. The conductor lifts his baton and the orchestra, which consists entirely of wind instruments, bursts forth with a deafening salvo. Tucked away among the musicians is a girl. I can see her as clearly as if I'm studying a photograph of the orchestra through a magnifying glass. She plays the cymbals, even though she's next to the flautist. In each raised hand she holds a huge brass cymbal, poised to clang them together. Shoulder-length blond hair falling from a centre parting. With each crash of the cymbals her hair billows up on either side of her face, lifted by the blast of air from the collision.

Her head looks as if it has wings. Her glazed eyes are fastened on mine. Abruptly, the orchestra falls silent, with the exception of the flautist. The girl clearly belongs to him. This is confirmed by a deafening crash of the cymbals, which wakes me up.

My eyes open quite easily, but they're the only part of me that hasn't gone completely stiff. I haul myself into a sitting position. My watch doesn't tick, not even when I shake it. Kaput. I have visions of the steel mechanism being cancerated by rust until only brown dust remains.

A bolt of lighting fractures the grey slab of sky. One, two, three, four seconds later comes the thunderclap. It's raining already in the environs of Vuorje: a rainbow over-arches the mountain, as though signalling some highly sacred event taking place on the summit. I have never seen a rainbow of such dazzling brightness. I feel I'm levitating, suspended in a soap bubble. My goal surrounded by a halo. With excruciating effort I stand up, open my flies and aim a jet of urine exactly at the centre of the arc. More thunder.

At my feet lie the contents of my rucksack. Not a soul for miles and miles around to take any notice. The seventeen matches aligned on the flat stone are now dry. The flattened matchbox cover – four rectangles joined together: blue, black, yellow-and-red, black – is dry. Seventeen cigarettes, their surgical white tubing stained brown: dry. Maps: dry. Notebook: dry. Sleeping bag . . . ?

I shake it out, plump it up, try teasing out the lumpy swansdown. Still too wet. I also check my camera in case the film has miraculously got unstuck. It has not.

I squirt half a tube of honey into my mouth, drink some water and smoke a cigarette. The wind is rising and between gusts the mosquitoes' buzzing intensifies. It isn't raining yet, although the sky has turned black save for a small patch of blue overhead. If only I knew where I am on the map, I could use my position plus the mountain to align the map properly, and then I'd be able to work out what time it is on the basis of the sun. All the stuff I've learnt is useless. But why do I need to know what time it is?

I gather up my belongings with deliberation, packing each item away as safely as possible (the matches go into my breast pocket wrapped in a bit of plastic – the least chance of them getting wet if I sink into a bog).

When I've finished packing I load my rucksack and take a last look round. No, haven't left any traces. No clues to my ever having been here. Not such a good idea, perhaps. I tear a sheet out of my notebook and write:

I am on my way to Vuorje. Alfred.

I fold the note in four and leave it lying on top of a large stone with a small stone as a paperweight.

36

Mount Vuorje has three flanks: one facing south, one north-west and one north-east.

I am approaching the mountain from the south, but won't be able to climb that side because it's too steep.

Judging by the indications on the map, the north-west flank will present the least difficulty.

The terrain I am walking on now is already rising steadily. The rain has reached me, or I have reached the rain. Fat drops – actually hailstones that have only just melted – fall on my plastic mac, rapidly forming rivers running down to my trousers and into my shoes. By now the note I left on the big stone will be soaking wet, reduced to pulp, vanishing without trace.

My thoughts are becoming as monotonous as the rain, as boring as my aches and pains. My fear of Mikkelsen being on the scent of a major discovery is a suppurating sore.

And yet, despite the fear, there are moments when I realise with a shock that I've been going for several minutes (how many?) without scanning the stones at my feet for meteorites.

Round holes containing only water don't occur at this altitude, nor do lakes.

I can now see the south side of the mountain in its entirety.

A blue-black wall encrusted with ribbons of eternal snow. Trickles of whitish shale run down from the top like tentacles widening into enormous suction pads. I stay out of harm's reach. My progress is slow, but it's progress. In the face of my diligence even the clouds give up and drift away. The sun floods the landscape with russet and red.

I tell myself I'm keeping to an altitude of 720 metres. In any case, I'm taking the left way round the mountain. My horizon changes from one moment to the next. At last! Lake Lievnasjaurre! I can see the Obbarda-elv winding towards it. Another two kilometres and I'll have a view of the whole lake. Qvigstad and Mikkelsen must be somewhere around here. Where's their green tent? With each step I take – and my steps are small – I can see a bit more of the lake, some three hundred metres down from where I am now.

At last there's no need to lift my weary head up high each time I want to survey my surroundings.

But the green double-roof tent is nowhere to be seen.

I sit down, stare at the mountain, stare at my map. I could, possibly, save time by not walking all the way to the foot of the north-western flank first. The sooner I get to the top the better. From there I'll have a view to all sides, and I'll spot Qvigstad and Mikkelsen, assuming they haven't yet left.

Striking diagonally across the base in the direction of the summit means gaining altitude early on.

The north-western flank is surprisingly easy to climb. It isn't bare rock, rather an undulating cover of stones and sand – originally mud flow, presumably, after which compaction was supplied by plants, creating the wrinkled effect of the skin on boiled milk.

There are some puzzling horizontal gullies running across the slope, dividing it into terraces. Probably gouged out of the mountainside by ice ridges in former times, creating an amphitheatre for giants with fifty-metre-long shins. But when I reach the uppermost rank I'm still a long way from the summit. Mountains always increase in height once you start climbing.

The vegetation peters out. I now come to a vast expanse of cobbles the size of cannon balls. The foot must be placed exactly on the middle of each stone or it slides off. Each step requires calculation, not the slightest move must be made without considering the consequences of a false step: foot jammed between cobbles, falling over, leg snapping like matchwood.

Every twenty paces or so I pause unsteadily to look about me. I do not dare to sit down, for fear of losing my balance when I get up again and being flung to the bottom at a dizzying speed, a gob of flesh and splintered bone spat out by Mount Vuorje.

Now and then I inadvertently dislodge a stone, at which it bounces up, comes thundering down, then bounces up even higher before crashing onto the cobbles further back. I can only breathe through my mouth now. My limbs are draped in sweat-drenched curtains. I have never read a description of what it's like to climb a mountain such as this. That all you can see ahead of you is ten or twenty metres of slope ending in a sharp ridge, beyond which the sky begins. And that as you climb further the distance to the top of the ridge increases. Like being on a treadmill, some gigantic cylinder made to revolve under your feet. Is there no end to it? Why do I keep thinking I have reached the top when I haven't? Maybe the people who have done this sort of climbing don't want to admit how harrowing the experience was. Or they simply forget. Nobody can recall precisely what the dentist's drill feels like. The pain is so excruciating and the sense of powerlessness so overwhelming that it is not something you dwell on, never mind put down in writing.

Another pause. I am panting heavily. A cloud comes drifting my way. Which it has every right to. I have ascended to the land of clouds, I am an intruder in their domain. The cloud sidles up to the mountain much as an airship in the old days, a zeppelin looking to use a church spire as a mooring-post. The cloud begins to envelop me. It is not nearly as dense as I had expected. Not a cloud, really, more like eddies of white mist. I take a deep breath and start walking again. A thin white deposit has formed on the crowns of the stones. Hoarfrost. The slope grows gentler at last, and then, abruptly, ceases to be a slope at all. I am at the summit.

Something stirs on the ground close by. Stirs, then stops. Some animal. A polar fox. White fur with brown markings on its back. It is standing right in front of me, wide-legged, head lowered between the shoulders, boxer-fashion, tufted ears pricked up. What does it want? Has it never seen a human being before? I wish I could coax it to come closer, like a dog. Suddenly it turns and trots away at a leisurely pace, as though dissembling its fright. Tail down, the tip almost touching the ground, it vanishes into the mist.

The summit.

What do I see? Nothing. White fog whichever way I turn. I can only see the small patch of level ground where I'm standing. I pace around in anguish: precipices on all sides, fringed in vapour. Where can Mikkelsen and Qvigstad be? They may be close by, but I can't see them. The mist swirls past me as if I'm sitting in an aeroplane. The density of the cloud varies, but it appears to be endless, endlessly prolonging my blindness.

I screw up my eyes with frustration and it's as if my spirit has already taken leave of this mountain. So where is it now? Somewhere in space, where the stars, such as there are, belong. For the most part there aren't any stars in space, for the most part there's nothing at all. Out there in that void somewhere there's me, gazing on the earth, a planet no bigger than a football. I can see the white mould of polar ice and snow-capped mountain ranges.

Never have I been so acutely aware of the thinness of the atmospheric layer that sustains human existence. Man finds life hard all over the planet, but we need only travel to the extreme north or the extreme south, or climb a mountain for that matter, for us to reach our limits. It has taken cunning, brute force, conspiracy, shiftwork, centuries of scientific endeavour and billions of man hours to launch one manned spacecraft. I know I am nothing but a chemical compound in a particular state of equilibrium, strictly confined within distinct, incontrovertible boundaries. In my mind's eye I see the world as a globe, a sphere covered by a thin membrane, which is the substance within which I am able to exist to the exclusion of all else. The membrane thins out towards the poles . . .

Jesus had an easy time of it – taking it for granted that fig trees grew all over the world.

But the other planets, a bit further away from the sun, or a little closer . . . what have they got? Dust storms, maybe, as on Venus. Or ice crusts of pure ammonia, as on Jupiter. What difference would it make if there were people living on other planets? I have never heard of Europeans feeling less lonely after Columbus discovered America and its population.

Seen from a distance, my globe looks as if it is supposed to be covered in ice. Warm winds have blown it off in places, but the poles and the tallest mountains are still ice-bound, for the ice has not been defeated. It expands underground. In the next Ice Age it may get as far as the tropics. The end of the world. Ragnarok. All it would take is for some object to come between us and the sun, screening us from the heat. A cloud of cosmic dust, say, or a dense swarm of meteorites.

I am standing with my feet on different stones, one in front of the other, leaning forwards with my head down and my left arm, with which I am holding my left knee, propping up my upper body. I can hardly bring myself to cast my eyes yet again over the small area that I can see: stones and mist and little else. I do not feel sad, only profound pity for all those people who are so distant from me, and even if I had a radio transmitter at my disposal there would be no point telling them what I think. They are beyond my understanding, and I am beyond theirs. Stamped indelibly on their minds are the craziest fairy tales, variations on megalomaniac notions dating back to their caveman ancestors, for whom a cave stood for the entire universe. And even if they do not believe in fairy tales, that doesn't mean they have given up hope of gaining spiritual revelations from manifest mumbo jumbo. Because, they say, we cannot go on living like this, we are lost souls and we need consolation. (I go on living, don't I? And who's consoling *me*?)

So they put popes in palaces and feed diamonds to the Aga Khan. They never think of the abuse suffered by millions in the name of their false consolations, they turn a blind eye to the preposterous religious laws existing in even the most civilised countries, because all they want is to lose themselves in fairy tales, and the more bloodshed there is the firmer their belief. For blood is all they possess, and the only incontestable existential fact is their insatiable thirst for the blood of others.

I would rather die a victim of the elements than of people. If I were struck by lightning, or hit on the head by a falling meteorite, or if I fell down the mountain from sheer exhaustion, it would be weeks before anyone discovered I had gone missing. That would suit me fine. It is even possible that I would never be found. A gratifying thought, but to savour the gratification I would have to survive for a while in spirit, or I wouldn't know they hadn't found me. Vanishing from the face of the earth like that would at least mean that *my death* is in keeping with what I know. *Because my life will never be in keeping with what I know.*

Never . . . I can't stay here. I begin to walk, down into the mist.

Eva would say I had gone to heaven.

But I do not fall down the mountain. I duck under the cloud, and a moment later I have left the stony summit behind. I am treading on moss, low heather. The slope is cushioned in mosses of every shade, black, blue, pale green, even orange and red. A flock of wild geese skims overhead.

I look out over the lake and recognise the far-off shore where we pitched our tents before. No Mikkelsen and Qvigstad.

Here, where I am standing now, is where we saw the immense herd of rumbling reindeer. The person herding them must have been here too, at some stage. But there is no sign of either now.

There is no doubt about it: in my current state of destitution the most sensible thing to do is to get back to civilisation. What will come of my scientific research? I didn't even get hold of the aerial photographs. Mikkelsen has them. He can see what I can't. If I ran into him now I'd kill him. But I don't run into him.

Compass lost, camera broken. Bleeding and bruised, feverish from lack of sleep, empty stomach. My mind is a blank. I don't even know the time.

The best thing now would be to head back to Skoganvarre, twenty-five kilometres away. But of course I can't do that, because of Arne. He could go on looking for me for weeks. And I'm pretty sure he's still waiting for me at the ravine.

Fantasising about ways of letting Arne know I'm heading back to Skoganvarre (walkie-talkie, carrier pigeon, sighting some Lapp I could ask to pass the message on to Arne, seaplane, helicopter – which I could hail, but there haven't been any flying overhead), I plod on towards the shore of Lake Lievnasjaurre. I sit down and peer at my map through my magnifying glass. At least I know exactly where I am now. Here, right near me, the water discharges from the lake into the Lievnasjokka. This is the stream we crossed in our socks. If I keep to it, along the right bank, then the fourth tributary will be the Rivo-elv. And if I continue down the Rivo-elv valley, I'll arrive at the ravine. It's a long way round, but my best bet if I want to avoid all risk of getting lost again. How far? About twelve kilometres, I think. I can easily get there by tomorrow evening.

In the meantime I have finished the last of the knäckebröd. I light a cigarette and spend the next twenty minutes staring at the ripples. Then I take the fishing net out of my rucksack, untangle it and carry it to the water's edge. I might be lucky, who knows? Now I have to unroll the net as I walk along the bank in search of a spot where it can cut off a small bay. But it keeps snagging, so I have to keep stopping to loosen the meshes from leaves and twigs. This is no good. Better to wade. I take off my shoes and my trousers. Having done that, I feel an irresistible desire to undress completely, despite the mosquitoes settling on my legs. My clothes smell foul as I pull them over my head. My trunk is streaked with tidemarks of sweat and pimpled with dried blood covering the bites of carnivorous flies. My right leg is swollen and has turned a purply blue all the way up to and over the knee. The sight of my own decrepitude disgusts me, and on an impulse I plunge my hand into the depths of my rucksack and bring out my soap to brandish it in the midnight sun. Oh, I know everything that I am and own appears incongruous in this setting. Yet the bar of soap in my hand bears a marked resemblance to the stones on the ground. A smooth green stone, a bezoar, an amulet. Clutching it as if it has magic powers, I stumble towards the water's edge, suffering hellish pain to the soles of my lacerated feet. Then I bend down, soap myself all over, wade into the lake up to my knees, drop forward and swim. Dirt and soapsuds instantly vanish. In water as pure as this, the traces are diluted a million times.

Floating in the blissful embrace of water is effortless, painless, even better than sleeping. A completely new sensation after these long weeks of forcing my attentions on the earth's crust only to be rebuffed by fists of rock: the boulders on which I lay, the precipices I teetered along, the stones that tripped me up. Through filaments of copper I swim towards the sun, while birds circle overhead in apparent welcome. There is no sound but the flurry of wings and the water rippling around my arms.

37

The mosquitoes have taken due account of my ablutions, which has made me even more enticing to them than before. They mass together around my head-net, which I have taken care to tie firmly under my chin before lying down.

Several hours must have gone by, because the sun is in the south. I do believe I've been asleep. I'd still be asleep if I weren't so hungry. My hand slides under my shirt and slaps flies on my bare skin. The hand comes away with fresh blood on the fingertips.

I get up, take my magnifying glass and try lighting a cigarette with it. Grey smoke billows from the tobacco, soon I can see it glowing too. The sun is brighter than it has been for weeks, and I feel my confidence mounting. I will find Arne at the ravine and, who knows, I may even find a meteor crater on the way. Go back to Skoganvarre? What for? Go back to Amsterdam? What would I tell Sibbelee? And what would I tell myself? Going back now would mean throwing away all the experience I have gained so far.

I lace up my shoes and walk to the lakeside. A duck and her five young have alighted on the water. Would there be a fish in the net? I go to the shrub where I fastened one of the lines and run my eyes over the row of corks floating on the surface. It looks as if there's an extra cork at one end, but when I jerk the line I hear the flapping of wings. One of the young ducks has got its feet caught in the net. I untie the line and take it along the bank to the shrub where I attached the other line. Cautiously I begin to draw in the net. What a catch! I pull the net towards me as gently as I can, folding the sections zigzag fashion as they emerge from the water. The creature is so panicked I'm afraid it will break its legs trying to escape. Enter Alfred, ravenous, self-styled poultryman. Promptly wrings the creature's neck. First time in his life he has killed anything this size. Twists the head round a couple of times, like winding up clockwork. Plucks the feathers off the small corpse, cuts it open. Entrails spill out: dark yellow, liver-brown and a lot of red. Hardly anything in nature is red, except blood and guts.

But before the young duck comes within my reach there is a violent tug on the net and a frenzy of thrashing. A trout! I free its gills from the nylon mesh, stamp on its head with my heel, then draw the net further in until the young duck is close enough to seize. Well, hello, my little friend! I have to sit down to disentangle its scaly feet from the net. Then I put it on a cushion of moss about a metre from the water's edge, where it remains, motionless.

Just before I finish hauling in the rest of the net the water starts heaving and boiling again: another trout.

The duck stays put on its cushion of moss, wings slightly raised, panting with fright, but apparently unharmed.

I make a pile of twigs close by.

I clean my two fishes, cut them up, stuff the pieces down the neck of the coffee kettle, fill it with water, scrape a bit of salt off the petrified lump with my penknife, set fire to the twigs.

The young duck observes everything I am doing, because it happens to be sitting with one eye facing in my direction.

No, I wouldn't say it is keeping me company, although I do talk to it kindly from time to time. I wish I had a crust of bread for you, but I count myself lucky to have caught those fish. The young duck's bill curving up at the corners is even more comical than the adult version. Its eyes are of the kind that see, not look. It cheers me up with its company, at no effort on its part.

Mmm! This is very good! Barely pausing to pluck fish bones from my lips, I fill my stomach with the tenderest, noblest fish ever caught! I also drink the remaining fish stock with its nutritious spots of grease floating on the surface.

The young duck has closed its bill. It shakes its head, twists round to preen the feathers on its back, then waddles off towards the water. Without visible exertion, blown along like a toy sailing boat, it heads straight back to its mother and siblings.

38

The terrain around here is so uneven that it is difficult to gauge the average distance covered by one step. Holes, bosses, brief stretches that are fairly level followed by a rise and then a dip and so forth. No two paces are of equal length.

I have unrolled the measuring tape and laid it on the ground with a stone weighing it down at each end. I try working out how many normal steps correspond to two metres. Three and a half. I pick up the measuring tape, let it spring back into its case and stuff it in my trouser pocket. Holding the map with both hands, I go and stand where the lake feeds into the Lievnasjokka. From here it is roughly five kilometres to the Rivo-elv, which according to the map is the fourth tributary on the right. Five kilometres, that's two thousand five hundred times two metres, which is . . . which is eight thousand, seven hundred and fifty paces. Approximately. Could be a margin of five hundred or a thousand each way.

Inaccurate as my estimate may be, counting my steps will help me decide whether I have reached the Rivo-elv or not. I don't know by which criteria my map was drawn, but the chances of one or more tributaries not having been included are considerable. So are the chances of the fourth tributary I come across not being the right one. What if I take the wrong valley! The idea makes me want to howl with terror.

Because how will I ever find Arne then? Here I am, spending all my precious time trying to find my way instead of concentrating on my research, and in the end I suppose I'll be grateful to be back in the civilised world having escaped death by starvation. And I will have achieved nothing. I will have survived, that's all.

I tear a page out of my notebook, fold it in four, clutch it in my left hand, take a pencil in my right and begin walking.

Counting aloud, I make my way through the Lievnasjokka valley. This is the where we saw the herd of reindeer moving down towards the water. I notice their droppings here and there. They could almost be taken for meteorites.

Metereorites! Won't find any of those this close to the water, where the ground is spongy and thickly overgrown.

So as not to miss the least opportunity, I move further up along the side of the valley, where the ground looks dry and stony and there is less vegetation. But the stones turn out to be rubble that has rolled down from the top.

Seventy. Eighty-seven, eighty-eight. Stumbling on a *thufur* and taking two or three steps in panicky succession – how many paces would that add up to?

I take a guess, just to give myself something to do.

Each time I reach a hundred I put a vertical mark on the paper I'm holding in my left hand. And start again. My mouth is getting parched from talking – does counting aloud rate as talking? The scrap of paper is becoming damp with sweat. While I am counting I am keeping my eyes peeled for remarkable stones, and at the same time I haven't lost hope of meeting up with Qvigstad and Mikkelsen. I keep hoping, against my better judgment. Because Arne told me they would be going to Skoganvarre by way of Vuorje, and I am heading south-east. Almost diametrically the opposite direction!

One thousand seven hundred and fifty. I have just crossed the first tributary. Which seems right. One thousand seven hundred and fifty paces works out at one kilometre. According to the map this watercourse comes to an end a little less than one kilometre from Lake Lievnasjaurre. Well I never! It all seems to work out remarkably well! I didn't know I had it in me. I might even get quite good at this kind of thing – finding my way across Norway without so much as a compass. To celebrate my success, I sit down for a rest and take out a cigarette. I have eight left. It's turned misty again and the sun is as pale as the moon. I light my cigarette with one of my last five matches. Not to worry, Arne has plenty. Another nine kilometres – oh all right then, ten. Four to the Rivo-elv, and five or six to the ravine. The map is very vague. You can't tell exactly where the ravine begins. Not that I know exactly where Arne is either. Ten kilometres, that's an hour and three quarters on a footpath in Holland. How much is it here? Five hours? Four maybe, because I don't have to cross mountains. Arne won't be surprised. He's been expecting me to turn up for days. He won't hold it against me, and he's not the type to bear grudges. Nor will he belittle me. I feel small enough as it is.

To think that Nansen was roughly my age when he crossed Greenland on foot from east to west, three thousand kilometres over ice at fifteen degrees below zero. Entirely alone. No sahib-venerating Sherpas for him!

I wonder what sort of life I should have had to render me capable of such feats of achievement. To begin with, my father should not have got killed when I was seven years old. But if that hadn't happened I might not have studied geology, I might not have gone to university at all. I might have become a flautist. A great flautist? Not necessarily. Regret? No. I am long past regretting. Playing the flute would not have vindicated my father's death, it would not have given me a chance to go right where he went wrong.

I stand up. Better get cracking. At least I can still walk, I'm still on my feet. Even if I do get lost, make a complete fool of myself, bungle everything, I'll still be hanging on and that's the only thing that matters.

That is all that matters. Until now there hasn't been a challenge I have not risen to. Everything is going to be fine, success is round the corner. I will discover a meteor crater in due course, and may even return with some meteoric stones. I can see myself showing them to Sibbelee. 'Ah well,' he says with his most condescending smile. 'Of course men like Nummedal made a valuable contribution to science in their day. But when they grow old they become resistant to new ideas. It seems to me that the best time for Nummedal to have resigned would have been forty years ago, when he was at the height of his fame.' We laugh heartily. I place the precious meteorites on his desk one by one. Next I'm facing five professors in academic robes across a green baize table. I'm wearing my tailcoat and my head is bowed, not out of deference but to decipher the PhD certificate lying on the table, upside down from where I am standing. A huge, handsomely calligraphed document bearing a red seal the size of a fried egg. *Cum laude.*

The score on the scrap of paper in my left hand is three rows of five tally marks and a final row of four. Ninety-five marks! Nine thousand five hundred paces. Multiply by two and divide by three and a half and I'll have the distance in metres: roughly five thousand. I was right! I can stop counting now. I've crossed three tributaries already, and the one I'm reaching now, the fourth, flows down into a deep valley. This must be the Rivo-elv. There's no need, really, to keep to the water in this case. I couldn't possibly get lost now, so I might as well take a short cut up the side.

Having climbed sixty metres, I'm on a crest from which I can see both the Lievnasjokka and the Rivo-elv. Foaming currents interspersed with shallow rapids.

I try to imagine what the valley of the Rivo-elv will look like further along, where it narrows into the ravine where I'll find Arne. But how am I to find him? I must now take a crucial decision: keep to the river or walk along the top of the left flank of the valley. Which is best? Taking the high route means I may not see Arne if he's down in the valley or on the opposite side of the river. And vice versa: keeping to the river means I have a good view of the slopes, but then he may have pitched his tent in a spot you can't see from the bottom of the valley. But he wouldn't do a stupid thing like that. He'll be doing everything he possibly can to make it easy for me to find him. Of course he will. And as it's so much easier for me to walk along the river, and as Arne will realise this, that's what I decide to do.

The valley grows deeper and narrower, the sides get steeper, too steep for plants to spread their roots. Some of the rock strata protrude like book shelves. They are lined with snow, which won't melt all summer. Snow. Speckled with black. But also red snow. I gather a handful and study it through my magnifying glass, but it melts before I get the chance to see the microbes that stain it red. They probably wouldn't be visible anyway. Shouldn't be wasting my time. If I keep up a steady pace I may come upon Arne within the next hour or two. Two hours – an irrelevant measure of time if you don't have a watch. Before nightfall – equally irrelevant in a place where it never gets dark. As soon as possible, then.

What will I say when we meet? 'Doctor Livingstone, I presume,' of course.

Doctor Livingstone, I presume! Laughing comes easily on an empty stomach. And it isn't even funny, because it was Qvigstad who made the joke in the first place, and I haven't found him either.

I reach into my trouser pocket for the tube of honey and squeeze it into my mouth as I walk. The last vestiges of doubt evaporate: this is certainly the right valley, although I can't say I recognise anything in particular from last time. Yes, the bed of the valley is lush and marshy as I remember it, and then suddenly my eyes light on the glacier on the left bank! The same glacier! The rush of water becomes louder, compounded now by the streams running down from the thawing glacier. It won't be long before I see Arne, surely. Doctor Livingstone, I presume.

'My compass indicated a different direction from yours. I'm sorry. You were right.'

'Where is it?'

'Lost.'

'That beautiful compass? Pity.'

'Good riddance, I'd say.'

'You must have misread it.'

'Don't worry. I have only your compass to go by now. Mine was given to me by my God-fearing sister. A typical present from her! I wonder where she got all those funny ideas from. My father was not a believer, my mother isn't one, and I'm not either. But she has taken it upon herself to point us in the right direction!'

'Where to?'

'Don't ask me! To the North Pole, like a compass, who knows? A bit cold, but then she makes up for it by being crazy about Negro spirituals.'

'Ha, ha, ha.'

Treading with care, I walk on, keeping as close as I can to the side of the valley so as to avoid the marsh. Three enormously fat Negresses, each weighing at least 200 kilos, clap their hands, sway from side to side, stamp their high-heeled shoes and scream hallelujah. I'm seized with pity for the Negroes, who even at the best of times are likely to be pictured in stupid, ridiculous or vulgar poses: yelling and screaming, leaping about, rolling their eyes, setting the place on fire, sweating profusely as they play their trumpets, clobbering each other in boxing rings, demanding equal rights under the guidance of a reverend minister of the very religion that oppresses them. On television or in the newspapers you never see a black scientist in a laboratory, or a black astronaut, or a Negro reading from his poetry – and yet they exist.

Is that Arne's tent? No, the man-made object in the distance is not his tent. It is something else. I stop in my tracks, at once joyful and puzzled.

It is the tripod with the theodolite fixed on top. Arne must be somewhere near here, that much is certain. Where else could he be? I have been worried sick for days, and there was absolutely no need. Shielding my eyes from the sun with my hands, I scan the area around the theodolite for a sign of Arne. Nothing. No tent either. But why worry, he is bound to be taking measurements around here somewhere. He will turn up in no time.

Walking towards the theodolite feels like cocking a gun at a sleeping animal.

Damn, I'm exhausted, but it has been worth it. All in all I haven't done too badly. Found him without a compass. Simple. As simple as finding a meteoric stone right under my nose, which will happen in a day or two.

Taking care to place my feet on matted willow roots, I venture into a stretch of peat alongside the water. The tripod is on the far side, at the base of the other slope. Must not lose my footing now, not a good time to go falling into the river or getting stuck in the mud . . . *Doctor Livingstone, I presume* – and a great pool of water collected around his feet.

I laugh so hard it hurts.

I cross the shallows without any trouble and without having to take off my shoes. Reaching the tripod, I look about me in all directions: no-one. In a reflex, I bring my right eye to the telescopic sight. A snow goose comes into sharp focus in the centre of the cross-hairs: alighting on the slope ahead, flapping its wings and pecking at something on the ground before taking off again.

Hesitantly, I make my way towards the place the instrument is directed at.

'Hey, Arne!'

He is lying on the ground a few paces off.

'Hey, hey,' I stammer.

Sprawled on his back, one leg bent, the other flung out. I can clearly see the smooth, worn-down sole of his boot, which has come loose. His head lolls against a rock, which is smeared with a custardy substance. Swarms of flies, of a sort I have never seen before, big and blue. Blue like the hands of a clock.

His mouth is closed in a strange manner, with his decaying upper teeth resting on his lower lip as in a final grimace of pain. For the rest his face looks exactly as it did in his sleep: unaccountably old and tired, wrinkled like the bark of an oak tree. But this is not sleep. This is beyond sleep.

My hand, clapped to my mouth, seems intent on preventing me from breathing.

There are also flies on his beard, his forehead, his half-closed eyes. Not a single mosquito, though.

39

How many times have I run up and down the slope where Arne fell to his death?

First I climb to the top, where I spied his tent. Looking down from there, I notice the notebook lying near Arne's body. He must have been holding it when he fell. I go down, retrieve the notebook and pocket it. Back up again, to the tent. Pull out the pegs and the supporting pole. I can use the canvas to cover Arne's body, so down I go again. Then it's back to the top once more, with the idea that I should do something with the rest of his gear. Can't think what, so end up wrapping his rucksack and sleeping bag in a groundsheet. Come upon the case belonging to the theodolite. Can't bear the thought of leaving the instrument on the tripod in all weathers. I go down, unscrew the theodolite, put it back in its case, collapse the tripod. Place both items on the ground beside Arne. Up one more time – don't know why. Better walk along the river if I'm to locate the trail to Ravnastua, I tell myself, so it's down yet again. I spring from one stone to the next, my shoulder intermittently grazing the rock face, but it's as if an invisible parachute keeps me from falling. Falling is the last thing on my mind.

Now and then I look over my shoulder. I am making my way through the valley, and the place where Arne is lying is no longer in sight. Carry on walking. Stop again, squat, pull down trousers. Horrendous belly ache. Diarrhoea. My diet of fish and honey.

Was it stupid of me to leave Arne's food supplies behind? I'm past caring. Don't feel hungry. It's beginning to rain. I plod on. The ravine narrows even further, then comes to a dead end. I clamber out of the cul-de-sac and continue in a straight line. The rain intensifies and I draw my plastic mac over my shoulders. On and on, down into another valley, almost blinded in the downpour. I stumble and manage to regain my balance, but in doing so step on the hem of my mac, causing a huge tear in the plastic. I rip off the dangling flap and toss it away.

40

The trail to Ravnastua is no wider than a shoe, and barely visible in the stony terrain.

Not a dry stitch on my back since I don't know when. It's been raining nonstop for at least two days. My eyes are running, my throat is so swollen I can hardly breathe, I cough with each step and my head is pounding. Still, I do pause now and then to put a pebble on top of some larger stone along the way. That'll be a help to anyone using the trail after me.

Not to Arne. When I take a break – and when the rain lifts somewhat – I leaf through his notebook. All those wonderful drawings going to waste. All those neat entries which I can't read because they're in Norwegian, although I try deciphering the occasional word. I see my own name twice in the last of his entries. What did he say about me?

Coming upon a small round lake, I dump my rucksack on the ground. I take out the fishing net and hang it in the water, which is fringed with tall bushes. Not far from the shore I lie down on my side and screw my eyes up tight. I need to sleep.

I open the door to the sitting room and hear an agitated film dialogue in a language I can't understand. Somebody must have forgotten to switch the television off, because there is no-one in the darkened room. I don't turn on the ceiling light, as I plan to watch television. Not only is there no light in the sitting room, the screen goes blank, too. Guided by the sound, I make my way to the television in the corner, sink to my haunches and twiddle the knobs to restore the picture. Without success. An assailant creeps up on me from behind, pounces on my back and claps his hand over my mouth. Father! I shout, shaken awake by fear.

Waking from a nightmare in broad daylight is hideous. What has come over me? Why call for my father? Me, father-less for eighteen years, calling for a father who has been dead too long for me to remember ever having called his name!

It was my own hand on my own mouth.

The rain has stopped, but there is a strong wind and the sky is overcast. I stay on my back staring up at the clouds for a long while. Then, having reconsidered all the angles I have considered already, I get to my feet, walk to the lake, untie the net and start pulling it in. A trout. Another trout. When the net is about half way out of the water it becomes incred-ibly heavy. A gust of wind blows the part that's above the surface into the bushes. I tug hard to get the rest out of the water, which is in commotion close to the net, as if it's boiling. Another fish. I take a few steps back and pull with all my might. The net is choked with fishes, there's one caught in each mesh, it's like a carpet of glistening, wrig-gling fishes, hundreds of them. What am I to do? I can't pluck them off one by one, I haven't the energy. I must eat first.

How many matches have I got left? Four. All the bushes are dripping wet after the prolonged rain. I set about building a small pyre, taking care to shake the drops off each twig before adding it on top. I strike the first match. It goes out: too much wind. The second and third go out too. The fourth keeps going long enough to light a thin twig, but the flame dies almost immediately. The twig continues to smoulder. I blow on it. No good. It stops glowing altogether. I look on in despair, chew the knuckle of my thumb, then cut the trout into pieces, roll them in salt and eat them. Tastes almost like pickled herring.

When I feel I have eaten enough I go back to the lakeside to try to disentangle the net from the bushes. But each time I have laboriously extricated a few meshes, the wind blows them into other branches. The fishes have fallen still, except for the occasional twitch at unexpected moments. Frantic now, I pull so hard that the net gets torn in places, but still it won't let go. In the end I leave it there, draped over the bushes, looking like the tinsel deposit of a tidal wave. The web of a gigantic spider.

41

I now stop on each rise to look at my map. It is raining again, and visibility is very poor. But I know that Ravnastua is not far away. It is afternoon, or evening. Not morning, at any rate.

Every hundred paces I have to rest, and my strides are becoming shorter all the time. I'm too tired to keep track of how long they are. Not sixty centimetres, for sure. The sole of my left shoe has come loose. I've already tried going barefoot, but found it too painful. I tear a strip of plastic from my mac and tie it round the shoe, but it keeps coming undone. The longer it takes me to get to Ravnastua – and truly I've been trying to make haste – the less it seems to matter. No-one knows I'm here. Where are the Lapps, the last wild men of Europe? I haven't come across a single one. It could just as well have been me that got killed instead of Arne. Strange, what happened to Arne is exactly what I was so afraid of happening to me. I almost feel left out.

The last time I wrote in my notebook was the day before yesterday. That was five days after finding Arne. By then I was already beginning to feel there was no need to hurry, as if it might be better if he were left lying there, undisturbed. One month in the wilderness is enough for the standards of civilisation to become those of the wild. A dead reindeer left in the open changes into a skeleton, until only an antler, a rib or a vertebra remains, and what difference would it make to Arne if the same happened to him? Funerals, eulogies and wreath-laying are the concerns of people who live on paved streets and who gather ten to a room in ten-storey tower blocks, a charade strictly bound to time, place and community.

The prospect of a square meal doesn't arouse me, nor the prospect of a proper bed. Even the fear that consumed me before to the point of hysteria – getting killed in an accident like my father – has turned to indifference.

Because, what am I bringing back with me? Not a discovery. Just bad news: that someone has got killed.

As if I'm not exhausted enough already, I have the added burden of the message I must deliver. I can't think about anything else. God Almighty! The mere thought of having to tell people what has happened makes me dread my return to the civilised world.

But return I must. Staying right where I am is not an option. So I draw up my knees, lean on my left hand and push myself up. There I stand, unsteadily but on my own two feet, as befits the crown of creation. Slowly I start up the next rise.

For some time I have noticed the narrow trail becoming more clearly defined. It's quite easy now to distinguish it from the surroundings. It even looks maintained. A sure sign: Ravnastua can't be far away.

It is not far to the top of the hill either. And what do I see when I get there? The largest animal I have seen for many a long day. A horse.

Dun-coloured, with a tufted black mane sticking up like the hackles of a hyena. The horse is grazing, and lifts its head when it hears me. It goes brrrr with its lips and shifts a foreleg. It is tethered to a stake in the ground with a long rope. What can it be eating? It is nibbling at a straggly shrub. There is no grass. Horses can't survive here on their own. So there must be people nearby.

Going over yet another hill I catch sight of a wooden house – no, three cabins painted reddish-brown. From the roof of the main one sprouts an enormous FM antenna, twenty or thirty metres high. Near the cabins I notice trees, the first I've seen in a long time. Proper beeches, although they're not very tall.

My progress is extremely slow. I keep having to sit down and rest. I'm long past caring where I sit. On a peat boss preferably, but mostly I don't bother to look for a spot that's dry. Not that I'm in a hurry. As I approach the main building I notice there are some steps up to the front door, which I'll have to negotiate somehow. I manage to haul myself up them, but my head's swimming as if I'm drunk. I reach for the door handle, but can't put a hand on it: I have to grope like a blind man.

The door opens. There's no-one there, just a sort of timbered hallway with a telephone and what looks like a large black filing cabinet against the wall. And another door.

The living room. Wooden walls. Seated by the window is a very pregnant woman with black hair in two short plaits and sallow, wrinkled skin. She looks ancient. I blurt a few words in English. She smiles, gets up and leaves the room. Isn't she much too old to be pregnant? The ceiling is hung with those strips of sticky paper that flies settle on, never to come unstuck.

The walls are bare except for three large calendars. Three. Along the base of the walls the floor is strewn with household goods: stainless steel pans, small chests, a sewing machine, bundles of clothes. Children appear, naked and dark-skinned. They don't make a sound, huddle behind each other, suck their thumbs. Through the door to the next room, which is ajar, I glimpse bunks. The children hover in the doorway, ready to slam the door in my face should I do something to alarm them. I freeze, but sway all the same. One, two, three, a lot of naked children.

The woman returns with a fair-haired man in tow, who speaks quite good English. As for me, I can barely speak at all. I show him on my map where I found Arne. He takes the map from me and turns away, motioning me to follow him into the hallway. He goes up to the black metal cabinet I saw when I arrived. It's a small radio transmitter. He cranks it up and talks on the telephone.

When he has finished he returns the map to me.

'They're sending a helicopter to search for him,' he says.

Together the woman and the man escort me to one of the other cabins, which has a sign saying STATENS FJELLSTUE.

I am sitting on a stool at a white wooden table in a room with bunk-beds against the walls.

On the table in front of me are a plate, a knife, a stainless steel frying pan containing reindeer mince with gravy, a steel pot containing potatoes boiled in their skins, a loaf of bread a metre long and a pitcher of milk.

Minced reindeer tastes almost like venison.

My hand goes back and forth between my plate and my mouth in slow motion. I chew in slow motion, too.

So many things I haven't seen or heard for ages. Such as

the drone of an aeroplane. The noise grows louder and louder, how can it take so long to get so loud? Must be a slow aircraft. When the noise is at its peak I look out of the window and see a helicopter skimming the treetops.

I can't keep my eyes open any more. I can just stagger to the nearest bunk.

When I open my eyes again the light is as weak as when I shut them. I am lying on reindeer hides and am also covered by one.

But it is twenty-four hours later.

I get down from the bunk and wash myself in a bucket of cold water. With soap!

42

I didn't catch his name, of course, and keep wanting to ask him what it is, but don't get round to it. He's a biologist and mycological expert working for the Natural History Museum in Tromsø. He has stopped asking questions about Arne.

While I pay the woman for my food and lodging, he says:

'She is only thirty-nine and expecting her fifteenth child. Many children, Lapps like many children. See how the house is furnished? As if they are still living in a tent: everything is kept on the floor.'

He presses a glass tube of aspirin into my hand and lends me a pair of rubber boots. How I wish I'd had them from the start!

He has been on the phone to arrange for a Lapp with a motor-powered canoe to take me down the Karasjokka to Karasjok.

From here it's a twelve-kilometre walk to the river. It will be easy to find. I say goodbye to the woman and the man and set off.

After a few paces he calls out and comes after me:

'Are you sure you're up to it? Walking to the river, I mean?'

'Yes, yes, I can manage.'

'Do the boots fit all right?'

'Yes, they're excellent.'

'I hope so. Because of course you could stay here if you prefer, then I'll ask them to send a Weasel from Karasjok to collect you.'

'Thanks, but no. I'm fine. Thank you very much!'

I have no problem finding the way to the river. There's a proper road, albeit knee-deep in black mud and puddles, but evidently wide enough for a Weasel, because the tracks of caterpillar tyres are still visible in places.

All of a sudden everything is much more normal: the road, the clumps of trees – I am now a hundred metres below the treeline. I won't get above it any more, because it's downhill all the way to the Karasjokka valley. The bend in the river where the canoe will be waiting is only a hundred and sixty metres above sea level.

This is not an expedition any more. This is a walk in the woods.

Suddenly, a harsh yellow glow lights up the cloud bank to my left, followed by a boom like a jet breaking the sound barrier. The glow fades, leaving the sky as grey as before, but the boom is followed by a prolonged rumble as if there's a goods train crossing a viaduct nearby.

I stop to listen, and remain standing quite still until after the din has subsided and there's nothing to be seen or heard save great flocks of screeching birds winging into the distance.

When they drop out of sight I turn off the road and climb to the top of a rise. But I can't see anything because of the trees, and there's no trace of fire or smoke.

*

Arriving at the river, I come upon a small house. There is little else, only green marshy plants and the canoe with the outboard motor close by, its prow hauled up on the bank. The Lapp appears at my side. He speaks a few words of German and offers to carry my rucksack to the canoe. I ask him if he heard that booming noise a while ago.

Yes, he heard it, and he also saw the yellow glow in the sky.

What did he think it was? A plane crash? Did he hear the roar of engines before it happened? I didn't.

No, nor did he.

The Karasjokka is very wide. Is this a river? More like a huge body of shallow water, barely navigable by canoe, with branching streams and gravelly sandbanks which are too low to qualify as islands.

I sit in the canoe, facing backwards. Not a building in sight, nor any other craft.

The river meanders across the plain, and we must meander within the meanders. The wooden hull scrapes over the bottom with a hollow, growling sound. From time to time, when the motor fails to propel us forwards, the Lapp motions me to stand up and rock the boat to dislodge it.

Karasjok. Timber houses on the waterfront. The Lapp steers the boat onto the bank near a steel arch bridge. We both step ashore.

A herd of brown cows troop across the steel bridge, baulking and jostling. Not far from the bridge rises a reddish-brown timber structure, all of three storeys high, with a pitched roof. Out in front there is a tall flagpole flying the Norwegian flag. This is the state-run hotel.

The Lapp takes me to a small shop where I buy myself

278

a shirt and a pair of rubber boots. I take off the biologist's boots, give them to the Lapp to be returned to the owner at the first opportunity, and pull on the new ones.

At the hotel I take a hot bath, shave off my beard and climb into a bed with clean sheets.

Next morning someone from the police comes to see me. He asks how long I had been separated from Arne when I found his body. I tell him exactly what happened and show him Arne's notebook. He reads the page with my name on it with interest, nods, hands the notebook back to me and asks whether I want to see Arne.

Together we walk to the clinic where his body has been taken.

A doctor receives me, after which the policeman leaves.

'Are you a relative?' the doctor asks.

'No, a friend.'

'Are you acquainted with his family?'

'No, never met them.'

'Would you like to see him?'

'I don't know.'

'I don't advise it, sir, I really don't advise it.'

'Then I'll be off.'

'No, don't go yet. Why are you having such difficulty walking?'

The doctor examines my legs, then rings for a male nurse. He cleans my wounds, ties a neat bandage round my knee and sticks plasters on the cuts.

Half an hour later I am on a bus. It begins by going north to Russenes, then turns west to join the coastal road to Alta, after which it continues southwards.

The bus halts for a good half hour at Russenes, because it's a port of call for the North Cape ferries.

At the stop I see a girl in a headscarf and long trousers, with a small cardboard suitcase on the ground at her feet. I hobble around her. Her right trouser leg has been mended on the knee, and her eyebrows are unevenly plucked. She returns my look, but that may be simply out of pity for my limp.

When the bus starts up again I wait for her to get on first so that I can occupy the seat beside her.

'Are you going to Alta?' I ask.

'No, further than that.'

'Did you come from the North Cape?'

'No.'

'So what brought you here?'

'I live in Honningvåg.'

'Where's that?'

'On the same island as the North Cape.'

'That's very far north.'

'Yes, it is.'

'So your winters are very dark.'

'It's dark all winter.'

'So what do you do to pass the time? Go to parties?'

'No. I do my lessons.'

I have no doubt she does, because her English is excellent, but I put the question anyway:

'Are you still at school then?'

'Of course.'

'How old are you?'

'Fifteen.'

'Fifteen? You're joking. Nineteen.'

'No, fifteen,' she says, glancing away.

I wish I hadn't asked! She'll think I look down on her, which will make her even less willing to talk to me. It's a while before I dare to break the silence.

'I'm from Holland.'

'Oh.'

'I was in Finnmark for a long time.'

'What were you doing? Fishing?'

'No. Studying soil conditions.'

'Are you a student?'

'Yes.'

'Was it interesting?'

'So so.'

She puts out her hand and points at the compass case hanging from my belt.

'What have you got in there? A gun?'

'No, nothing.'

I open the case, show her it's empty and say:

'It's my compass case. I dropped the compass into a fissure between some rocks. Stupid of me.'

'Shame. Such nice leather. It looks quite new.'

'Would you like to have it?'

'Of course not!'

'It's no good to me any more.'

'You could buy a new compass.'

'You can have it as a souvenir.'

'What could I do with it?'

I have no idea what she could do with it either. A souvenir? Of me? She doesn't even know my name.

*

Now I am truly stumped, and for the next couple of hours I sit next to her more or less in a daze, not saying a word, as if our conversation had never taken place.

Skaidi. A stop on the mountain plateau, by the wooden stall selling snacks. I get off the bus and hobble about aimlessly. She gets off too, and, somewhat to my surprise, walks along beside me, on the side of my bad leg. So she does want to be friendly after all. She even seems eager to support me.

The touristy Lapp emerges from his tent, brass-bowled pipe clenched between his teeth, reindeer antlers in his hands. An exact reprise of his appearance on the scene when I stood here with Arne, shivering under a dark wintry-looking sky. That was before everything started to go wrong. *Before Arne died*.

I stop in my tracks and take the girl's arm. She's smiling.
'Why are you smiling?'
'Why aren't you?'
Moved by fatherly emotion, I buy her a bar of chocolate at the stall.

When the bus sets off again I rack my brains for something we could talk about, but can't come up with anything better than:
'You still haven't told me your name.'
'I'm Inger-Marie.'
The only response left for me is to tell her my own name: one word. So much for having a conversation.

After a pause I take out Arne's notebook, look up the page with my name on it and pass the book to her.

'There,' I say, pointing, 'can you read that? Can you tell me what it says?'

She reads slowly, moving her lips and tracing the lines with a nail-bitten index finger. When she reaches the bottom of the page her finger goes back up to my name, and she translates:

'*Alfred headed off in the wrong direction. I thought he was joking. Fifteen minutes later he still hadn't come back. Spent the whole afternoon looking for him. Went back to the ravine. I will wait for him here.*

'*Some gabbros crumble easily into loose debris. 33.P.234 . . .*'

Inger-Marie's voice falters.

'Oh, you can skip that part.'

She skips a few lines, then goes on:

'*Alfred not back yet. Have decided to stay here, a week if necessary. I noticed he was having trouble with the rough terrain, which he isn't used to. I admire his perseverance. Never complains, although he has had some nasty falls. And I keep him awake at night with my terrible snoring. Anyone else would have packed it in long ago.*

'*Gradient . . .*'

I nod, take back the notebook and shut it, lost for words.

The bus drives on through clouds of dust.

'Are you Alfred?' she asks.

'Yes.'

'Is your leg very painful?'

'No, it's much better now,' I lie.

'I hope I translated it properly. I want to go on to university, but my father says I'm mad. By the way, did you know there was an incredibly loud bang yesterday? Somewhere around Karasjok. It was on the news this morning. First they thought there had been a plane crash, but nothing was found. I wonder what it could have been.'

'I haven't a clue.'

'I don't believe in flying saucers. Do you?'

'No, I don't.'

'Maybe it was ball lightning. Have you ever seen ball light-ning?'

'No, never.'

'I have. Once. I was sheltering from the rain and there was house nearby with a pitched roof. It was as if a ball of fire came rolling down the roof. But there was only a hissing sound.'

We arrive in Alta. I get up and put out my hand, but she ignores it. Instead, she throws her arms around my neck and gives me a long kiss. My hand is on her back and I can feel her thin shoulder blades. Finally I kiss her twice on each cheek and get off the bus in a daze.

The driver has alighted too. He climbs onto the roof to unload my rucksack.

Inger-Marie is watching me from her window. She isn't smiling, in fact her expression is quite blank. I wave feebly, without any particular hope or expectation. The driver gets in again.

When the bus drives off, she goes to the window in the rear door and watches me from there with the same blank expression on her face. The last thing I see of her is that she's gesticulating. Waving? Blowing a kiss? There's also the possibility that seeing me framed by the window reminded her of a shape chalked on a blackboard, and that she was wiping me out, so to speak. That would be by far the best for her.

43

Arne's friends are still on holiday. I call at the neighbours for the key and find the house in exactly the same state as we left it. My suitcase under the sofa in the living room, and so forth. I undress and put on my ordinary clothes again: shirt, tie, jacket. When I'm done, I ring the Geological Survey in Trondheim. Direktør Oftedahl isn't in, nor is Direktør Hvalbiff or whatever his name is. But the secretary has a message for me. She tells me that the aerial photographs have been loaned to the university in Oslo. They do not have copies, but they do have the negatives. A fresh set of prints? Yes, that would be possible, but no, there is no point in calling round tomorrow. I cannot count on the prints being ready for a very long time. It will be two, three months at least, and there is considerable expense involved. Do I want her to make a note of my address?

Next I phone the university in Oslo and ask for Professor Nummedal. Oh. Professor Nummedal? He's not here. He's gone to Hop, which is a suburb of Bergen. When he'll be back? He didn't say. Not for some time anyway. Are you on your way back to Holland? Then you could try in Bergen. Shall I give you his address? Hop: Troldhaugensgate 5, phone number 3295.

Finally I ring for a taxi and leave two ten-kroner notes by the phone. My feet are too swollen and thick with plasters to get into my shoes, so I'm still wearing the rubber boots.

I take my suitcase and rucksack and get in the taxi that will take me to the seaplane dock. In the cramped ticket office I dictate a telegram to my mother, telling her I'll be back in three days' time.

44

Blue skies, bountiful sunshine. Here I am not surrounded by sounds, but by fragrances, and there are no mosquitoes at all, nor bloodthirsty flies. The gardens have jagged rocks erupting from lawns and beds of flowering rhododendron.

Troldhaugensgate number 5 is on a narrow asphalt road so steep that cars have to climb it in first gear. The path leading up to the house is even steeper – part of it is stepped, roughly hewn out of rock.

Once again I find myself having to climb before I can speak to Nummedal, which seems full of significance. What the significance might be, though, I can't imagine. I clamber up the steps and ring the doorbell.

'Professor Nummedal,' I blurt to the maid. 'He's expecting me, I spoke to him on the telephone this morning.'

She smiles – only speaks Norwegian probably – and takes me through to a conservatory where Nummedal is sitting in the sun. He is not wearing his ingenious spectacles, the ones with the extra lenses that can be flipped up and down. Just ordinary sunglasses.

Nummedal has not risen, but mutters something in Norwegian. The maid utters a long string of words, of which I catch only 'professor', then leaves.

I limp towards him.

'Herr Professor Nummedal . . .'

'Bitte, bitte. Take a seat. Why are you walking with such difficulty?'

'I fell.'

'You too? Did you both fall at the same time?'

'No, I wasn't there when it happened. I had got lost, and didn't find Arne until afterwards.'

The chair nearest to Nummedal is still quite far away – at the other end of the conservatory. I seat myself facing him. Beside me stands a potted palm with fronds pressed up against the ceiling.

Pondering what I shall say, I stare at my feet. Ludicrous, those rubber boots under pale grey flannel trousers.

Nummedal has fallen silent. The vertical wrinkles are now so deeply etched as to give him a sliced appearance, and his skin has the dingy shade of old newspapers. At last I say:

'I have Arne's notebook.'

'So you told me on the phone. How did you get on in Finnmark?'

'I wasn't very successful, I'm afraid.'

'What do you mean? Success cannot be measured until one has processed one's findings.'

'I believe that my starting-point was wrong. I also believe that I lack the proper training for research into my subject. I was trying to follow up a suggestion of Professor Sibbelee's, but have come to the conclusion that it's not leading anywhere. I would like to carry on the research Arne was engaged in. I want to learn Norwegian. Redo my courses where necessary. I would like to study with you in Oslo, for two or three years maybe, and then go back to Finnmark. For a foreigner like me, being so unfamiliar with the polar terrain, that is the only way forward.'

'Is that what you think? But then you are far too

pessimistic. I can understand you being distressed. But before you came to Norway Professor Sibbelee sent me a letter expressing his high opinion of your abilities. Surely you are not saying you found Professor Sibbelee's teaching lacking in any way?'

'Perhaps Professor Sibbelee's expectations of me were too high.'

'That is the most preposterous thing I have heard in years. Why would Professor Sibbelee recommend you to me if you were insufficiently prepared for your task? I don't know what you are talking about, sir.'

'Before my departure Professor Sibbelee told me about certain ideas he had. Suppositions he wanted me to verify.'

'They must have been very interesting suppositions!'

Haltingly, I reply:

'I didn't find anything to substantiate them.'

'But my dear fellow! There's nothing unusual about that! What would the world be coming to otherwise? You seem not to have the faintest idea of the number of suppositions people work on.'

I make an attempt at polite laughter, but fail to produce the proper sound.

Nummedal doesn't laugh either.

'After the holidays,' he says, 'I will not be returning to Oslo University. My successor has not yet been named.'

Holding Arne's notebook in my hand, I go up to him and say:

'Here is the notebook. It might be interesting to know how far Arne progressed with his research. Maybe you have another pupil who could continue his work. I would like to have kept it as a souvenir, but then I don't know Norwegian. Besides, the information might be useful to someone.'

Nummedal reaches out to take the notebook, but his hand gropes wide of the mark. He is totally blind! I have to take his hand and press the book into it. Then I say:

'I'm awfully sorry that you will be leaving the university.'

'Did you ever get those aerial photographs from Direktør Hvalbiff?'

Yes, that's what he said, I heard it clearly.

'I didn't get the photographs, and I discovered later that your student Mikkelsen had them. That was another setback, but I'm not blaming anyone. I realise that I was an outsider, there was no way I was going to belong. Which is why I want to study in Oslo. I want to start a new life.'

'Start a new life, you say?'

He gets up from his chair with great difficulty. He doesn't seem able to tell where I am by ear, either. Addressing the palm tree more than me, he continues:

'There were no aerial photographs at my institute. Hvalbiff has them, Geological Survey in Trondheim, as I told you. The Geological Survey, that is the place to go for aerial photographs. Direktør Hvalbiff. But that man has been getting in my way ever since his appointment there! You should be grateful you don't live in this country! Such a big country and fewer than four million inhabitants. But all they do is quarrel! Start a new life? Here in Norway? Starting a new life is always a continuation of the old life! I challenge the whole Salvation Army to prove that I am wrong! I suggest you think about that long and hard before you take up residence in this country!'

Clutching Arne's notebook, he gestures in the direction of the potted palm. As if it were me standing there, me pressed up against the ceiling!

Why did Arne ever make me jealous? He was such a good

draughtsman, his notes were so meticulous, he could climb the steepest slopes without effort and cross rivers without getting his feet wet. Now his work, unfinished, is in the hands of a blind man.

Hvalbiff, was what Nummedal said. No doubt about it.

Nummedal hates the man. Blind hatred – surprise, surprise.

Damn! It could just be a *nickname* Nummedal invented for the director of the Geological Survey. How they must have laughed behind my back . . . Hvalbiff. That means whale meat, Arne had said. Funny eh, Qvigstad had said, not a trace of fat in it, just like beef.

Like a crash of thunder, it comes to me: the pink, fleshy face of the man I spoke to in Trondheim and who, when I asked for Direktør Hvalbiff, introduced himself as a geophysicist by the name of Direktør Oftedahl.

Could 'Hvalbiff' and Oftedahl be one and the same person?

I am not going to bother to find out.

45

The maid shuts the door behind me as I begin making my way down to the gate. The lushness of the vegetation, the mild weather, the scattering of villas, all this affects me with unreasonable self-reproach at having left Finnmark. When I was there I didn't experience any longing to be back in the world of buildings and trees, I actually felt more at home among the ice and the abundance of shrubby plants, the birds and the fishes. Having left the rugged upland behind feels like defeat.

In the meantime I have noticed a signpost nailed to a tree on the other side of the road:

TROLLHAUGEN

The name sounds familiar, but there's something odd about it. I have the feeling I'm on the brink of discovering what it is, as if I have just one page to go before the end of the book containing the answer.

A large open convertible comes towards me over the quiet road. The driver is a woman. She is hatless, her gleaming auburn hair like a cowl over her head, her eyes hidden by a long fringe. Her immaculately made-up face looks like a parchment copy of a face I have seen before, so who can she be? She looks at me intently and stops at the gate.

'Hey! I knew I'd run into you again,' she says. 'How's it going?' She has an American accent.

It is the woman I met in Tromsø, in the light of the midnight sun.

'Got any plans?' she asks. 'I'm on my way to Troldhaugen. You know, the home of Edvard Grieg, the famous composer. Why don't you come along?'

Grieg!

I limp around the car and get in beside her.

She is wearing a very low-cut dress and a multi-strand pearl necklace.

'Such a lot has happened since we last met. I've had a face-lift, you know. Left the clinic last week. They did a pretty good job, I think.'

She puts the car in gear and we spurt off.

'Jack's on a binge, he's been drunk now for three days. I tell myself why sit around moping? Might as well spend some time visiting the sights. And what have you been up to?'

'I've been in the High North.'

'Doing what?'

'Searching for meteorites, but I didn't find a single one.'

'Is that how you got that limp?'

'I hurt my knee when I fell.'

'And those rubber boots you're wearing . . . you look like a plumber on his way home from work.'

'I can't get into my ordinary shoes.'

'You look a mess! All those blotches on your face – what happened?'

She tilts the rear-view mirror a fraction towards the windscreen so she can see me in it.

'That's the work of mosquitoes and flies up north,' I reply.

'Good Lord, you poor kid.'

She pulls up at the entrance to Troldhaugen, which was spelled with a double 'L' on the sign. A white house can be glimpsed beyond the trees.

'Why don't you just stay in the car. Better not strain yourself. I won't keep you waiting for long, back in no time.'

She twists round to reach for something on the back seat. Did she get her figure lifted too? It is shapely and gorgeous.

'Too bad,' she says. 'But I'm going to go right ahead and do what we Americans are always ridiculed for, or you'll be sitting here for nothing while I have a look round.'

The object she reached for is a cine-camera, which she now raises to her eye and swivels round as if she's mowing the whole place down with a machine gun.

Indeed, she is back in no time!

'Nothing unusual about the house. Inside there's a big grand piano, with a whole lot of photos on it. You can't imagine a single note of Grieg's music having been written there. But you can go down to the bottom of the garden, where there's a cottage with another piano. That's where he did all his composing, in full view of the beautiful lake. Shall we go for a drive?'

We drive around.

'Grieg,' she says, 'Grieg must have been truly great to have written all that music while being obliged to live in a house like everybody else. Perhaps that's a characteristic shared by great men. The first humans who took it into their heads to live differently from other animals had no idea what an awful adventure they were embarking on in their awful houses. If they hadn't turned to building, man would have remained a rare species, like the okapi or the bird of paradise.'

She pulls into a parking area at a promontory jutting out over the fjord, so that we can admire the view.

'So weird,' she says, 'us being here together, now. I can't believe it. I often think there isn't really that much difference between living and dreaming. The difference is illusory, because when we're awake we're too busy interpreting all the sights around us to see that life's a dream, too.'

I lean back with my arms folded across my chest. I'm all ears. She tells me she is a music critic, and that she writes about music for several leading weeklies.

'No-one is more painfully aware of the demise of human culture than the American in Europe. There are plenty of landscapes like this in the States, but all of them are ruined. You wonder why that is. There are buildings here too. The trees are much the same as back home, and they're sawn into the same kind of planks. But it's as if Americans keep getting the proportions wrong by about two inches. You can't imagine how irritating it is to find a big nation like the United States being copied the world over in the silliest of ways. All those cigarette brands with American names, in countries where they don't speak English. Why? South State Cigarettes. I ask you. What does it mean? It's the most banal name you could think of. But calling a European packet of cigarettes South State apparently improves the taste. And then all those youngsters getting together in pathetic little jazz bands with crazy English names, singing American songs in crazy accents. Hipsters, beatniks, real gone guys. It's so incredibly sad to see all those kids busting their guts for the sake of mere imitation. Just as sad as a Texan oil millionaire displaying a fake Picasso in his lounge, no, even sadder, because millionaires don't deserve any better. Those kids are wasting their energy on a sort of spiritual enslavement, because they're trying to become Miles Davis or John Coltrane in ways that'll never work. And then there are more and more people nowadays writing poems, and even novels, in the most awful broken English. Of course, I can see why Europeans speak English with an accent. I have profound admiration for anyone who knows a second language. But the moment people find out I'm American they start speaking English with a strange throaty accent which they take to be American. It's the same all over Europe. The other day I was in a restaurant having dinner and there were two Germans at a neighbouring table. I don't understand much German, but I could clearly hear one of them larding his conversation with the English expression "so what!" He obviously thought he was very clever. So what!'

It was not the shortest route back to town by any means. I confided in Wilma that my first ambition was to be a great scientist like my father, and that I had wanted desperately to possess a meteorite from the age of six, but that after my father died I was set on becoming a flautist instead of a scholar – that is, until I was fourteen and discovered I had learnt to play the wrong kind of flute.

She commiserated. Said I could still become a flautist if I wanted, mentioned great musicians – Americans I've never heard of – who turned to music full-time later on in life.

'But it's hardly a good sign that I didn't even get out of the car to visit Grieg's home, now is it?' I say. She retorts that we'll go back there as soon as my leg is better.

What is she thinking of? And isn't this at odds with her

theory about living and dreaming? I can't imagine chance meetings with the same person happening three times in a dream.

She occupies a plush suite with a wide balcony on the top floor of the hotel. A waiter comes in bearing a silver platter covered by a napkin and an ice bucket containing a bottle of champagne.

We stand together on the balcony looking out over the town. Here in Bergen you can actually speak of darkness falling. Not black darkness. Blue. Impossible to describe the shade: a blue that is almost incandescent.

An illuminated cable car rises against a black mountain-side.

Down on the pavement in front of the hotel three Salvation Army soldiers strike up a tune on a tambourine, a guitar and a banjo.

'It's very hot,' Wilma says. 'Hold on a moment.'

She retreats from the balcony. I wonder what brought those Salvation Army people here. Do they know I am about to start a new life? Did Nummedal send them after me?

I too go back inside, switch on a small lamp and lie down on the divan. The rumble of traffic, the Salvation Army singers, the shower splashing close by.

Wilma emerges from the bathroom. She has on a kind of pyjama suit of tea-rose satin. A short top and long narrow pants, low-waisted and with a showy zip-fastening on the front.

Smiling at me, Wilma goes to the door, turns the key and then crosses to the side table. She uncorks the champagne and fills two glasses.

With a glass in each hand she says:

'The zip's pretty neat, don't you think? Men usually find this sort of thing very sexy.'

'Because it doesn't . . .' I mumble

She perches at the end of the divan.

'Sköl,' she says, and drinks.

I find her beautiful, like an exotic doll.

She says:

'I know exactly what you were going to say. A zip fly on a woman's pants is just decoration, because it doesn't serve the same purpose as for men.'

I laugh, realising that she amuses me and, unknowingly, comforts me too.

Wilma says:

'But the real explanation lies elsewhere. I'm sure the designer of these pants sought advice from a psychoanalyst. You know why?'

'I don't know anything about psychoanalysis.'

My eyes linger on her thighs in the slinky skin-tight trousers with tiny, almost invisible creases in the side seams. The straining fabric is even sexier to me than her fly fastening, but what would be the psychoanalytical explanation for that?

It's too complicated to ask her.

Wilma says:

'A thinker with a simplistic outlook once told me it's because a fly fastening on a woman's pants resembles what's underneath. Gross, don't you think? And not very psychoanalytical either. It's the actual fastening that it's all about. We must think in terms of repressed homosexual components in the psyche of the normal, heterosexual male.'

'Must we?'

'Let me explain. Heterosexual men are sent into a panic by the mere thought of opening another man's flies. That's what defines them as heterosexual. That sense of panic. The sight of any zip fly immediately rouses unconscious fears in them, which are promptly allayed by their consciousness when they realise that the fastening in question belongs to a woman. What it comes down to, you understand, is that a woman appeals more fully to the male heterosexual psyche in pants like these than in a skirt – more even than if she's completely naked. Because it's not only the heterosexual component in his psyche that is prevailed upon, it's also his repressed homosexuality. Therefore the stimulus is far greater.'

'Rather complicated, isn't it?'

'Not at all. What does a normal man think? That other people's flies are taboo. Taboos invite breaking. What happens if the man breaks the taboo when it's a woman wearing the pants? Not the dreaded forbidden fruit is his reward, but the garden of paradise. It's as simple as that.'

She takes my hand and strokes the inside of my wrist with the tips of her fingers. She settles back on the divan, folds one leg beneath her and stretches the other in a long slanting line down to her varnished toenails.

'So now you know. A detail on a woman's clothing that appears to be merely decorative can turn out to serve a purpose that is, to some extent, rationally evident.'

I want to touch her, anywhere, but I'm not thinking straight. I find her beautiful, like a precious Egyptian mummy.

'I just remembered something about Grieg,' she says. 'I forgot to mention it earlier. He was buried in his own garden. His tomb was sealed into the sheer cliff overhanging the path, with a simple slab engraved with his name to mark the spot.'

She jumps to her feet, goes over to the side table and takes up the silver platter.

'Know what this is?'

She folds the napkin back and holds the platter out to me.

'Looks like smoked salmon.'

'Yes it does, but that's not what it is. It's gravlachs.'

Gravlachs! The delicacy Nummedal made such a fuss about back in Oslo, saying it was so hard to find!

'You know what gravlachs is? It's very special. Raw salmon, which is buried in the ground for some time – I don't know how long – and then dug up again. The taste is very refined. Go on, try some.'

At that very moment there's a great thud against the door and a deep, hoarse voice roaring 'Wilma, Wilma! Open this door!'

He hammers his fists on the door, kicks it violently, then hurls himself against it.

Fred Flintstone!

It is exactly like the cartoon: the door bends forward in the middle, causing great gaps to appear on either side, after which it springs back into the frame.

'Yes, Jack, I'm coming!' Her voice sounds unconcerned, languid, as if she has been asleep. He goes on pounding the door.

She replaces the platter on the table, takes the napkin in one hand and removes the champagne from the ice bucket, then tips the contents of the bucket onto the napkin. The ice cubes remain in a heap, the water drips down to the floor. Holding the ice cubes wrapped in the napkin, she goes to the door and turns the key.

I have got up from the divan.

Flintstone staggers into the room, groaning. His mouth is so turned down at the corners that he must have spent the last couple of hours with a dinosaur bone clamped between his jaws.

The look in his eyes is both helpless and menacing. He snorts, splutters, sprays vaporised aquavit.

Inaudible in my soft rubber boots, I manage to slip past him towards the door, which he left open. In the corridor I glance over my shoulder.

Flintstone lolls on the divan. Wilma, in a shaft of light from the corridor, dabs at his head with the ice-pack as though extinguishing a fire in a wastepaper basket. Her free hand is raised to me. She opens and closes it a few times, gives me a rueful smile and says:

'Bye-bye!'

46

The stewardess comes past with the basket containing duty-free spirits. I buy a half bottle of whisky. The newspaper I have just been reading slides off my lap. There is a brief item in it about a bright glow in the sky followed by a loud bang, reported in the vicinity of Karasjok. The Geophysical Survey dispatched a reconnaissance aircraft to measure the magnitude of the magnetic field, and a strong magnetic deviation was indeed recorded locally. This may have been caused by a meteor striking the earth. A team of geologists is on its way to Karasjok to investigate.

I immediately open the whisky and have a few swigs.

Meteorites, pieces of broken-up planets. So will the earth break into pieces at some stage – and I don't care. It could happen any time, it seems to me, as I stare out of the window at a few tiny islands set in a wrinkly sea far below, so far away that I can't even seen the wrinkles move. This is how God sees the earth, and also how my father sees the earth, if Eva is to be believed. So they don't care any more than I do. God looks down from heaven and views the world as an aerial photograph. And Nummedal, Lord of aerial photography, is blind.

I do not have aerial photographs, I am not God, and I can't even get a clear view of my surroundings after I have reached the top of a mountain after a tremendous struggle.

The bottle is empty by the time the plane reduces speed and prepares for landing at Schiphol airport.

The cosmos is a gigantic brain and the earth a tumour within the mass of grey matter. That just about sums it up, I tell myself. Pity I can't tell Qvigstad. No smoking, fasten seatbelts.

I leave the empty bottle on the plane.

Eva waves, but my mother holds a handkerchief to her mouth as I limp towards them, suitcase in one hand, rucksack in the other. It drags over the floor, but I didn't think it worth hoisting it onto my back for the short distance to the exit, which I estimate at thirty-two paces.

It was by counting my paces – which I have done since I was a boy, in imitation of Buys Ballot – that I was able to find my way without a compass. How's that for success? How's that for the ultimate achievement I've been living towards all my life? Finding the corpse of my friend and finding the way home. Nothing else. But it's no good trying to explain that to my mother. She hasn't a clue about my studies, anyway. She's sobbing with emotion at her clever boy's homecoming. I cannot, must not disappoint her.

I almost lose my balance when my mother throws her arms around me.

In the taxi I sit next to her. Eva sits facing us on the folding seat.

My mother's sobbing intensifies.

'Oh, Alfred, you gave me such a dreadful shock, I'm sorry, never mind me.'

'What was it that shocked you?'

'Seeing you limp like that.'

'But I'll be fine in a week or two. I just hurt my knee, that's all.'

'That's not the point,' my mother says.

'The things is, Alfred,' Eva says, 'she didn't sleep for three nights after she read the news about Brandel.'

'Brandel?'

'Yes, Brandel. Haven't you heard? He and his team reached the summit of Nilgiri, but he came back with frozen feet. Ghastly, isn't it? I saw his picture in the paper last week. In a wheelchair, next to the plane. And then Mummy got it into her head . . .'

47

My mother and Eva have lovingly installed me in the largest armchair in the house, with my injured leg propped up on a footstool.

'Tell me, Alfred,' Eva asked a moment ago, 'what happened to my compass?' To which I replied: 'Dumped it, because it indicated the wrong direction.'

The lamp is lit over the round table bearing my mother's typewriter. But she is not working. After enquiring in detail as to the circumstances of Arne's death, she heaves a deep sigh and offers her personal summary of the events:

'A terrible accident, but at least you are safe. I am proud of you.'

Outside it is dark, really dark. For the first time in weeks I can be assured of the light of day being relieved by dark-ness, the pitch darkness of night, during which sleep is possible – unless you're tormented by thoughts of having to catch up on all the things you didn't do during the day and better your ways.

I wonder if Arne's funeral has already taken place. There was no point in my attending it, as I've never met his family. His father presses a handkerchief to his eyes, laments to an aunt or uncle: 'He wouldn't take anything from me! He was so hard on himself. Never touched the money I sent him, just kept it in the bank. I told him a hundred times to get himself a new pair of boots.' The aunt or uncle just think: 'That wouldn't have done any good. What he needed was seven-league boots to keep up with your success.'

I also wonder if Qvigstad and Mikkelsen are still trekking through Finnmark, unaware of Arne's death and my departure. Strange that I will probably never see them again, any more than I will see Arne again.

Brandel comes to mind. Two years ago the pair of us took part in an excursion to Lake Rissajaurre in Swedish Lapland. The Swedish geologist in charge had told us the lake was forty metres deep and the water so clear than you could see the bottom when you swam in it.

When we got there Brandel and I were the only ones to jump in. The water coming from the snow on the surrounding slopes was only a few degrees above freezing. Which was why the others preferred to keep their clothes on.

I swam across the lake and back, and so did Brandel. Later on, long after we'd got dressed again, Brandel asked me 'Well? Did you look under water? Did you see the bottom of the lake?'

I had forgotten to look down.

As in a nightmare, I then said to myself: You know, you're not cut out for this line of work. Yes, you try, you're a virtuoso performer during exams, you don't mind plunging into freezing water, but then you go and forget the most important thing.

Maybe it would have been better if I had failed in my first year at university. Now it looks as if I am the victim of my own virtuosity.

But then what? What would I have done? Become a flautist after all? How will I ever find out? No-one can start at the same point twice over. If an experiment can't be replicated, it ceases to be an experiment. No-one can experiment with their life. No-one can be blamed for being in the dark.

To all their questions (What was the rest of your trip like? Any interesting discoveries?) I reply: Not bad, or: Nothing much.

'Oh, Mummy,' Eva says in the end, 'why don't you give it to him now? He looks so miserable.'

My mother goes to the oak cupboard in which she keeps her newspaper cuttings and comes back with a small parcel.

Dear old Mum! I bet she's bought me a new watch!

'How did you know my watch got wet?' I ask.

'It's not a watch,' she says as I unwrap the parcel.

The paper parts to reveal a jeweller's box covered in blue velvet.

The box contains a pair of cufflinks. The bar and chain are made of gold, but the cufflinks themselves look like raw stones.

'Do you know what they are?'

I study them closely. I have never seen stones quite like these before. They are surprisingly heavy. If I'm not mistaken, each cufflink is set with half of the same stone.

'An expert like you should be able to tell right away!' Eva says.

'It looks like some mineral,' I mumble, annoyed at my blindness – yet again. 'A chunk of mineral matter, I think, cleaved in two. Look, they fit together.'

The sides are highly polished and gleam like steel. I demonstrate how perfectly they fit together.

'Well, Alfred,' my mother explains. 'Remember you were so keen on having your own meteorite when you were little?

You wanted a stone that fell from the sky. I never told you this, but your father bought one for you before he died, as a present for your seventh birthday. I kept it hidden away all these years, never said a word. I couldn't bear to give it to you, because it wasn't my present but your father's. Then it suddenly occurred to me to have a pair of cufflinks made, as a gift for your doctorate. I think your father would have approved. I think he'd have approved if I gave you your present now, too.'

'A gift from heaven, that's what it is, Alfred,' Eva says, 'truly, a gift from heaven.'

I look at her, crushed. She can't help it. She's a fool. Heaven. What does she mean by heaven? If I asked her for a definition she'd be tongue-tied.

I also look at my mother. I will never make her understand the cause of my misery. She is proud of me. And it's not as if there are any demands being made on me that go against what I myself want and have always wanted. Here I sit, holding a cufflink in each hand. Put the two together and I have one whole meteorite. But not a shred of evidence for the hypothesis I had to prove.

THE END

Groningen, September 1962 – September 1965

AUTHOR'S NOTES

The report on the Himalayan expedition on pp. 37–40 appeared in *Algemeen Handelsblad*, 3rd October, 1962.

'Jane Mansfield' on p. 51. The author of the graffito was referring to Jayne Mansfield, an American film actress with a very large and at the time very famous bust.

NOTE TO THE FIFTEENTH PRINTING

There is, I believe, a growing trend among authors to rewrite or thoroughly revise novels that were first published many years ago. An excellent idea.

Some reviewers object to this – no doubt because their criticism of the original book no longer applies to the altered version.

All the better, I'd say.

There are two sides to everything, and more than two to novels. Not for nothing is the story of Jesus told four times over in the Bible.

Writing a novel can in some respects be compared to playing chess. The difference is that writing is not a competition. A bad move on the part of one player is an advantage to the other. A weak passage in a novel is no use to anyone.

If a chess player thinks of a better move thirteen years after a particular game, it is too late.

For a novelist it is never too late to substitute a full stop with a question mark, a comma with a colon, one word with another, or to expand a paragraph that has proved too succinct in the original to be properly understood.

In this new printing of *Beyond Sleep* there are about two

hundred and fifty changes. Most of them will seem very minor. But the book is still the same, that is to say: what it should have been when it first came out.

Paris, 30th July 1978